PRAISE FOR DECE

"Lourey creates a splendid mix of humor and suspense."

—*Booklist*

"Lourey, who keeps her secrets well, delivers a breathtaking finale."

—*Publishers Weekly*

"Lourey pulls out all the stops in this eighth case."

—*Library Journal*

PRAISE FOR *NOVEMBER HUNT*

"It's not easy to make people laugh while they're on the edge of their seats, but Lourey pulls it off, while her vivid descriptions of a brutal Minnesota winter will make readers shiver in the seventh book in her very clever Mira James mystery series."

—*Booklist* (starred review)

"Clever, quirky, and completely original!"

—Hank Phillippi Ryan, Anthony, Agatha, and Macavity Award–winning author

"A masterful mix of mayhem and mirth."

—Reed Farrel Coleman, *New York Times* bestselling author

"Lourey has successfully created an independent, relatable heroine in Mira James. Mira's wit and fearlessness enable her to overcome the many challenges she faces as she tries to unravel the murder."

—*Crimespree Magazine*

"Lourey's seventh cozy featuring PI wannabe Mira James successfully combines humor, an intriguing mystery, and quirky small-town characters."

—*Publishers Weekly*

"Lourey has a knack for wholesome sexual innuendo, and she gets plenty of mileage out of Minnesota. This light novel keeps the reader engaged, like one of those sweet, chewy Nut Goodies that Mira is addicted to."

—*The Boston Globe*

PRAISE FOR *OCTOBER FEST*

"Snappy jokes and edgy dialogue . . . More spunky than sweet; get started on this Lefty-nominated series if you've previously missed it."

—*Library Journal* (starred review)

"I loved Lourey's quirky, appealing sleuth and her wry-yet-affectionate look at small-town life. No gimmicks, just an intriguing plot with oddball characters. I hope Mira's misfortune of stumbling over a dead body every month lasts for many years!"

—Donna Andrews, *New York Times* bestselling author of *Stork Raving Mad*

"Funny, ribald, and brimming with small-town eccentrics."

—*Kirkus Reviews*

"Lourey has cleverly created an entertaining murder mystery . . . Her latest is loaded with humor, and many of the descriptions are downright poetic."

—*Booklist* (starred review)

PRAISE FOR *SEPTEMBER MOURN*

"Once again, the very funny Lourey serves up a delicious dish of murder, mayhem, and merriment."

—*Booklist* (starred review)

"Beautifully written and wickedly funny."

—Harley Jane Kozak, Agatha, Anthony, and Macavity Award–winning author

"Lourey has a talent for creating hilarious characters in bizarre, laugh-out-loud situations, while at the same time capturing the honest and endearing subtleties of human life."

—The Strand

PRAISE FOR *AUGUST MOON*

"Hilarious, fast paced, and madcap."

—*Booklist* (starred review)

"Another amusing tale set in the town full of over-the-top zanies who've endeared themselves to the engaging Mira."

—*Kirkus Reviews*

"[A] hilarious, wonderfully funny cozy."

—*Crimespree Magazine*

"Lourey has a gift for creating terrific characters. Her sly and witty take on small-town USA is a sweet summer treat. Pull up a lawn chair, pour yourself a glass of lemonade, and enjoy."

—Denise Swanson, bestselling author

PRAISE FOR *KNEE HIGH BY THE FOURTH OF JULY*

Lefty Finalist for Best Humorous Mystery

PRAISE FOR *JUNE BUG*

"Don't miss this one—it's a hoot!"

—William Kent Krueger, *New York Times* bestselling author

"With just the right amount of insouciance, tongue-in-cheek sexiness, and plain common sense, Jess Lourey offers up a funny, well-written, engaging story . . . Readers will thoroughly enjoy the well-paced ride."

—Carl Brookins, author of *The Case of the Greedy Lawyers*

PRAISE FOR *MAY DAY*

"Jess Lourey writes about a small-town assistant librarian, but this is no genteel traditional mystery. Mira James likes guys in a big way, likes booze, and isn't afraid of motorcycles. She flees a dead-end job and a dead-end boyfriend in Minneapolis and ends up in Battle Lake, a little town with plenty of dirty secrets. The first-person narrative in *May Day* is fresh, the characters quirky. Minnesota has many fine crime writers, and Jess Lourey has just entered their ranks!"

—Ellen Hart, award-winning author of the Jane Lawless and Sophie Greenway series

"This trade paperback packed a punch . . . I loved it from the get-go!"

—*Tulsa World*

"What a romp this is! I found myself laughing out loud."

—*Crimespree Magazine*

"Mira digs up a closetful of dirty secrets, including sex parties, cross-dressing, and blackmail, on her way to exposing the killer. Lourey's debut has a likable heroine and surfeit of sass."

—*Kirkus Reviews*

PRAISE FOR *THE TAKEN ONES*

Short-listed for the 2024 Edgar Award for Best Paperback Original

"Setting the standard for top-notch thrillers, *The Taken Ones* is smart, compelling, and filled with utterly real characters. Lourey brings her formidable storytelling talent to the game and, on top of that, wows us with a deft stylistic touch. This is a one-sitting read!"

—Jeffery Deaver, author of *The Bone Collector* and *The Watchmaker's Hand*

"*The Taken Ones* has Jess Lourey's trademark of suspense all the way. A damaged and brave heroine, an equally damaged evildoer, and missing girls from long ago all combine to keep the reader rushing through to the explosive ending."

—Charlaine Harris, *New York Times* bestselling author

"Lourey is at the top of her game with *The Taken Ones*. A master of building tension while maintaining a riveting pace, Lourey is a hell of a writer on all fronts, but her greatest talent may be her characters. Evangeline Reed, an agent with the Minnesota Bureau of Criminal Apprehension, is a woman with a devastating past and the haunting ability to know the darkest crimes happening around her. She is also exactly the kind of character I would happily follow through a dozen books or more. In awe of her bravery, I also identified with her pain and wanted desperately to protect her. Along with an incredible cast of support characters, *The Taken Ones* will break your heart wide open and stay with you long after you've turned the final page. This is a 2023 must read."

—Danielle Girard, *USA Today* and Amazon #1 bestselling author of *Up Close*

PRAISE FOR *THE QUARRY GIRLS*

Winner of the 2023 Anthony Award for Best Paperback Original

Winner of the 2023 Minnesota Book Award for Genre Fiction

"Few authors can blend the genuine fear generated by a sordid tale of true crime with evocative, three-dimensional characters and mesmerizing prose like Jess Lourey. Her fictional stories feel rooted in a world we all know but also fear. *The Quarry Girls* is a story of secrets gone to seed, and Lourey gives readers her best novel yet—which is quite the accomplishment. Calling it: *The Quarry Girls* will be one of the best books of the year."

—Alex Segura, acclaimed author of *Secret Identity*, *Star Wars Poe Dameron: Free Fall*, and *Miami Midnight*

"Jess Lourey once more taps deep into her Midwest roots and childhood fears with *The Quarry Girls*, an absorbing, true crime–informed thriller narrated in the compelling voice of young drummer Heather Cash as she and her bandmates navigate the treacherous and confusing ground between girlhood and womanhood one simmering and deadly summer. Lourey conveys the edgy, hungry restlessness of teen girls with a touch of Megan Abbott while steadily intensifying the claustrophobic atmosphere of a small 1977 Minnesota town where darkness snakes below the surface."

—Loreth Anne White, *Washington Post* and Amazon Charts bestselling author of *The Patient's Secret*

"Jess Lourey is a master of the coming-of-age thriller, and *The Quarry Girls* may be her best yet—as dark, twisty, and full of secrets as the tunnels that lurk beneath Pantown's deceptively idyllic streets."
—Chris Holm, Anthony Award–winning author of *The Killing Kind*

PRAISE FOR *BLOODLINE*

Winner of the 2022 Anthony Award for Best Paperback Original

Winner of the 2022 ITW Thriller Award for Best Paperback Original

Short-listed for the 2021 Goodreads Choice Awards

"Fans of *Rosemary's Baby* will relish this."
—Publishers Weekly

"Based on a true story, this is a sinister, suspenseful thriller full of creeping horror."
—Kirkus Reviews

"Lourey ratchets up the fear in a novel that verges on horror."
—Library Journal

"In *Bloodline*, Jess Lourey blends elements of mystery, suspense, and horror to stunning effect."
—BOLO Books

"Inspired by a true story, it's a creepy page-turner that has me eager to read more of Ms. Lourey's works, especially if they're all as incisive as this thought-provoking novel."

—Criminal Element

"*Bloodline* by Jess Lourey is a psychological thriller that grabbed me from the beginning and didn't let go."

—*Mystery & Suspense Magazine*

"*Bloodline* blends page-turning storytelling with clever homages to such horror classics as *Rosemary's Baby, The Stepford Wives,* and *Harvest Home.*"

—*Toronto Star*

"*Bloodline* is a terrific, creepy thriller, and Jess Lourey clearly knows how to get under your skin."

—Bookreporter

"[A] tightly coiled domestic thriller that slowly but persuasively builds the suspense."

—*South Florida Sun Sentinel*

"I should know better than to pick up a new Jess Lourey book thinking I'll just peek at the first few pages and then get back to the book I was reading. Six hours later, it's three in the morning and I'm racing through the last few chapters, unable to sleep until I know how it all ends. Set in an idyllic small town rooted in family history and horrific secrets, *Bloodline* is *Pleasantville* meets *Rosemary's Baby.* A deeply unsettling, darkly unnerving, and utterly compelling novel, this book chilled me to the core, and I loved every bit of it."

—Jennifer Hillier, author of *Little Secrets* and the award-winning *Jar of Hearts*

"Jess Lourey writes small-town Minnesota like Stephen King writes small-town Maine. *Bloodline* is a tremendous book with a heart and a hacksaw . . . and I loved every second of it."
—Rachel Howzell Hall, author of the critically acclaimed novels *And Now She's Gone* and *They All Fall Down*

PRAISE FOR *UNSPEAKABLE THINGS*

Winner of the 2021 Anthony Award for Best Paperback Original

Short-listed for the 2021 Edgar Awards and 2020 Goodreads Choice Awards

"The suspense never wavers in this page-turner."
—*Publishers Weekly*

"The atmospheric suspense novel is haunting because it's narrated from the point of view of a thirteen-year-old, an age that should be more innocent but often isn't. Even more chilling, it's based on real-life incidents. Lourey may be known for comic capers (*March of Crimes*), but this tense novel combines the best of a coming-of-age story with suspense and an unforgettable young narrator."
—*Library Journal* (starred review)

"Part suspense, part coming-of-age, Jess Lourey's *Unspeakable Things* is a story of creeping dread, about childhood when you know the monster under your bed is real. A novel that clings to you long after the last page."
—Lori Rader-Day, Edgar Award–nominated author of *Under a Dark Sky*

"A noose of a novel that tightens by inches. The squirming tension comes from every direction—including the ones that are supposed to be safe. I felt complicit as I read, as if at any moment I stopped I would be abandoning Cassie, alone, in the dark, straining to listen and fearing to hear."

—Marcus Sakey, bestselling author of *Brilliance*

"*Unspeakable Things* is an absolutely riveting novel about the poisonous secrets buried deep in towns and families. Jess Lourey has created a story that will chill you to the bone and a main character who will break your heart wide open."

—Lou Berney, Edgar Award–winning author of *November Road*

"Inspired by a true story, *Unspeakable Things* crackles with authenticity, humanity, and humor. The novel reminded me of *To Kill a Mockingbird* and *The Marsh King's Daughter*. Highly recommended."

—Mark Sullivan, bestselling author of *Beneath a Scarlet Sky*

"Jess Lourey does a masterful job building tension and dread, but her greatest asset in *Unspeakable Things* is Cassie—an arresting narrator you identify with, root for, and desperately want to protect. This is a book that will stick with you long after you've torn through it."

—Rob Hart, author of *The Warehouse*

"With *Unspeakable Things*, Jess Lourey has managed the near-impossible, crafting a mystery as harrowing as it is tender, as gut-wrenching as it is lyrical. There is real darkness here, a creeping, inescapable dread that more than once had me looking over my own shoulder. But at its heart beats the irrepressible—and irresistible—spirit of its . . . heroine, a young woman so bright and vital and brave she kept even the fiercest monsters at bay. This is a book that will stay with me for a long time."

—Evelyn Little, *Los Angeles Times* bestselling author of *Dear Daughter* and *Pretty as a Picture*

PRAISE FOR *SALEM'S CIPHER*

"A fast-paced, sometimes brutal thriller reminiscent of Dan Brown's *The Da Vinci Code*."

—*Booklist* (starred review)

"A hair-raising thrill ride."

—*Library Journal* (starred review)

"The fascinating historical information combined with a storyline ripped from the headlines will hook conspiracy theorists and action addicts alike."

—*Kirkus Reviews*

"Fans of *The Da Vinci Code* are going to love this book . . . One of my favorite reads of 2016."

—*Crimespree Magazine*

"This suspenseful tale has something for absolutely everyone to enjoy."

—*Suspense Magazine*

PRAISE FOR *MERCY'S CHASE*

"An immersive voice, an intriguing story, a wonderful character—highly recommended!"

—Lee Child, #1 *New York Times* bestselling author

"Both a sweeping adventure and race-against-time thriller, *Mercy's Chase* is fascinating, fierce, and brimming with heart—just like its heroine, Salem Wiley."

—Meg Gardiner, author of *Into the Black Nowhere*

"Action-packed, great writing taut with suspense, an appealing main character to root for—who could ask for anything more?"

—Buried Under Books

PRAISE FOR *REWRITE YOUR LIFE: DISCOVER YOUR TRUTH THROUGH THE HEALING POWER OF FICTION*

"Interweaving practical advice with stories and insights garnered in her own writing journey, Jessica Lourey offers a step-by-step guide for writers struggling to create fiction from their life experiences. But this book isn't just about writing. It's also about the power of stories to transform those who write them. I know of no other guide that delivers on its promise with such honesty, simplicity, and beauty."

—William Kent Krueger, *New York Times* bestselling author of the Cork O'Connor series and *Ordinary Grace*

DECEMBER
DREAD

OTHER TITLES BY JESS LOUREY

MURDER BY MONTH MYSTERIES

May Day

June Bug

Knee High by the Fourth of July

August Moon

September Mourn

October Fest

November Hunt

December Dread

January Thaw

February Fever

March of Crimes

April Fools

STEINBECK AND REED THRILLERS

The Taken Ones

The Reaping

THRILLERS

The Quarry Girls

Litani

Bloodline

Unspeakable Things

SALEM'S CIPHER THRILLERS

Salem's Cipher

Mercy's Chase

CHILDREN'S BOOKS

Leave My Book Alone! Starring Claudette, a Dragon with Control Issues

YOUNG ADULT

A Whisper of Poison

NONFICTION

Rewrite Your Life: Discover Your Truth Through the Healing Power of Fiction

DECEMBER DREAD

JESS LOUREY

THOMAS & MERCER

Text copyright © 2012, 2018, 2024 by Jess Lourey
All rights reserved.

Published by Thomas & Mercer, Seattle

www.apub.com

Amazon, the Amazon logo, and Thomas & Mercer are trademarks of Amazon.com, Inc., or its affiliates.

ISBN-13: 9781662519369 (paperback)
ISBN-13: 9781662519376 (digital)

Cover design and illustration by Sarah Horgan

Printed in the United States of America

To Christine, who always brings the sunshine

Chapter 1

It's sixty-eight degrees inside the car. The core-heated air smells sharp, like pine freshener and coffee. Outside, a winter sky the color of lead blends with the snow-slush roads, morphing the landscape into a blurry daguerreotype day. The radio is set to AM. An announcer squawks about a history-making fifty-seven-yard Hail Mary. The game took place last Sunday. The show is a replay, its urgency offensively fake, a mystery already solved, shelved, and forgotten.

The killer stabs the radio button and cruises past the woman's house for the second time in thirty minutes. It isn't difficult to blend in, even in a rural area. Silver sedans are a dime a dozen, especially borrowed older models with a rouge of rust rimming the wheel housing.

The killer's target is removing snow from her sidewalk, her dog alongside her. A quick pass reveals her wide-mouthed shovel digging deep into the drifts and coming up loaded. Her shoulders are strong, her concentration absolute. She tosses the snow to the side. Her mutt tries to catch it before it lands. They've been at it for a while because the dog is more snow than animal.

Shovel. Toss. Catch.

Shovel. Toss. Catch.

The killer isn't worried about the dog. Animals are easy to subdue, if a person is quick. The woman likely won't put up much of a fight, either, despite a toned upper body. Fear is an effective paralyzing agent.

Although her ski cap is tucked low, the killer knows that underneath she's a brunette, just like the rest. She likes to travel and has visited Italy twice. She loves a good debate, Ben & Jerry's Chunky Monkey is her guilty pleasure, and she tends toward the sarcastic side, though she doesn't mean anything by it.

Also, she lives alone.

The last point, the killer uncovered by walking past her house and, twice, riffling through her mail while she was at work. The rest was revealed in her online-dating profile.

"Quiet," the killer snaps. "I know she shouldn't have put all that out there. A woman who advertises shouldn't be surprised when a buyer shows up, right?"

The only response is the hum of the heater. The twelve-inch plastic doll strapped into the passenger seat has nothing to add. She sits in her perfect Jackie O dress suit, her immaculate brown hair scraped into a bun. Her face poses a frustrating half smile, always.

The killer turns the radio back on.

Chapter 2

Friday, December 11

The cartoon elf grinned at me from my fossil of a Zenith TV, a row of bowlegged appliances dancing behind him. Flashing lights crawled across the bottom of the screen. The soundtrack featured a helium-voiced singer belting out "Deck the Halls."

"Did you know there are only thirteen shopping days until Christmas?" the elf squealed. His eyes begged me to say no.

"Yes," I told the TV, "and did you know that every time a television set is turned off, an elf dies?"

I clicked the power button on my remote and showed my back to the tube. I didn't hate Christmas. In fact, you'd find no bigger fan of twinkle lights, old-fashioned peppermint candy, and holiday cards. It was the Christmas *advertising* that rubbed me raw every year, starting before Halloween and ending only when every American was corpulent with credit card debt and buyer's remorse.

That was why I only turned on the TV this time of year to quickly check the weather report. If that made me a Grinch, so be it.

I stretched and glanced around the double-wide I'd called home since last spring. I was trailer-sitting for Sunny, a friend who'd fled to Alaska the previous April to fish salmon with a monobrowed lothario. She'd planned to return in the late summer, but when the time came, she couldn't leave Rodney or the great white north.

That left me to hold down the fort in Battle Lake, a gorgeous jewel of a Minnesota town where I'd had the unfortunate luck to cross paths with a corpse each month since May.

The people were nice, though—the live ones—and in an odd way, I was beginning to feel like I'd finally found a home. Sure, it was a prefabricated double-wide trailer, and there were no Asian restaurants within thirty miles unless you counted the gas station that sold fried rice and egg rolls in a shiny buffet warmer near the live bait, but on the whole, Battle Lake and I were growing comfortable with each other.

I sipped my jasmine tea and regarded Luna, the German shepherd mix who came with the trailer. She was one of my favorite things about living here, but sometimes I wished she weren't so smart. I needed to come clean about a touchy subject, and I wasn't sure the best way to approach it. I finally decided to come at it from the side.

"I forgot to pick up eggs and toast again last night." I trailed my finger along the countertop and watched her out of the corner of my eye.

She cocked her head.

"And you know breakfast is the most important meal of the day . . ."

She whined. She knew exactly where I was going with this.

"You're wrong," I protested, setting down my tea. God, she made me feel defensive sometimes. "I *really* forgot to buy groceries. If I don't grab you-know-what out of the snow-emergency kit, I've got nothing to eat."

She glanced away, sadly. She would not be party to my addiction.

I turned to my calico kitty, Tiger Pop. "You understand, don't you?"

Tiger Pop lay in a patch of winter sunlight, not even bothering to flick her tail. I studied her for a good minute before deciding she was ignoring me with approval. That was all the encouragement I needed. I tugged a winter coat on over my pajama T-shirt and slipped my bare feet into boots before opening the front door.

The double-wide was perched within throwing distance of Whiskey Lake on 103 acres of oak forests and undulating hills. All I had to do was step outside to be afforded one of the most gorgeous views in the entire state.

I paused to suck in a deep, cauterizing breath. It was one of those beautiful December mornings where the air felt so clean it scrubbed your lungs. It was bracing but temperate compared to what had been Minnesota's bitterest November in decades. The wind licked at but did not slice my bare knees. Glittering diamonds of light sparkled off the rolling sea of snowdrifts that made up my massive front yard.

I crunched down the steps and over the path I'd recently shoveled toward my beloved Toyota Corolla. The two of us had been together for nearly a decade, and except for a bunk thermostat that I'd had replaced last month, she'd never let me down.

In this part of the country, people didn't lock their cars at night, and I knew a handful of neighbors who didn't even bother securing their houses. I was a house locker—I'd lived in the Cities too long to be anything else—but there was nothing in my car worth stealing.

Well, *almost* nothing.

I flipped open the trunk and reached for the Folgers can tucked in the far corner. I peeled off the lid: two fat candles, a box of matches, a flashlight, a Leatherman, a survival blanket the size and consistency of a sheet of tinfoil that I hoped had magical properties, and a single Nut Goodie. The contents of this can were all that stood between me and a hypothermic starvation death in the event that my car went into a ditch and disappeared under a towering snowdrift on some lonely country road.

Wait, only *one* Nut Goodie? I scrabbled around the bottom of the can. I'd stuffed in a half dozen of the candy bars when I first created the winter-survival kit three weeks earlier. How could there be only one left? I dumped the contents into the trunk and sifted through them, but there was no changing the facts: only a single Nut Goodie remained.

The Minnesota original candy bar was my fix, my love, my chocolate ecstasy. As big as the palm of your hand, it was a delight of chocolate and nuts wrapped around a maple candy center and encased year-round in a frenetic Christmas package of red, white, and green. I refused to keep them in the house because I couldn't stop eating them once I started. I'd hoped the inner reaches of my car would serve as a demilitarized zone.

I'd been fooling only myself.

I glanced guiltily at the house. Maybe Luna was right. Possibly, I wasn't doing myself any favors with the Nut Goodie breakfasts. The thing is, the candy was my heroin, and I was weak.

I held the Nut Goodie in my hand, confronted with a *Sophie's Choice* moment: immediate gratification or long-term survival? My knees and fingers were growing stiff with the cold, but I couldn't decide. On the one hand, I was already heavy on saliva imagining the frozen chocolate melting into a warm pool of happy in my mouth. On the other, some sane part of me knew I shouldn't snarf down *all* the food in the emergency kit. Then I remembered: I had granola bars in the house! They could be my survival food. Why hadn't I thought of that before? I pocketed the candy, repacked the coffee can, and charged toward the house before my nibbly bits froze off.

Luna forgave me my weakness, greeting me at the front door with an energetic wag like I'd been gone for a week. I patted her head, doffed my boots and coat, and planted myself at the kitchen counter to enjoy my chocolate breakfast while I read yesterday's mail. I'd come home too late to peek at it the night before, putting in extra hours at the library as well as finishing up a front page article for the *Battle Lake Recall*, the local newspaper where I freelanced. Both jobs had toppled into my lap after I'd moved to town from the Twin Cities, the library job as a result of a murder in May and the reporting gig due to my having a bachelor's degree in English and, subsequently, low income expectations.

The top letter was a plea that I become a contributing member of Minnesota Public Radio. For the millionth time, I promised myself I'd do that. Soon. I hated feeling like a public radio parasite, but money was tight for those of us at the bottom of the food chain, even when working two jobs.

Using a side tooth, I pried off a chunk of hard, frozen Nut Goodie and continued reading. Next on the pile was a holiday card from Peyton Bertram and her mom, Leylanda.

Peyton, a precocious eight-year-old, was one of my favorite attendees at the library's children's reading hour every Monday. The card I held was dominated by her gap-toothed smile, and a tongue-lolling golden Lab wearing a Santa hat reclined between her and her mom. They must have gotten a dog.

I showed the photo to Luna. "Think we should do something like this next year?"

She licked my still-cold knee.

I made room on the fridge for the holiday photo and sifted through the rest of the mail: phone bill, Victoria's Secret catalog, and a card rimmed with red-and-white-striped candy canes, promising me a free box of the peppermint treat if I signed up for a one-year subscription to *Healthy Holidays*. I tossed it. Seemed like a mixed message, and besides, I could already feel the Nut Goodie knocking out a wall in my stomach so it could add on. I also trashed the catalog, wrote a check for and stamped the telephone bill, and got ready for work.

Freshly showered and brushed, I offered Luna one last chance to paint the snow, made sure both animals had clean water, snagged the granola bars to restock my emergency car kit, and headed to town, a smile on my face.

My instincts must have been taking the day off.

Chapter 3

Otter Tail County hadn't had fresh snow since Wednesday, so the roads were clear. I planned to arrive an hour early to the library so that I'd have time to finish the book ordering I'd begun last night. Come to think of it, I still had a delivery to catalog. I was high on the thoughts of all the organizing I'd accomplish when I pulled onto the Battle Lake main drag and spotted the mob outside the police station.

I slowed the Toyota to a crawl and hand-cranked the window. The odors of car exhaust and winter air washed in. The crowd of twenty or so was dressed for the weather, mostly female, and appeared abuzz about something. I recognized a friend I hadn't seen in a while. "Gina!"

She caught sight of me and made her way to my car, no mean feat given the size of the crowd shoving against her burgeoning pregnancy belly.

Sunny had been best friends with Gina before taking off to Alaska with her Bert-browed man. It'd felt natural for me to step into the friendship. Gina was raunchy, funny, and outspoken, three qualities I admired. Me, I talked big in my own head, but I rarely walked the walk.

"Mira! Did you get one, too?" Her cheeks and the tip of her nose were rosy, and white puffs of air accented her words.

"One what?"

"This." She held up her mittened hand. It clutched a candy cane–rimmed card promising her twelve free candy canes if she signed up for a year of *Healthy Holidays*.

"Yeah. I tossed it into the trash this morning. What of it?"

She raised her eyebrows so high they disappeared under the edge of her knit cap. "Cripes. I know you live in a trailer, but is it under a rock? Haven't you heard about the Candy Cane Killer?"

"Sure," I lied. "Candy. It's a killer."

"Gack." She reached in to slap my forehead. Her woolen mitten cushioned the blow. "I'm not talking about candy. I'm talking about the Candy Cane *Killer*, the guy who only murders in December and only kills slender brunettes who are between five four and five six? He started his spree two Decembers ago in Chicago. Last December he targeted central Wisconsin. They think he's hunting in Minnesota now. Two days ago a bunch of women in White Plains got his calling card—a single candy cane—and yesterday, one of them was murdered."

White Plains was a little over an hour directly southwest of Paynesville, my hometown. I'd attended track meets there. My stomach was twisting, so I self-soothed by focusing on the details. "OK, but that's not an actual candy cane." I pointed at her card. "It's an advertisement for a magazine."

"You think you know more than the police? They want to speak with all the folks who got one of these." She shook the card for emphasis, and it made a rippling noise in the wind. "If you have one, you better go get it. *Now.* You have time before the library opens."

She forced her way back into the crowd, and I rolled up my window and motored away. I had three things on my mind:

1. Yes, I often did think I knew more than the police—at least the local chief of police, Gary Wohnt.
2. I'd scented hysteria brewing in that crowd, a faint sulfur smell that took only a single match to ignite.
3. I didn't want to be the dumb bunny in the horror movie who ignored everyone's warnings.

Unsure of what to do about one and two but confident that I didn't want to die stupid, I pointed the car toward home. I'd snag the card, show it to one of the officers at the police station, and still have time to open the library before ten.

I pulled into my driveway on autopilot, left the car running, and hurried toward the house. I was so deep in thought that I'd yanked open the outer glass door and walked halfway through the interior steel door before I realized it'd been unlocked. Had I been in such a hurry this morning that I hadn't closed it tightly? That would be a first.

I examined the doorknob. It seemed fine. I glanced around the living room. Everything appeared in place, except for one thing. No dog had greeted me.

"Luna?"

She met everyone at the door, tail wagging, no exceptions. If she was inside, she was too hurt to move.

My eyes swept the kitchen, the open door to my left leading to the main bedroom, and the hallway to the right leading to a bathroom, office, and spare bedroom. No movement.

My heart trip-thudded.

The outer glass door I'd had installed for the winter was weighted and self-closing, meaning that even if I'd accidentally left the interior door unlocked, there was no way Luna could have exited the house unless someone opened the outer door for her. I suddenly felt hollow.

"Luna?" This time it was a whisper.

Chapter 4

Across the room, a corner of the candy cane card winked at me from the kitchen garbage, the frolicking border a lurid red.

"Luna?" I called again.

This time, I heard whining from the direction of the spare bedroom. My heart soared. She was alive! But then, what was keeping her from coming to me? My ears felt like saucers, twirling, searching for any alien sounds in the house. Was the Candy Cane Killer here, now? Had he hurt Luna?

I reached behind me without looking, sliding my hand down the cool wood of the Louisville Slugger I kept just inside the door. Stumbling across seven murders in as many months had shaped me into a strange cross between paranoid and desensitized. (It'd also forced me to start pursuing my PI license before I earned a nickname like Mortuary Mira.) The bat felt solid in my hand. I left the interior door open in case I needed to beat a quick escape and inched toward the spare bedroom, keeping my back to the wall. While walking, I reached into my coat pocket with my free hand. I touched two Nut Goodie wrappers, a hair tie, and a calculator I'd borrowed from the library so I could balance my checkbook.

Bingo.

I pulled out the black plastic rectangle, made some movements on it with my thumb, and held it up to my ear.

"Drake? Yeah. No, definitely come over. You'll be here in two minutes? Perfect. Come right in. I left the door open."

I slipped the calculator back into my pocket. "Drake" had been a good choice, I thought, considering my heart was beating so loudly I could hardly remember my *own* name. "Thor" or "Brutus," the first two options that'd come to mind, might have given me away as a fake. Sure, it would've been nice if I owned a real cell phone and if someone were actually on their way here to save me, and if wishes were pennies, I'd be rich.

Then I could afford a real cell phone.

Sweat trickled down my neck. I still wore my winter coat, but with the door open, the room was chilling quickly. Fear provided its own furnace, however. If not for my concern for Luna, I'd be halfway to Battle Lake by now. Funny thing, I wasn't worried about Tiger Pop. Cats really did land on their feet.

I reached the hallway that led to the spare bedroom, a bathroom, and an office. I couldn't see around the corner into the other two rooms, but the office door was wide open in front of me. Winter sunshine poured into the room, spotlighting all the angles. Nothing more evil than dust bunnies in there.

Before I could chicken out, I whipped around the corner, my back still glued to the wall. The bedroom door was partially closed, but I could see into the bathroom. The only illumination filtered in from the snowed-over skylight, but it was enough to reveal that the tiny room appeared empty. I darted forward and used the bat to push aside the blue-and-green shower curtain.

Nothing.

My breath came in shallow bursts.

I heard the whining again, this time closer. It was definitely coming from the spare bedroom, and the sound was so mournful that it twisted my heart. I attempted to weigh stealth against speed, but Luna made another sad sound, and my instincts overrode my brain. I kicked open the partially ajar door and charged in, swinging the bat like a helicopter blade.

I tried to see everywhere at once.

A bed.

Pivot.

An empty dresser.

Pivot.

A chair.

Pivot.

A cat.

Pivot.

A closet.

Pivot.

That was it. Wait, a cat?

"Tiger Pop?"

She lay in front of the closed closet door, licking her front paw in a patch of sunlight. She didn't seem particularly agitated. I, on the other hand, was coiled as tight as a spring. I could feel my eyes wide and the fear veins throbbing on each side of my forehead.

"Where's Luna?" I asked.

Tiger Pop tossed me a cool stare. I forcibly slowed my breathing. As I did, awareness began to dawn on me, and my shoulders unclenched. I thought I knew what was happening, and it had nothing to do with a serial killer.

I'd actually witnessed Tiger Pop practicing for this.

She would stroll into a room, completely relaxed and cool. Luna would follow, always up for a good time. Tiger Pop would hang out just long enough for Luna to lie down, then she'd dart from the room and rub her back against the door, trying with all her might to close it before Luna wised up and escaped.

It was a mean trick, one that had gotten Luna stuck in a bedroom more than once, which was why I tried to keep all the doors wide open.

But how had the *cat* convinced the *dog* to check out the spare bedroom closet?

I nudged Tiger Pop out of the way with my foot. "You're a bully."

I had barely turned the closet knob a full rotation when Luna leaped out, pushing me to the floor and licking me like I was on fire.

"S'okay, Luna. I'm here now." I couldn't help but smile, my blood pressure dropping with each lick. "You gotta stop trusting that cat. Really."

I'd been scared for nothing and felt more than a little foolish. Just to be on the safe side, though, I examined every corner of the house, peeked under every piece of furniture and in every closet, until I was satisfied that it was only me and the animals inside. Hands on hips, I stood in the living room and examined the front door. For the life of me, I couldn't remember not locking it, but I must not have.

After a stern lecture to Tiger Pop and a few minutes spent resting a book against the base of all the doorjambs so she couldn't close them on poor Luna again, I retrieved the candy cane card from the garbage and made my way back to my car.

The thing was, despite my outward smiling, I couldn't shake the tingly sense that I was being watched the entire time.

Chapter 5

By the time I reached Battle Lake, the crowd had mostly dispersed, all except for Gina and two other women. Judging by the angry set of Gina's shoulders as she spoke with an officer outside the station, he'd had the poor judgment to get on her bad side.

I parked my car and ambled over.

I didn't recognize the officer she was arguing with but thanked my stars that it wasn't police chief Wohnt. He and I'd had a series of run-ins since I'd moved to town. I could understand why he'd take a professional interest in me, given that the murder rate in the county had increased 700 percent since I'd relocated here, but had the man never heard of a coincidence?

Plus, he always wore those mirrored cop shades that drove me to confess irrelevant and often embarrassing personal facts. As if all that weren't enough, he'd lost a pile of weight a few months ago and now bore an uncomfortable resemblance to Chief Wenonga, the sexy-hot twenty-three-foot fiberglass statue that graced the north side of town. Good thing I had a boyfriend and was as loyal as the day was long.

". . . don't know that," Gina was saying.

"Yes we do. Look, Gina, I realize that you're worried, but you have Leif at home. He'll look out for you."

I thought I spotted smoke wisping out of the knit holes in her ski cap. I put my hand on her shoulder, hoping to ward off a fistfight. "What's up?"

"What's *up*," Gina said, crossing her arms but not taking her eyes off the officer, "is that Eric here says the candy cane cards are legit, not connected to the killer, and that we should all go home and bake something nice for our husbands."

The other two women puffed up behind Gina, and Eric glanced at them uncomfortably. "Now, that's not fair. I didn't say all that." He reached under his hat to scratch at his scalp. "But yeah, we did get a hold of the *Healthy Holidays* office, and they confirmed that they're running this candy cane promotion right now. There's no reason to believe the killer is anywhere near Battle Lake."

His words didn't appease Gina. "Maybe if he was killing off policemen with more hair than brains, you'd be a little more concerned."

The officer gave in to the strain. "Unless you're planning to grow four inches and dye your hair brown, you don't have anything to worry about, either. Short blonde nurses don't fit the profile."

Gina balled her mittened hands into fists. I stepped between her and the cop. "Come on, Gina. None of this is his fault."

It was only when I was up close that I noticed the tears in the corners of her eyes. She wasn't angry. She was scared.

She rubbed her nose and stared at the ground. "The news just reported he killed her *dog*, too," she said quietly. "The woman in White Plains? He murdered them both."

I sucked in the icy air and glanced over my shoulder at the police officer and then at the other two women. They didn't deny it. I felt the blood drain from my face.

A woman had been murdered only two hours away. I'd known that, and I'd imagined her last moments had been horrifying. Then I'd pushed any thoughts of her out of my mind and returned to the regular programming that made up my stupid, mundane life. So what was it about this new detail that made the murder seem suddenly personal? Certainly the victim had friends and family suffering terrible grief. But somehow, it was the detail about her dog that really drove it all home.

"Jesus," I said.

"Yeah," Gina agreed. "Jesus." Her shoulders slumped, all the fight knocked out of her. "I should probably go home."

I nodded, feeling deflated myself. "And I should get to work," I mumbled. "You're gonna be all right?"

She shook her head as she walked away. "None of us are gonna be all right, Mira. Not until this guy—and everyone like him—is caught."

The other two women followed her. I stood my ground for a moment, feeling the officer's eyes on me. I couldn't meet them.

I knew what he was thinking.

Brunette, five six, around 130 pounds. Watch your back.

I walked to my car and drove it the four blocks to the library.

Chapter 6

Normally, the Battle Lake Public Library was soothing, a haven of leafy green plants, seasonally appropriate twinkle lights, and the inky, promising smell of books.

Not today.

Today, I felt like I was dragging bricks as I entered.

I flicked on the lights, grabbed a stack of novels and two DVDs out of the book-return bin, and made my way to the front desk. The library was scheduled to open in ten minutes, and I didn't have the energy to do much more than sit. I kept picturing the last moments of that poor woman and her dog.

Acting on the theory that knowledge was power, I fired up the front desk computer and went online. The White Plains murder was front-page news on every major site. I clicked on the least grisly headline.

> A serial murderer, nicknamed the Candy Cane Killer for his practice of sending candy canes to his victims before his attack and sometimes leaving them at the scene, is believed to have struck in White Plains, Minn. On Saturday, Dec. 12, police found Lisabeth Hood, 34, dead in her home after a coworker alerted them that Hood had missed two days of work. The body of her dog was found lying across her.

The Candy Cane Killer's first victim is believed to be Monica De Luca of Chicago. Her body was discovered two years ago this December, in her apartment, under a pile of candy canes. Since then, police have tied eight more murders to the killer—four, including De Luca, in the Chicago area during the same month, four more a year later in central Wisconsin, and now the single killing in Minnesota.

All the victims were women, ages 27 to 46, brunette, of average height and slender build. The murder weapon in all cases was a knife. With the exception of De Luca, all victims are known to have received an unexplained candy cane 12 to 72 hours before they were killed. In Hood's case, it appears that six other White Plains women also received candy canes, resulting in a curfew being placed on the town, population 9,814.

Police have found no connection between the murder victims other than their appearances and have no leads at this time. The FBI's Violent Crimes Task Force, headed by SAC Walter Briggs out of Quantico, is working closely with local law enforcement to catch the killer.

Blood thumped loudly in my ears. No wonder Gina had been freaked out. Some monster had declared open season on Midwestern brunettes, and the police had no leads? If his past murder sprees were any indication, he had three more women to kill before he met his grisly Minnesota quota.

I closed the news site and headed to the stacks to reshelve books, but it was difficult to concentrate. I was grateful when the front door opened and hurried to the front to see who it was.

"Mira James! I do declare, you get prettier each time I see you."

I scowled at Kennie Rogers, Battle Lake mayor, faux-southern-accent wielder, busybody, constant schemer, and repeat winner of the "most likely to dress like a zaftig Britney Spears" award, all gratitude melting out of me. She was hardly a reprieve from dark thoughts. We'd formed an uneasy truce the past few months, but we mixed like orange juice and toothpaste. Her tone alone was enough to set my teeth on edge. She'd sounded friendly, and I knew her well enough to know that if she was being nice to me, she wanted something. I stepped behind the front desk to put it between us. "Other than hat hair, I look exactly the same as the last time you saw me."

"That must be it, then," she said, pinning a conservative smile to her face. The expression complemented her sensible down jacket, matching hat and gloves, and plaid-rimmed Sorel boots.

Wait a minute.

"Why are you dressed for winter?" I asked suspiciously.

She fluffed the platinum hair peeking out from under her hat. "Because last time I checked, it's December."

"Yet when I saw you last week, you were wearing a tiara with earmuffs, a pink pleather coat, and three-inch-heeled boots." And I'd considered that modest for Kennie.

"That pink pleather coat was lined," she purred, avoiding eye contact.

I stared at her until she met my gaze, ignoring the cloud of yeasty gardenia perfume that seemed to habitually envelop her.

"Fine," she huffed, removing her gloves one finger at a time. "Times are tough. I didn't want to appear extravagant while I was laying people off." She smiled brightly. "I'm caring that way. You might want to take notes from me on proper people management." She waved a hand in the general direction of the bookshelves. "If you ever want to promote yourself beyond your current station, that is."

I'd stopped listening three sentences earlier, right after she'd said "laying people off." As mayor of Battle Lake, Kennie held the power over three jobs in her manicured little hands: the manager of the municipal liquor store's, Chief Gary Wohnt's, and mine. Since rumor had it she was knocking boots with the chief, and since the liquor store was the town's linchpin on sanity in the winter months, that left the library.

The words tasted like chalk coming out of my mouth. "You're laying me off?"

"Hmmm?" She glanced at me out of the corners of her eyes. "Did I say that?"

I nodded. "You pretty much did."

She slapped her gloves on the counter between us and tsked. "I certainly did not. I wouldn't lay off a friend, would I?"

She paused.

When I said nothing, she answered her own question, faux hurt in her voice. "Of course I wouldn't."

I was suspicious. There was more to this. "For real?"

"Real as Rice Krispies." She smiled so wide that I had to blink against the brightness. "Only thing is, I *do* need to close the library for three weeks. Budget cuts and all that. This book shack isn't too busy over Christmas, anyways." Her nuclear smile softened. "Close up after today, reopen on January 2, and we meet our budget shortage without firing anyone. Easy peasy." She grabbed her gloves, swiveled on her heel, and scampered toward the door like the yellow-livered ferret she was.

I couldn't believe it. "Wait! Three weeks without pay? How am I supposed to cover my bills?"

She shrugged without stopping. "With your savings?" she called over her shoulder.

"Savings?" I yelled. "I barely make above minimum wage. The city council voted to keep me at an assistant's salary because I don't have the librarian degree. You know that."

"Go home and visit your mom for the holidays, then, and be glad you have a job to return to," she said as she sailed out the door.

I watched her go, knowing I had no recourse. "Curse words," I muttered.

Money was tight all over Minnesota, I knew that, and we'd all have to do our part. Yet I was barely scraping by.

I sighed.

Go home, indeed. Kennie knew better. I couldn't have escaped Paynesville any faster after I'd graduated high school if I'd had a jet pack strapped to my back. My dad had been the town drunk. One of them, anyway. He'd gone out in a blaze of shame, killing himself and the driver of the other car in a head-on collision. I imagined his blood alcohol level must have been so high that he hadn't felt a thing. At least, on my good days I imagined that.

I'd had to hurry past the tin-can wreck of his car, purchased as a cautionary example for the driver's ed students, my last year and a half of high school. I grew wild and bitter pretty quickly, shunned by people I'd called friends, whispered about behind hands, judged wherever I turned.

Manslaughter Mark's girl, people called me.

Huh. Guess death had marked me at a younger age than most.

Once I'd graduated high school, I'd shot to the University of Minnesota in Minneapolis without looking back. None of it'd been my mom's fault. She'd always been a quiet, consistent housewife and stable mother.

Except she also hadn't left him, which I'd begged her to do for the year leading up to the accident, the year his drinking had really spiraled out of control. I'd had a hard time forgiving her for that.

We'd kept up a superficial relationship when I lived in the Cities, but that changed when she drove to Battle Lake in August to tell me she had breast cancer. She was going to be OK, but she wanted me back in her life. We'd been phoning each other regularly since then, rebuilding our relationship. I found I liked it, but at a distance. No way could I spend three weeks in a row with her, in the hometown I hadn't seen in more than a decade. I'd get the reverse bends.

There must be some other way to fix this.

As soon as lunchtime rolled around, I hoofed it over the snow-packed streets to the *Battle Lake Recall* office, a new plan percolating. Maybe Ron could give me more work during the lean times. It'd help me to cover my heating, phone, and electric bills, keep me in groceries, and allow me to make the minimum payment on my school loans.

The earthy smell of paper greeted me when I entered the office. "Knock knock!"

I hated when people said that when walking into a room. That I'd just done it myself demonstrated my current level of stress.

Ron grunted from behind the front counter, where he was tapping away on a computer. He and his wife ran the paper. He was the editor, publisher, layout guy, and head writer. His second and current wife sold ad space. She also spent an inordinate amount of time making out with Ron in public. I'd come to terms with this tic of theirs but was always deeply grateful when I caught one without the other.

"Nice to see you, too, Ron. You heard about the candy cane card scare in town?"

"Not much of a scare," he said, not glancing up from his iMac.

"I don't know about that." I ran my hand across his counter. "Seems like there's a story there, if someone wants to do some digging."

This earned me a glare over the top of his bifocals. "Someone like you?"

"I'm the only other reporter here, aren't I?"

He returned his focus to his computer screen, sliding a sheet of paper across the countertop.

"What's this?" I asked.

"Read it."

I did, out loud. "Private Investigator Training. This fifteen-hour course covers all the necessary topics set out by Rule 7506.2300 and Minnesota Statute Chapter 326.32 regarding certified training of private detectives." That was followed by a lot of small print, which I pretended to skim. I'd already worked one case under the supervision of an attorney, as required by Minnesota law, but I had yet to take the required certification class. "Thanks, but this doesn't do me any good. This class is in Willmar, and it starts next week. That's a two-hour drive from here, one way."

"But only a thirty-minute drive from Paynesville."

My eyes narrowed. "Have you and Kennie been talking?"

He tugged his glasses to the tip of his nose and leaned back in his chair, studying me from beneath his bushy eyebrows. "I'm on the city council. I know the library is closing for three weeks."

He reached for a pencil and twirled it in his fingertips, visibly weighing whether he should tell me more. In the end, he decided to lay it all on the table. "It was going to be longer, except Kennie fought for you."

"What?" My brain was trying to make sense of his words. I must have misheard him, and he'd actually said "Kennie caught the flu," or "Kennie bought four ewes."

"Believe it," he said, a smile tugging at the corner of his mouth. "There were council members who thought it'd be more fiscally responsible to close the library entirely during the winter months. Kennie held strong that if it had to be closed at all, it should only be for three weeks."

I didn't know where to fit the revelation that Kennie might have done something nice for me of her own volition, so I opted for an offensive move instead. "Why didn't *you* fight for me?"

"Who says I didn't?" He pushed his glasses back up his nose. "It ultimately came down to closing the library for three weeks or turning off the Christmas lights early. Some people choose popular over smart."

I groaned. "So you knew I'd be coming here looking for extra work?"

He nodded. "And I knew I wouldn't have it. Go home. Visit your mom. It'll do you both good. While you're there, find out why their local paper is doing so well and get this class out of the way so you can start earning more PI money."

I hated being told what to do, especially when it was for my own good, so I kept on the attack. "Most people can't afford time off, you know. Most of us have to work. I couldn't pay for the class if I wanted to."

He opened his desk drawer and pulled out a prewritten check. "Thought you'd say that. Good thing you've got your Christmas bonus coming."

I took the check: $425. Exactly the cost of the class, made out to Willmar Community Education. I wasn't used to people doing nice stuff for me and didn't know if I was angry or happy. I kept my head down so he couldn't see my flushed cheeks.

"James?" His voice was soft.

"Yeah?" I asked.

"It's a favor to me." I'd never heard this note of concern in his voice before, and he'd had me cover some dangerous stories. "Now's not a good time to be a woman living alone, especially one who looks like you. Merry Christmas."

I tossed him a furtive glance, but he'd returned his attention to his computer. I think I'd just experienced our longest interaction ever.

"Thank you," I murmured, and backed out of the office with the check and class information in hand, feeling both cornered and cared for. It was uncomfortable in a way I liked.

Outside, a gust of wind blew the edges of my scratchy purple scarf into my face. To my left and to my right, the streets of my adopted hometown were bustling with people rushing to lunch at the Turtle Stew, or into the post office, or out of the dentist or attorney offices. I caught snatches of their conversations over the thin notes of Christmas music rolling out every time someone opened the door of the apothecary across the street. I thought I caught a trace of the metallic scent of an approaching snowstorm.

Somewhere in those moments, I made up my mind.

There it was, then. Settled. The day had finally arrived.

It was time to return to the small town that had formed me, scars and all.

Here I come, Paynesville.

Chapter 7

Sunday, December 13

If there's a phrase scarier to a twenty-nine-year-old woman than "Your room is just as you left it," I have yet to hear it.

Yet this was exactly what my mom uttered to me—after much hugging and clucking—as she walked me, Tiger Pop, and Luna up to the second floor of the old farmhouse. I couldn't help but acknowledge her Ants in the Pants physique—skinny legs, round belly and butt, mysteriously absent chest, just like the blue pants that came with the game of the same name—as I followed her up the narrow stairs. Somehow, her perfectly curled and dyed brown hair, sweet bland face, and eternal smile complemented her body.

She'd lived in this slope-ceilinged farmhouse my whole life, in this desolate spot ten miles from Paynesville, the nearest neighbor a country mile across winter-buried fields.

She and my dad had bought the farmhouse plus fifteen acres back in the '70s to "get away" from the cosmopolitan life of Saint Cloud, the smallish city they'd been living in when Mom found out she was pregnant with me. Even as a child, the isolation had made me feel claustrophobic rather than free. Yet just last spring, I'd fled Minneapolis for the countryside outside Battle Lake. How did that make sense?

These thoughts raced through my head at jackrabbit speed as I pushed open the door of my childhood bedroom, a place I hadn't visited since I'd moved out. When we got together, my mom came to me in Minneapolis. The last place I'd wanted to come was home, the source of my darkest pain. Yet here I was. There was no turning back.

I pushed open my door, no longer listening to my mother's chatter.

I watched with dread and anticipation, sucking in my breath as all was revealed.

Yup. Exactly as I left it.

Imagine gathering the most embarrassing person you've ever dated, a supposedly secret videotape of you acting out every 1980s MTV music video, and your junior high diary. Got those three things? OK, mash them into one big pile of shame, stir it with a crimping iron, and pour the resulting liquid into a paint can. The color you get is Time Machine Teal.

That's what my bedroom walls were painted with.

The trim was Mortification Mauve.

On top of that were Led Zeppelin and *Footloose*-era Kevin Bacon posters. Below were loaded bookshelves, a multicolored dresser with Garbage Patch stickers down the front, a worn quilt on a wrought iron bed with my childhood sock monkey perched in the center, all bathed in the lingering stench of Aqua Net and Love's Baby Soft.

It set me back on my heels.

"Jeez, Mom, you could have redecorated."

"It's not mine to redecorate." She'd always been a yes-woman, my mom. That also hadn't changed. "Would you like some supper?"

Chapter 8

The snow settles softly onto the killer's hat, plump, glistening flakes so large and whimsical that they make a tiny sound when they land.

The town is asleep, or close to it.

Ten o'clock on a Sunday night is considered late in farm country, where the animals rise before the sun. Even in town, where the farm-work gave way to waitressing, office, and health care jobs decades ago, people still live by the rhythm of an agricultural clock.

It is odd for the killer to undertake this mission in such familiar territory.

This hunt has taken longer than the rest to plan because the killer must decide whether to build the snowmen in advance or create them from scratch in the women's yards.

In the end, the most sensible route is a compromise.

Snowman starter kits.

The trunk of the sedan, this time a blue four-door Dodge, is packed with three huge white globes of snow, each as large as a prized pump-kin. Six more are balanced in the back seat, three basketball size, three cantaloupe size.

It takes only moments to roll each ball across the virgin snow to pick up more girth, then construct the three-foot-tall snowmen in the center of each yard, wind a scarf around their necks, pop in two button eyes and stick arms, and balance a candy cane on the edge of each branchy claw.

Even if people were out and about, few things are less threatening than stumbling upon a person building a snowman.

Targeting multiple women is a recent addition to the master plan, something introduced in Minnesota.

Seven women in White Plains received a candy cane.

Only one, along with her mutt, drew the short straw.

Sending out seven calling cards for one killing was accidental. Previously, in Chicago and then Wisconsin, there had been only a single calling card, followed by a single death. But in White Plains, there were so surprisingly many viable candidates, so many beautiful, trashy brunettes selling themselves so cheaply online, that in the end, it had been necessary to educate more than one.

Killing seven would have been ridiculous, but *contacting* seven, forcing the misguided females to reflect on the error of their ways?

That was a good idea.

It'd been a happy accident, the effect that the seven calling cards had had. It'd be a while before any White Plains woman exposed herself freely to the world, and wasn't that the point? So the killer adjusted. More women threatened equaled effective behavior changes, so more women would be targeted.

Building seven snowmen, however, simply is not practical. Fortunately, only three women in this town truly need the wake-up call.

The killer pats the last bit of snow into place on the third and final snowman of the night. It's a little small compared to the other two snowmen, but extra buttons provide a smile for this one. The other two had only eyes.

The killer reaches for a tissue. The night wind is bitter, the snow-man-building tedious, especially when she's so loud and demanding inside the killer's winter jacket. Her complaints are constant even though she's well bundled in her Jackie O winter gear.

Don't jostle so much.

Hurry, I'm cold.

Don't be so stupid.

The nagging becomes grating.

When the job is finally finished, the killer steps forward to knock on the front door of the final house, then melts into the shadows around the corner. The snowflakes fall more softly here.

Inside, footsteps sound. She's been watching the ten o'clock news. She should know better than to answer the door in her pajamas. She pulls back a curtain and glances out the window first, maybe, surveying the landscape of her front yard before deciding to let down her guard.

In any case, she opens the door and spots the smallish snowman with its button smile. She laughs and claps her hands. Does she think a secret admirer has left a surprise? If so, she's right, in a way. She slides her feet into slippers and skips through the snow.

Is it her childhood she's thinking of? Fresh, fat snow, hot chocolate, sleigh bells?

She's standing immediately in front of the snowman when she notices the candy cane hanging from its stick finger. Her hand goes to her throat. She stumbles as she backs away, half crawling and half running into the house.

She leaves a slipper behind in her terror-rimmed haste.

But it's too late.

The killer has already slipped inside.

Chapter 9

Monday, December 14

My mom had left me to reacquaint myself with my blast-from-the-past bedroom, giving me space until the morning, when she couldn't stand it any longer. She woke me up at 7:00 a.m. and began stuffing food into me, peppering me with questions, stroking my arm as if to make certain that I was actually sitting at her dining room table. It became annoying, but I had to admit her scrambled eggs were even better than I remembered.

"Thanks, Mom." I accepted the pancakes and orange juice she passed my way. "Fattening me up for the oven?"

She stood with her hands clasped in front of her, the same beaming smile that had lit up her face since Tiger Pop, Luna, and I had arrived.

"You could use some thickening," she said. "You're skin and bones."

"Check this out." I pulled up my shirt and pooched out my belly. I could pull off lean with the right clothes, but I had an Uncle Fester stomach. "Pretty impressive, huh? No bones there."

She shook her head like she didn't know what to do with me. It was a gesture as familiar to me as my own face growing up. I was surprised by how loved it made me feel. "Are you sure you have to go to that detective class today?" she asked. "We've hardly had a chance to visit. You haven't even been into town yet."

"Town" meant Paynesville, and she was right. Because her farmhouse was so far into the country, I'd easily and purposely skirted Paynesville to get here. I wasn't ready for it yet.

"I'm going to be here for at least a week." I'd told her this several times already. I think she just liked to hear me say it. "We'll have plenty of time to catch up."

"You sure Johnny can't join us?"

I sighed involuntarily. Hot, sexy Johnny Leeson and I'd been seriously dating for a few weeks. He was a blond Adonis with lean hips and large hands, and he got my blood humming like nobody's business. He was also smart, sweet, and supportive, which was exactly why I was sure I was going to mess up the relationship. To stall the inevitable crash and burn, I'd put up boundaries. No telling each other we loved each other or sleeping together for six months.

It was tough work, a first for me, really, and I couldn't say that I liked it. I did like *Johnny*, though, and I wanted to keep him around as long as I could, even if it meant pretending I was someone I wasn't.

"He and his mom flew to Texas to stay with his aunt. He won't be around this Christmas."

She fluffed the edges of her hair. "Maybe he can join us for Easter, then?"

"Mom, I'm here now. Let's just focus on that, 'kay?" I could feel my blood pressure rising. She hadn't changed at all, which was both good and bad. Good because she'd always been an attentive parent. Bad because *I* had changed, and it left me feeling older than her somehow. It was uncomfortable.

She shook her head, her voice sad. "I was just asking. It'd be nice to see him, you know. And his mother. We had such a nice visit in Battle Lake in August." Mom cupped her elbows while she spoke. "What about Mrs. Berns? What is she doing for Christmas?"

Mrs. Berns was the first ride-or-die friend I'd ever had. She was under five feet tall, over ninety years old, and she lampshaded everything. I missed her something terrible, which just added to my annoyance at my mom's line of questioning.

"Visiting family in Fargo."

"Hmm. It would be wonderful to see her," Mom said dreamily, totally missing my mood, like she always had. "And Mrs. Leeson and Johnny. Just wonderful."

"All right," I said, my tone unexpectedly harsh. "I'll see what I can do. Is that good enough?"

It felt like the little farmhouse was closing in on me all of a sudden, and my world was shrinking with it. I hadn't even been here twenty-four hours. It didn't help that I'd slept so poorly last night. I kept tossing and turning and waking up to find Kevin Bacon staring at me.

I sucked in a deep breath and rubbed my face. "Look, I'm sorry, but I have to head out, all right? The class starts in an hour, and all the roads might not be plowed yet."

She disappeared into the kitchen and returned with a brown paper sack. "I packed you a lunch."

"Of course you did." I stood and gave her a peck on the forehead. "You're going to be fine with Tiger Pop and Luna?"

She patted Luna's head. The dog had clung to her side since we'd arrived. "I'll relish the company." Her lips drew tight. "When are you going to be home?"

"Mom."

She held out her hands. "I want to know if I should cook supper for one or two, that's all. I'm not trying to track your every movement."

I forced my voice to be even. "I'll be home for supper, OK?"

Her smile was bright enough to read by. "I'm making your favorite."

She was my mom. *Everything* she cooked was my favorite. Still, I couldn't escape that house fast enough. It wasn't just her, or even my room. *None* of it had changed. The kitchen had the same blue-flowered wallpaper, chipped cupboards, and Goodwill plates. The dining room table was the same one I'd chipped a tooth on when I'd fallen into it when roller-skating in the house—against the rules—at twelve. Dad's record collection in the den was exactly as I'd last seen it.

Even their bedroom was the same, a dusty little space with a single photo of them together the day my dad returned from the Vietnam War holding his honorable discharge papers and a Purple Heart. The picture was in color, but a weird 1969 version that was both brighter and less distinct than current color photography. The photo showed him short and compact, maybe five seven to my mom's five four. His jaw was set, his eyes tired, a little scared, hopeful. He held my mom around the waist, close. She was grinning.

That was the only photo of him she displayed.

Altogether, it was enough to make any reasonable person climb the walls.

I offered to help with dishes, but she shooed me out of the house. I was ashamed of how grateful I was to go. Thirty minutes of driving southwest, and I located the Willmar Community Education center with little trouble, right off the main drag. The building was squat and gray, the classroom the first room on the right inside the doors.

I was surprised at the amount of apprehension I felt walking inside. Entering a classroom at the ripe age of twenty-nine, even if it was at PI school, was a little like taking your first step out of the bathroom at a nudist colony.

Is everyone else going to be naked, too?

Chapter 10

The classroom had the off-gassing smell of new carpet. It was modern, with a whiteboard consuming one wall, a podium and table in the front, and a couple dozen chair desks arranged in rows. An LCD projector hung from the ceiling like a mechanical uvula.

A man was writing on the board in black marker: WELCOME TO PI CLASS. I'M MR. DENNY. He appeared to be in his fifties but took good care of himself.

I chose the farthest seat in the rear, closest to the door without putting my back to it. You know—where all the smart kids sit. Six other students were already in their chairs. I was gratified to see that I was the only one under forty, but disappointed that I was the only woman. Two of the men seemed to know each other. The other four guys sat on the periphery, like me. I opened my notebook and began doodling, now wishing I'd never left the farmhouse.

A few minutes later, another woman entered. I watched her through the partial shield of my hair. She was about my height and weight, but blonde and a decade younger. Judging by her amazing dye job, the parade of trendy bracelets ringing her arm, and the expensive, orange blossom–tinged perfume that emanated off her, she either wasn't from the Willmar area or had left for a bit and only recently returned home. Her purse cinched it. I'd seen the soft black Coach satchel on Jennifer Aniston's arm in the latest issue of *People* magazine when I'd accidentally dropped it at the library, open to that page. (And then the next page. And the next.)

The woman grabbed a stack of papers from Mr. Denny's desk, smiled secretively at him, and walked out. Three minutes later, he began class.

"Welcome!" He made eye contact with each of us. His gaze was unnervingly direct. "You're all here today because you want to be private investigators in the state of Minnesota. To do so, you must complete a fifteen-hour certification course, which this is, and six thousand hours of supervised work. Does that surprise any of you?"

No one spoke.

"Good. I'd like to add a third qualification: to be a PI, you must also be observant. Who can describe the person who just removed your personal, private, highly detailed student files from my desk?"

Some of the men began buzzing. One spoke without raising his hand. "Young. Eighteen maybe. Blonde and blue-eyed. An office worker here?"

The man next to him nodded. "Same thing I saw. Except she wore a lot of jewelry, too. I heard it clink."

"Excellent," Mr. Denny said, nodding. "Anyone else have anything to add?"

You couldn't have paid me to volunteer my input. Not only was I the only woman in the room, but I also had a rule against drawing attention to myself. It never ended well. I slumped lower in my seat and, in doing so, accidentally knocked my notebook to the ground. Mr. Denny's hawk eyes found me. He glanced down at a sheet of paper on his desk.

"My-ra James, is it?"

"It's pronounced 'Mira,'" I corrected him, reluctantly. "Rhymes with 'can of beer-ah.'" *Wow. Totally unnecessary.*

His face spasmed. "Mira, then. Did you see the woman?"

"Yeah." I tipped my head at the clot of guys, forcing out the words. "They got it right. She was blonde, lots of bracelets but no earrings or rings, and I'd put her closer to twenty than eighteen."

He nodded approvingly. "You also think she's an office worker?"

"No. I think she's your daughter." Once I started, I couldn't stop. "Based on how she's dressed and smells, she definitely goes to college in a big city, probably on one of the coasts. You two gave each other a look like you'd done this before but not recently, so I'm guessing this is something of a tradition for the first day of class. At least until she went off to college. She's home on Christmas break?" I clamped my mouth shut. Too much. I had said too much.

He pursed his lips. "She goes to Berkeley. Any guess what she's studying?"

"Sociology."

He threw back his head, and to my great relief, he laughed. "Close enough. Psychology. And we'll save any psychoanalyzing of that choice. Very nice job, Mira. What made you think she was my daughter?"

I tried to form an invisibility shield, but that didn't work. In for a penny. "You both acted too familiar for her to be a colleague or an acquaintance. That meant she's either family or your girlfriend. I figured a woman who dresses like her would never date a guy who wears a corduroy blazer with corduroy pants, and gambled that you"—here I indicated his wedding ring—"are too decent a person to cheat on your wife. That leaves family, and since you two have the same nose, I guessed daughter."

Mr. Denny drew his hand over his face. The other students swiveled to stare at me as my cheeks cooked. When Mr. Denny finally pulled his hand away, his eyes were dancing. "Nice work. Gentlemen, take note. Body language and interactions can give you as much, if not more, information than written facts. Now, let's get down to business."

I was relieved that the rest of the class took the shape of a lecture, with Mr. Denny discussing the definition and goals of private investigation, other foundational terms, the limits of a PI's rights and jurisdiction, and case studies. There was no need to call myself out again. By noon, my wrist was sore from taking notes and my head was full, but in a good way. For the first time in my life, I was beginning to wonder if I had what it took to be a real-life PI.

The lecture wound down, and me and my fellow students were gathering our notebooks and reaching for our jackets when Mr. Denny made his last announcement for the day.

It was a doozy.

"Most of this class will be a combination of lecture and films, but I have one out-of-class project for you." His expression was grim. "There are seven students in this class. I'm about to reveal seven secrets. It's your job to match the secret with its owner by the end of Friday's class. The only way to earn an A in here is to connect them all accurately." He crossed his arms and stared at us.

The guy two desks to my right and one forward blanched, and not at the part about acing the class. The other five appeared mildly interested. I wondered if the whole world was about to find out I was sleeping in a room with a Kevin Bacon poster.

"Secret 1," Mr. Denny said, his voice booming, "is that someone here served in the military."

Harmless enough. My money was on the guy who wore his hair in a buzz cut.

"Secret 2," Mr. Denny continued, "is that someone in here is cheating on his wife." The blancher went so white he was almost blue. *Bingo.*

"Secret 3, someone here has a drinking problem. Secret 4, someone here was fired from their job a month ago but still pretends to go to work in the morning. Secret 5, one of you was born in Albania. Secret 6, someone in here has a prosthetic leg, and Secret 7, one of you is on the FBI watch list."

Shit. I hoped I was secret 3.

The fiftysomething student with unnaturally black hair raised his hand. He'd introduced himself as Leo and had been the one chatting with the buzz-cut older guy at the start of class. "Isn't some of that information private?"

"Exactly," Mr. Denny said, with no hint of sarcasm.

"What if we don't correctly match the seven secrets with the seven students?" asked Gene, Leo's buzz-cut friend.

"Nothing, except that the highest grade you can earn is a B. It won't affect licensing, as you just have to pass this class to fulfill the requirement."

Since I was inquisitive by nature, I was jazzed about this assignment, but I was clearly the only one. The guys' expressions ranged from annoyed to *something is crawling in my underwear.*

"Are there more questions?" Mr. Denny asked.

Nobody had any.

I grabbed my coat and casually strolled to the women's bathroom. I waited in a stall for six minutes. When I exited, the classroom was empty except for the teacher speaking at the front with the blancher. I stood to the side of the door so they couldn't see me and tried to eavesdrop.

I caught only the student's name—Edgar—and some mention of a lawsuit. The conversation ended abruptly, and I ducked into the nearest unlocked classroom. Fortunately, the lights didn't turn on when I entered, allowing me to watch Edgar storm out, followed by a calm Mr. Denny.

I counted to twenty-five before leaving, following the signs to the main office in the center of the building. I passed three classrooms on the way, all of them dark. The beige Berber carpet swallowed my footsteps. An office worker with a face as creased as a winter apple glanced up as I entered the office.

"May I help you?" she asked pleasantly.

"I hope so." I rested my purse on the counter and leaned forward with what I hoped was a friendly smile. "I'm taking the PI licensure class."

"How exciting!" She sounded genuine.

I kept my smile pinned in place. "Yeah, it's only the first day, but I really like it. Mr. Denny seems like a great teacher."

She nodded but didn't offer anything on that subject.

"The reason I'm here is kind of embarrassing," I continued.

She leaned forward. I had her.

"You see, everyone in class introduced themselves at the beginning, but I was sort of out of my element and too nervous to pay attention." It was true that everyone had introduced themselves, but only first names. I needed first *and* last names, correctly spelled, to begin researching. "I can't remember anyone's name. Of course they all remember mine because I'm the only woman in there."

She nodded knowingly. "You want the class enrollment list?"

"If possible," I said, nodding, but not too eagerly. "I don't need any student IDs or personal information, obviously, just first and last names so I don't feel like a loser when I come to class tomorrow."

"Not a problem." She typed swiftly on her keyboard, then swiveled in her chair to face the printer. "I can print names, addresses, and phone numbers, unless they're unlisted." She grabbed the paper from the printer and turned around.

"Thanks!" I took the hot sheet. "You've been a great help."

She smiled. "Happy holidays."

I waited until I reached my car to peek at the register. It was easy to place names with faces with the list in front of me. Next to Edgar's name, I wrote, *Cheater*. Gene received the label *ex-military*. There was no Leo on the list, but there was a Leotrim Hamza. Next to his name I wrote, *born in Albania?* It'd be fairly easy to confirm the origin of the name.

Three down, four to go.

I still wasn't sure if I was "drinking problem" or "FBI watch list." I definitely had a problem even though I'd been mostly dry for a few months; I just didn't believe my drinking history was public information, as I mostly imbibed at home. I penciled both possible secrets next to my name with a question mark and left the rest blank.

The rush from the class assignment put me in such a good mood that I drove to the Kandi Mall to buy my mom two Christmas presents: a set of navy-blue plates and a new quilt for her bed. It took half my savings, but I couldn't bear to have her use the same bedspread that she'd slept under with my dad.

I was walking out of Sears when I spotted Kent, one of the six guys from class. He hadn't said a word all day, which drew its own sort of attention. His hands were shoved in the pockets of his khaki pants, and he was meandering toward the appliances and tools section.

I decided to follow.

Tailing someone on foot was impossibly hard. It seemed easy in movies. You just stayed out of your target's sight line while keeping them in yours, yes? People were erratic, though, and sometimes you had to duck and hide, which allowed them to slip away.

Compounding the difficulty was the fact that I was lugging two unwieldy bags, one containing dishes and the other stuffed with a jewel-toned quilt. I darted behind racks of green and red sweaters, peered through mannequins' arms, and generally did my best Inspector Clouseau impression, but to my great disappointment, Kent didn't engage in any unusual behavior.

He peered at a price tag on a deep fryer, walked another ten feet before picking up a power drill, and ran his fingers over a table saw, but that was it. Christmas music jingled merrily from hidden speakers, and tinsel and festive ornaments accompanied every display. I was about to give up on him when he turned abruptly, forcing me to drop to my knees behind a table.

"Can I help you?"

I peered up. An angular, pockmarked teenager wearing a blue Sears shirt and a Santa hat stared down at me. I grabbed blindly at the nearest table and held up the first solid object I touched. "Can you tell me how this works?"

A puzzled line sprouted between his eyebrows. "A hammer?"

Kent strode past, his face forward. He suddenly seemed to have a destination in mind. I stood, setting the hammer on the hand tools table. "Sorry, I must have been looking at it upside down. Thank you."

I darted after Kent, but a group of women crowded the housewares aisle, cooing over a set of margarita glasses with stems shaped like cactuses. I pushed my way through, but my awkward bags held me up.

When I reached the other side, Kent had vanished.

Chapter 11

Back at home, Mom and I hand-decorated Christmas cards in her scrap-booking room. She had lots of questions about PI class, and I was excited enough about it that I answered them all. I didn't tell her about the seven-secrets challenge, though. It'd made perfect sense in the room but felt a little seedy outside it. Sure, much of a PI's job involves catching cheaters and liars in the act. It just seemed in poor taste to talk about it.

For supper, Mom and I ate her amazing Tater Tot hotdish and french-sliced green beans doused in a warm vinegar dressing. It was fabulous, and I ate too much. At eight o'clock, however, I realized I was suddenly crawling the walls.

Again.

I studied my mom. She was bent over the sink, washing plates that she then handed me to dry. She was a good woman who'd dealt with my father's alcoholism with tolerance and a truckload of head-in-the-sand, but she'd always been there for me. I loved her, but I was beginning to realize that four conscious hours in this house was my limit.

I decided I might as well take the leap and confront the rest of my past, if it'd get me out of here. "I think I'm going to run into town and see if there's anyone I know at Sir Falstaff's."

The fear-chased-by-disappointment look on her face shamed me, but I couldn't stay here any longer. The walls were closing in.

"Sure, honey. You know Patsy Gilver works there now? Just drive safely."

That'd always been our code, and we both knew what it meant: Don't drink and drive. Ever. I'd been stupid enough to violate that rule in the past. Actually, I'd made an Olympic sport out of assifying myself under the influence of alcohol, which was why last August I'd finally declared a moratorium on drinking. I'd done great through September and even refused the many temptations of Oktoberfest season. Come November, though, I'd slipped and had a beer plus done some shots.

Then I'd been shot *at*.

That horrible night had left me with occasional nightmares and an inclination to overreact to loud noises. Subsequently, I was feeling due for a tall cool one, and what better place for that than the town that had taught me to drink and then given me a reason to?

I brushed my hair and slapped on honey-flavored lip gloss before giving my mom a hug. The slicing December wind almost changed my mind, but I knew my car would heat quickly. I got her rumbling and took a left out of the driveway, wondering if I really wanted to head to Paynesville's only bar.

I could instead choose one of two in the nearby town of Lake Henry. Lake Henry's bars had sat on opposite sides of the street from one another since the dawn of humankind. I'd thrown back my first drink, a lime vodka sour the color of antifreeze, in one of them, back before they carded teenagers.

Sneaking into a bar was a rite of passage when I was in high school, an embarrassingly easy one, and after my dad's death, I found that the more I drank, the more friends I acquired, at least for the night.

That memory tasted lonely.

The idea of catching up with Patsy in Paynesville wasn't that much more enticing, however. She'd been a sweetheart in high school, kind to everyone, including Manslaughter Mark's wild daughter. I supposed she was the closest thing to a friend I'd had, but the thought of seeing her again filled me with dread. I didn't know which I feared more: her not remembering me, forcing me to flush my single positive memory from high school, or her knowing exactly who I was, which would in turn force me to face the person I'd been.

I slapped my steering wheel. I was behaving like a sissy pants, as Mrs. Berns would say. I was twenty-nine years old; I had a bachelor's degree and a decent job—no one had to know what it paid—great friends in Battle Lake, and a sweet boyfriend. For now, anyhow. I tapped my blinker, choosing the right turn to Paynesville rather than the left to Lake Henry.

The drive was hauntingly routine. I probably could have made it with my eyes closed. I counted off the houses, initially spaced far apart and then clustering as I neared town, remembering who had boarded the orange ISD #741 bus from each. I passed the Skjonsby house, the Notch house, the Miller house, crested the hill to the golf course as the landscape abruptly morphed from winter-scalded prairie to a hardwood forest and hills, and finally, there it was.

Paynesville.

The town was laid out in the small valley below, a flat plate of a village meandering along with no real plan, home to 2,300 or so people, five miles from the nearest lake. Christmas lights glittered like jewels scattered across the otherwise dull vista.

As I drove down the hill and into town, I spotted the familiar lit-up candy canes and wreaths festooning the streetlights, and huge snowflake lights strung across the main intersections. Saint Joseph Catholic Church's life-size nativity scene had been erected on the edge of downtown, ready for the actors to take their places for the three nights leading up to Christmas.

Amazingly, the predictability of it all thawed me a tiny bit.

I'd expected the opposite reaction.

Sir Falstaff's Bar and Grill had changed hands a few times since I'd left town, but I saw it still had the same knocked-back, small-town charm I remembered. The outside was plain, but when I stood before the entrance, warm laughter and the welcoming smell of french fries and fresh-tapped beer wafted out.

This was it.

I was going to step back in time and face my high school demons. I shored up my walls and pulled open the door.

Chapter 12

Walking through the tinseled doorway of Sir Falstaff's, I became aware that my shoulders were hunched and my face turned to the side as if anticipating a blow. I willed myself to relax. Nobody had even glanced up when I'd entered.

Immediately inside the door were a dozen or so tall tables circled by stools. Two pool tables and four dartboards made up the rear, and a huge circular bar dominated the far right.

Three women sat at a tall table nearby, drinking daiquiris and leaning in close as one of them shared what I gathered from their laughter was a racy story. In the rear, a couple played darts, smiling at one another in a carefree, constant way that suggested they were early in their relationship.

Four men posted spots at the bar, none of them sitting next to each other, all of them amiably watching one of three TVs and tipping their beer mugs. Shania Twain sang sassily in the background. I didn't recognize the bartender, or anyone for that matter, and I felt strangely let down. I was about to leave when the swinging kitchen doors opened, and Patsy Gilver sailed through cradling a plastic basket of steaming onion rings.

She carried herself as though she'd had a few hard years, but mostly, she looked the same. She still frosted her hair and wore it in a ponytail, though she'd grown out the scrunchy bangs. Good move. I don't know why America forgot to send rural Minnesota girls a memo back in the

'80s telling us to stop dividing our bangs into two equal parts, one a tube that curled upward and the other a claw that grasped down, but some of us still carried a grudge.

Patsy'd always been petite but pear-shaped and still was, carrying a few extra pounds in her hips. My belly nodded sympathetically. It could relate.

I opened my mouth to call out her name, but no sound came out. What if she turned that kind smile my direction, and her eyes stayed blank? What if she hadn't even liked me back in high school and had just been nice because she felt sorry for me? What if—

"NO! Miranda Rayn James, is that you?"

She actually squealed, and a big, dorky smile forced its way onto my face. "Patsy?"

"Whee!" She tossed the basket in front of one of the guys at the bar and rushed over to hug me. Her hair smelled like fryer grease and apple shampoo. "Do you know how long it's been?" she said.

I did. What surprised me was how good it suddenly felt to be here. I'd built Paynesville up into a mythical monster, the place that had chewed me up and spit me out and then backed up to drive over what was left. It was the tangible representative of everything bad that'd ever happened to me. Could it be that I'd given it too much power? That nobody here had thought about me nearly as much as I'd thought about them?

"Too long," I said. I felt my smile down in my bones.

"Come on over to the bar. Let me buy you a drink." She herded me to the spot farthest from the men sprinkled around it. "The kitchen closes in an hour, so I'm off soon. You have to stay here until then so we can catch up. What're you drinking?"

It was all happening so fast. The glass bottles glittered at me, some green, or blue, or clear, but all tantalizing. I could be grown-up and have wine, but my guess was they chilled the merlot here. "Tall vodka club soda, three limes." It was the adult version of my first drink.

She was staring at me and shaking her head. "You look great, Mira. Really. Just like you did in high school, only with better hair."

It was exactly what I'd thought about her, except in my head, it'd been judgy. Her face was guileless, though, sweet and open. Nobody would ever say that about me. I had a sudden thought. "Hey, remember when we dressed up like Jimmy Page and Pamela Des Barres for Halloween?"

My Led Zeppelin adoration had taken root my freshman year in high school. It had started because I had a crush on a boy who was a huge Zep-head, and it stuck once I listened to the music. Patsy didn't really know who they were, but she'd liked the idea of dressing up as a 1970s hippie groupie chick. (I'd been Jimmy Page, of course.) So out we'd gone, me wearing a velvet suit and pointy shoes, my long hair made wavy, and Patsy in a flowing dress with a flower in her hair.

She giggled. "Yeah. And how everyone thought we were Dudley Moore and Rhoda Morgenstern?"

I squeezed one of the lime wedges balanced on the edge of the drink I'd just been handed. A sour squirt landed on my lip, and I licked it off. "Forgot about that part."

She squeezed my arm. "It was still a fun night. So what have you been up to? Tell me everything. I heard you went off to live in the Cities."

Turned out, she'd never left town except for a handful of family vacations. She'd married and divorced and had two kids, replacing her dreams with theirs. My living in Minneapolis appeared a grand adventure to her, even though I'd spent most of it skipping class, waiting tables, and drinking too much.

I was halfway through telling my story and listening to hers when she bought me another drink and, ten minutes later, another. Then a fourth. By the time she punched out, I was putting the "tip" in "tipsy" and we were laughing more than talking.

I wiped the happy tears from my eyes. She'd just reminded me of the time we tried out for the Barkettes, the high school dance squad, claiming we were doing it as a protest when really, we wanted to learn how to dance. We'd failed the tryouts miserably.

"I don't think it helped that we called them the *Barf*ettes," I said.

"Probably not," she agreed, chuckling. "And the football team was so cute that year. We probably could have gotten a date if we'd made the squad. You seeing anyone now?"

I told her about Johnny, and just saying his name out loud made me flush with warmth. I couldn't stop gushing about how kind, and smart, and funny, and good-looking he was. Talking about him made me miss him terribly.

"Is he good in bed?" she asked, a mischievous glint in her eyes.

"I don't know. We haven't slept together yet."

She couldn't have looked more shocked if I'd told her that he was my brother. I knew why, too. You see, I'd partied like it was 1999 all through high school, or at least after my dad died, but I'd graduated a virgin. I hadn't wanted anyone to know that, however. It would have ruined my reputation.

So I talked big, and I put my hand in the back Wrangler pocket of my share of losers when the occasion called for it, but I kept my legs together. All that changed after I moved away from Paynesville, of course. But while I was in high school, except for some painfully unskilled and unproductive huffing and grinding, I'd been chaste.

"How come?" she asked.

It was a logical question. One I had a really hard time coming up with an answer for with my vodka-fogged mind. I knew that at one time, I must have had a good reason for not yet sleeping with Johnny, a really important one, but I couldn't for the life of me remember it.

Best to let it go and do what he and I both wanted to do, I decided. "Do you have a cell phone?"

She laughed like I'd just asked her if she had a car. Then she saw I was serious and apologized, handing over her phone. "Are you calling your mom?"

"Nope, Johnny. Excuse me."

I stumbled to a far corner, realizing even as I did so that my words were slurred, perfectly reflecting my critical-thinking abilities. I also felt ten feet tall, bulletproof, and as horny as a goat. It was *time*. What'd I been waiting for? I loved Johnny, and I was pretty sure he loved me. Plus, we were consenting adults. He could hop a plane out of Texas and be in Paynesville in a matter of hours. We'd get a hotel room. It'd be romantic. I'd tell him I loved him, and he'd be happy to hear it. We'd wake up in each other's arms on crisp white sheets, our smiles blissful, bluebirds braiding my hair.

Click.

"Hi, this is Johnny. Please leave a message."

I blinked, one eye closing a little later than the other. A message? Well, I supposed I could. "Johnny, this is Mira." I dropped my voice so it was breathy, husky. "Guess what I'm wearing?"

I tried to concentrate on my body from the neck down. Blue jeans and a T-shirt, only I saw four legs where there should have been two. I was disappointed. I'd hoped I'd have a better answer to my own question. "Um, I'm wearing *down*, that's what. I want you. I want you bad. We should consummate our relationship. Right now. I love you, baby."

Satisfied that my message was clear, I hung up. Or at least I wanted to, but I had no idea how to work the phone.

I swerved over to Patsy, who stared up at the TV. This drinking was super fun. Why had I given it up?

"Here ya go." I handed her the phone, but she didn't take it. Her eyes were glued to the set. I followed her gaze to the grim-faced reporter standing in front of a white house with black shutters, klieg lights casting a deep shadow behind him. The front yard was drifted with snow and contained a sad little snowman wearing a bright scarf and a lopsided smile.

Reflected police car cherries pulsated off the reporter. I closed one eye so I could focus. The ribbon underneath him read "River Grove, Minnesota."

"Police confirm a woman's body was found in her home this evening by her water-delivery service. We have learned from an unnamed source that police believe she is the most recent victim of the Candy Cane Killer, though no official information is being released until the family has been notified."

"Oh no," I said, feeling a sickening jolt. I went from drunk to sober with unnatural speed. "He got another one."

Patsy turned to me. Tears were coursing down her face. "I know that house. It's Natalie Garcia's. Mira, she was our homecoming queen!"

Chapter 13

Several glasses of water, three cups of coffee, and two hours of trying to calm down Patsy made me as sober as a nun and brokenhearted. See, not only had Natalie been homecoming queen, but she'd been my best friend back in sixth grade. She and I had practiced kissing with pillows and sworn we'd never tell anyone. She was the person with whom I'd first experimented with lip gloss and mascara, and the girl I giggled with on the edge of the playground the day I stole my dad's dirty magazines and smuggled them to school.

We'd started an underground newspaper that year, posting silly knock-knock jokes, ridiculous rumors about teachers ("Is it just me, or does Mrs. Thielen smell like Mary Jane?"), and made-up horoscopes. We'd called it the *Pee-ville Papers*.

It'd flown off the shelves.

After pinkie swearing to never get married unless it was a double wedding and that the only thing that would come between us was a war or maybe a really bad earthquake, we'd grown apart by seventh grade.

Natalie had discovered boys, and I'd stuck with books.

We stayed friendly, in a distant way. Come high school, Natalie became very popular. She was funny, always seemed interested in people when she talked to them, and was a good storyteller. She had charisma, I guess—that and a great head of wavy, dark hair.

My only clear memory of her those last couple years in Paynesville was at my dad's funeral. She and Patsy had both attended, the only two kids I remembered in that big, empty church. I'd felt too ashamed of my dad's car accident to talk to them, and after the funeral, I hung on to that feeling, shutting most everyone out. Patsy, on the other hand, had kept in touch with everyone from high school who still lived in the area, and she knew Natalie well enough to recognize her house. River Grove, where Natalie's place was located, was the next town over heading northwest on Highway 23, not more than a fifteen-minute drive from Paynesville.

"She was a nurse, but she threw those Coddled Cook parties—you know, the ones where they show you how to use kitchen gadgets? That's why I was at her house. She never married. She said she wanted to go to medical school someday and that her career was always going to be her focus." Patsy blew her nose again.

I nodded miserably. "It's terrible, Patsy."

"God, her parents! They must have just found out. I have to go to them."

That's exactly the kind of person Patsy was: golden, through and through. "Do you need a ride?"

"No. Want to come with?"

The thought made my stomach clench violently. At will, I could call up the autumn scent of rotting leaves and the Old Spice the reporting police officer had worn when he showed up at the farmhouse to tell us my dad was dead. I could hear my mom's wail, the thump as she fell to the floor in a sobbing heap. Me, left standing alone in front of the officer.

No, I wouldn't be coming with, though I hated my cowardice. "I can't, Patsy. I have to get back to my mom. I can check on your kids, though, if you want."

"They're with their dad. They're fine." She nodded reassuringly. "Thanks, though. I'll call you."

We embraced in a long, sad hug. She went in the kitchen to gather her coat and purse, and I walked into the frigid night.

In the foyer, I spotted a white sheet of paper with a red, blue, and black flag on it: WOMEN'S SELF-DEFENSE CLASSES. CERTIFIED INSTRUCTOR, FOURTH-DEGREE BLACK BELT. LEARN TO DEFEND YOURSELF IN ONE WEEK.

I ripped off a slip of paper with the phone number, location, and times, and shuffled to my Toyota.

Chapter 14

Day two of the PI class was supposed to focus on Minnesota statutes regulating private investigators and the ethical code of the PI field, but the classroom was vibrating with talk of the second murder.

"Should we just get it out of the way?" Mr. Denny finally asked, holding up his hands. It was the third time Gene and Leo's whispering had interrupted him. "It's the death in River Grove, isn't it?"

Leo nodded. "That's two dead women within sixty miles of here, and the police don't have anything to go on. And this wacko's been at it for three winters!"

The murmurs and nods passed through the class like a fever.

Mr. Denny crossed his arms and leaned back against his desk. "Before I opened my own PI firm, I used to be a police officer. In Minneapolis, twenty-three years. I can tell you they're doing everything they can, in partnership with the FBI. Once the killer crossed state lines, this became a federal investigation."

"But how hard can it be to catch someone who sends calling cards, for Christ's sake?" This from buzz-cut Gene. "Seven women in White Plains got targeted, three in River Grove."

"What?" I asked. It was the first thing I'd said out loud in class today. "*Three* women in River Grove were targeted?"

Gene turned to face me. Although he'd seen me before, he seemed to be finally *looking* at me, and I recognized his expression. I'd witnessed more of it in the last couple days than I'd seen in my life: concern and pity. Every brunette in the state was probably on the receiving end of the same stare and understood what it felt like to be a bull's-eye.

"It was on the news this morning, ma'am," he said politely. "The murderer left a snowman with a candy cane in front of the lady's house before he killed her. At least two other women in town had identical snowmen in front of their houses, and the police are checking to make sure there aren't more." He turned back to Mr. Denny. "Wouldn't it make sense for any woman who receives something strange to call the police?"

"It's December, the week before Christmas. Millions of unexpected gifts are being exchanged every day." Mr. Denny's voice was resigned. "This killer knows what he's doing, I'm afraid."

Leo clenched his fists. "Can you teach us something to help catch him?"

Mr. Denny shook his head. "On an investigation of this scale, the best thing any of us can do is stay out of the way and contact the police if we see or hear anything relevant. Back to work, OK?"

As he distributed the test, one of those fat, lazy winter flies started buzzing around my head, as noisy as a chainsaw. I swiped at it and glanced around, hoping no one would notice. It was like having a loud finger pointing at me, telling the world I was stinky. I shooed it again and sniffed my armpit. That's what I was doing when Mr. Denny passed me my test.

"Good luck," he said, his expression puzzled.

"Oh, I was just . . . thank you." I desperately wanted to tell him that I did not, in fact, smell, and that I'd showered and brushed my teeth this morning. Some things shook out worse in the explanation, though. Damn fly.

I watched with satisfaction as it flew toward Gene like a drunken marble, but the happiness lasted only a moment. My mind careened back to Natalie, as it had a hundred times since I'd watched last night's news. I remembered the sad, shy smile she'd had for me at my dad's funeral, her black blazer stuffed with shoulder pads in the style we all wore that year, the momentary sense that I wasn't alone that quickly disappeared under the permanence of the loss of a parent, no matter how shitty they were.

The test suddenly felt like an outrageous waste of time. I normally loved a written challenge, but I just didn't have it in me to care about abstract, multiple choice questions. I filled them in haphazardly and handed it back.

The rest of the class included a lecture accompanied by a short, pro-foundly cheesy film on PI ethics where the main actor wore a flasher's trench coat and violated one ethic after another, each ending with him turning to the camera and asking, "What would *you* do?" *I'd probably not swipe her red silk underwear while snooping through her drawer for incriminating photographs, buddy, but that's just me.*

The film's buffoonish tone seemed in particularly poor taste after last night's murder, and Mr. Denny appeared to realize it halfway through, shifting uncomfortably once or twice in his seat.

There was no mention of the seven-secrets assignment, but because I felt restless after class, I decided to follow Kent again. Sure as shoo-tin', he drove directly to the Kandi Mall, parked in front of Sears, and entered. He was acting very much like the owner of secret #4, a man who no longer had a job to go to but didn't want to go home. I wasn't sure how I'd find out for certain, short of coming right out and asking him, and I didn't feel like stepping inside the mall. I also didn't want to go home and help my mom with a sewing project, or pie making, or housecleaning, or building her time machine that would take the whole world back to the 1950s with her. Figuring I might as well get some work done to pay Ron back, I pointed the car toward Paynesville and specifically the *Reporter* office. The local newspaper had been around since the late 1800s, Ron had informed me, and was doing something right, because its circulation kept growing at a time when newspapers in the rest of the country were going the way of the dodo bird.

The office was unassuming, tucked near the two-screen movie theater in downtown Paynesville. The familiar scents of ink and paper washed over me as I entered, and beneath that, I caught a whiff of designer coffee or a vanilla air freshener.

The layout was similar to the *Battle Lake Recall* office. Visitors were tracked immediately to the front desk, where I imagined all business was done and ads were sold. Metal filing cabinets ringed the front room. Down a hall, two doors opened across from one another—I guessed one was a bathroom and the other was the editor's office—and the hallway ended in a spacious room filled with computers, a large table, and likely more filing cabinets out of sight.

"Something I can do for you?"

I didn't recognize the older woman behind the counter, but she had nice smile lines. "Yes, I'm Mira James, here on behalf of the *Battle Lake Recall*. My editor said he'd call ahead so you'd be expecting me."

"Ah yes. We weren't sure when you'd be arriving, but you're in luck. Lorne's here now, and he's agreed to give you a tour. You can just have a seat over there."

"OK," I said, choosing the least uncomfortable-looking plastic chair. I picked up the copy of the *Reporter* next to me. The paper's layout was clean, the articles well written. It reminded me a lot of Battle Lake's paper, except with more ads in the back. So many, in fact, that it had a separate insert for them.

"Mira?"

I glanced up guiltily, feeling like a spy. Which I was, in a way. The man walking toward me was in his late twenties if he was a day, with long, straggly hair pulled back into a ponytail at his neck.

"Lorne?"

"At your service." He glanced at his watch.

His body language was impossible to ignore. He had much better things to do. I couldn't blame him. "Thanks for making time for me."

He nodded once, abruptly. "This is going to be a short tour. We don't have a lot to show here. Mind if I ask why you're interested?"

"Didn't Ron tell you?" I asked, stalling for time. I didn't want to explain that Ron wanted me to snoop and find out the secret to their success.

"No," he said, his expression hooded, "but I figured it's because our circulation numbers just bumped and he wants to know our secret."

I immediately decided to like the guy. I didn't need to waste any good fibs on him. "You figured right. Are you one of the reporters?"

"I suppose I am." He tipped his head. "I'm also the editor and the publisher, just like Ron. I have two employees, one you met at the front desk and the other who sells ads for us. Keeping the overhead small is the only way to make a newspaper work in a small town."

I studied him some more as he led the way down the narrow hallway. "You look pretty young to have your own newspaper."

"My parents owned it before me. Didn't you graduate from here?"

"Yeah," I said, wondering if he knew my history. I hoped he didn't. "I didn't get out much, though. Grew up ten miles out of town, over past Lake Koronis."

He nodded in a distracted way. I got the sense he was a habitually busy man. "Well, this is the do-all room," he said, flicking on the light. "You'll recognize the layout table, computers, file cabinets. We don't have all our archives transferred into a computerized form yet, but we're working on it."

A fully extended copy of the newspaper's front and back pages caught my eye. "Your paper comes out tomorrow?"

"Yep. Deadline is Monday and the paper comes out every Wednesday."

I pointed at the headline article. "You're reporting on the River Grove murder."

His brow furrowed. "I had to arrange what I thought was the final layout to make room for that story. The victim graduated from here."

"I know." We both stared at the headline for a couple beats, the atmosphere in the room suddenly heavy. "Did you find out anything that they haven't aired on the news?"

He shook his head. "Not really. The same FBI crew that covered the case in Chicago and Wisconsin is handling it in Minnesota. The supervisory agent is named Walter Briggs. He's with the Behavioral Analysis Unit, and he's not big on answering reporters' questions."

I sighed. "So we all just wait."

"Yeah." He regarded me thoughtfully. "Some more than others."

I pushed back my hair. "I wonder if I should dye it."

He shrugged. "You can't change your life. If I were you, I'd make sure I wasn't ever alone, though."

"Thanks. I'm actually taking a self-defense class. Starts tonight." I didn't know that I'd reached that decision, but something melancholy in his gaze made me want to stay positive.

"Good idea," he said, walking back toward the front of the building. "That's about it for the tour. Got a bathroom over there, my office across from it, and you already saw the front desk. Not a lot of magic here."

"But your circulation, it's going up. Can you tell me the secret?"

He stopped and turned, offering me the first hint of a smile. "No secret. Good writing, clean layout, loyal community." His smile widened, going lopsided. "Oh, and the woman we hired two months ago to sell our ads? She looks like Angelina Jolie."

I couldn't help but laugh. Mystery solved. "I'll be sure to tell Ron the secret, though I don't know if it'll do us any good."

He led me out and told me his door was open if I had any more questions while I was in town. I thanked him and walked away, deep in thought.

The stores on the street were exactly the same as I remembered—small mom-and-pop gift shops, a Jack and Jill grocer, a Ben Franklin five-and-dime.

I'd almost reached my car when I spotted something that turned my blood to sludge: my mom, her jacket pulled tight around her ears, walking into an alleyway a block up, toward the rough part of town.

Chapter 15

OK, so Paynesville didn't really have a rough part of town. It was composed mostly of family-owned businesses, a car dealership or two, some churches, and row upon row of walk-out ramblers sprinkled among the colonials.

There was, however, a section on the edge of the small downtown area that was mostly rentals, and the serial killer scare had me imagining the worst.

"Mom!"

She didn't hear me, so I jogged toward the alley she'd disappeared into. My boots crunched on the salt littering the sidewalk.

"Mom?"

I peered down the alleyway that ran between the old creamery and the turn-of-the-century Paynesville hospital, both of which had been converted into apartments in the '60s. The alley featured a webbed series of stairs attached to the three-story brick buildings on each side.

Just a glance was all it took to ignite a surprisingly pleasant memory.

A summer night smelling of blooming peonies and fireworks. Me, Patsy, and another girl in this alley on a dare. Instructions to walk to the farthest set of stairs, climb up to the third floor, and knock on the blue door. A Ziploc bag of Minnesota ditch weed exchanged for a hot ten-dollar bill. I remembered getting more headache than high, but we did a lot of laughing that night. I half smiled thinking of it. Where had I been storing all these positive memories?

I pulled myself back into the moment, counting eight separate balconies and doors, four on each side of the alleyway. Mom could have disappeared into any one of them. Was it possible the town dealer was still living here? Unlikely, and even if he was, he'd be the last person my mom would visit.

Right?

I replayed the image of her in my head. Had she looked scared, or in a hurry? That's when I realized I hadn't been able to make out her face, and come to think of it, the black down jacket she'd been wearing was a generic design that everybody seemed to sport nowadays. I'd assumed it was my mom because of her height and build and something essentially Mom-like about her, but maybe it hadn't been her after all.

Still uneasy but lacking an alternative, I returned to my car. The decision that followed—to drive west—wasn't a conscious one, but I found my Toyota pointing that direction, and soon I passed the white-trimmed, green sign letting me know that I was entering River Grove, population 767. The town's streetlight poles were swathed in plastic green garlands and topped with Santa heads that I was sure lit up at night.

The layout was similar to Paynesville's, with two main streets that intersected. The downtown consisted of churches, grocery stores, and assorted offices surrounded by neat houses. A sprinkling of people walked the streets, but they all appeared to be in a hurry. Everyone's head was down.

I wasn't sure what I was looking for, so I drove up and down the streets. Many front yard fir trees were trimmed with Christmas lights, and one house had a giant balloon Santa tethered to its roof. Not a single snowman existed in any yard, though, despite the fact that today's sticky snow conditions would be perfect. Three large globes of snow scattered in front of a blue rambler suggested that any existing snow-people had been destroyed after the murder.

I took a right, away from downtown, and made my way to Oak Street, which ran parallel to the town park. The houses here were more lavishly decorated, with elves frolicking in the snow, deer silhouettes in various stages of surprise and bristling with twinkle lights, walks lined with huge colored bulbs in red, green, and blue. The effort at good cheer relaxed me marginally, and I stayed that way until I reached the end of the block and spotted it: a white bungalow, its entire lawn thick with candy canes.

My breath caught in my throat.

Red-and-white-striped canes rimmed the yard, a gingerbread play-house covered in candy canes was erected in the center, and candy cane lights decorated the roof, porch, and windows. It made my stomach cramp to look at them. Who lived there, and why hadn't they taken down their decorations when the Candy Cane Killer struck their town?

It was an unfair thought, one I quickly dismissed. Maybe an elderly couple lived here and they had no way of removing the decorations without help. Why should they have to change something that obviously brought them happiness just because of one twisted human? It certainly wouldn't bring anyone back.

Still, I couldn't flee the street fast enough and took the first right I could. I found myself in a sea of official-looking cars. Behind the row of sedans sat the house from last night's news, Natalie Garcia's sweet little black-shuttered home. Only now it was crisscrossed with yellow-and-black tape, a local news crew shuffling from foot to foot as they stood a respectful distance from the crime scene.

I drove to the end of the street and parked, my heart heavy. I supposed this was what I'd come for, to see her house, to feel a connection with her, to pay her back for the kindness she'd shown me thirteen years earlier. And maybe a part of me had even come for some reassurance that I or somebody I loved wouldn't be next. It was a fool's errand, for sure.

In my rearview window, I saw men in too-thin dress coats standing in her yard, their red cheeks and breath plumes revealing their discomfort. A pair in head-to-toe white traveled from a van in the driveway to Natalie's house, their face masks and full gowns rendering them genderless. This was the FBI, and they needed a small-town, aspiring PI around like they needed a toothpick in their eye.

"Hello?"

The voice was muffled, but still, I jumped. I'd been so intent on watching the scene play out in my rearview mirror that I hadn't noticed the man walk up to my driver's side door. I rolled down the window, figuring I was about to get reamed out for rubbernecking. "Hi."

The man was about five ten, and the way he carried himself suggested he was lean and rangy under his overstuffed blue jacket. His eyes were a friendly brown, and he didn't appear to be upset. "Hi. Sorry to startle you." He glanced over at the cluster of FBI agents. "Did you know Natalie?"

"Are you with the FBI?"

His mouth curved into a smile. "Nope. They don't get to wear the puffy jackets. They have an image to uphold, you know."

He yanked off his glove and offered me a handshake. He was a lefty with no wedding ring. "Adam De Luca. I'm a reporter for the *Chicago Daily News*. Did you know her?"

I immediately felt protective of my history with Natalie and avoided answering his question. "What are you doing all the way out here?"

A pained look crossed his face. He pulled his glove back on and stuffed his hands into his coat pockets, standing fully upright. I had to lean out to see him. "This is my beat, I'm afraid."

"Minnesota?"

He shook his head. "Crime, generally, and right now, the Candy Cane Killer. He began in Chicago." He rubbed his cheek. "That's where I started, too. Assigned to him almost since day one."

I swallowed past a lump in my throat. "That's a pretty gruesome beat."

"I agree. It's not all I do, but for the last three Decembers, it's become the focus of my life. Nobody'll be happier than me when this case is solved." He glanced to his right, a rueful smile on his face. "The FBI will probably be happy to never see me again, too."

I leaned my head the rest of the way out. A man had broken off from the group in front of Natalie's house and was making his way toward us. He was an inch or so taller than Adam but beefy, his shoulders poking through his coat like armor. His expression was as inviting as stone, but Adam seemed to know him.

"Agent Briggs," Adam said, when the man was within ten feet.

"De Luca. You still around?"

Adam smiled crookedly. "Looks that way. You can get rid of me anytime. Just solve this case." His voice was pitched light and easy, but his eyes and mouth were tight.

Agent Briggs grunted and brushed ice off his bushy mustache. "I'll see what I can do."

He turned his attention to me, and I felt reduced to the confidence and brains of a six-year-old. "Something we can do for you here, ma'am?"

"No. I mean, I don't think so." It felt important suddenly that he not think I was an ambulance chaser. "I went to high school with Natalie."

"So you're not a reporter like him?" He jerked his gloved thumb at Adam, balancing as much loathing as he could on one word.

Don't lie to the FBI. Don't lie to the FBI. "I'm here as a friend. I heard about Natalie on the news last night, and I'm concerned for her family. I'm worried about the rest of us, too. Do you have any information on the killer?"

"We know he's a bad man." He delivered this understatement in a flat voice.

I couldn't tell if he was being sarcastic or just tired of answering that question. Either way, his response made me defensive. "That wasn't information, it was *un*formation. As in, it was very unformative."

His eyes narrowed. "What'd you say your name was?"

Inexplicably, the words "Lola Clambaker" bubbled up in my throat. It was only through great effort that I was able to hold them back. "Mira James," I mumbled.

He shrugged. "Sorry, Mira James, for the *un*formation. I've got work to do."

I watched his retreating back, and it wasn't until the grinding sound of boots on snow disappeared that I realized Adam was chuckling. "I think you've made a friend for life."

I quirked my lips. "He's not a real people person, is he?"

"Supervisory Agent Walter Briggs is the best in the business. I think he's a good man, but no, he's not the warm and fuzzy type. So," he said, leaning back toward my window. I smelled the soothing scents of cinnamon and aftershave. "You *did* know Natalie."

I squeezed my steering wheel. "I haven't seen her since high school, but I used to know her." I shrugged. "As much as you can know anyone at that age, I suppose. Have they figured out how the killer targets his victims?"

De Luca's eyes grew pained again. "If they did, they'd have him. But no, other than their appearances, and some career choice similarities, none of the victims seems to have any connection with each other, though I heard Briggs is looking into a possible resort area in Mexico three of them visited at different times. You didn't happen to know the first Minnesota victim, the one from White Plains, did you?"

I shook my head.

"Good for you, bad for the case." He reached into his back pocket and pulled out a silver case. He slid a business card from it without removing his gloves, pulled a pen from his pocket to scribble something on the back, and handed it to me. "It's too cold to stay out much longer, don't you think? Here's my card. Give me a call if you remember anything that might be relevant. I put Briggs's number on the back, too. Like I said, he's not a man whose time you want to waste, but if you get something good, he should know. OK?"

"Sure." I took the card and considered telling him I was also a reporter, except it would be like telling Michael Jordan that I dribbled a little in my spare time. The *Chicago Daily News* was one of the biggest papers in the Midwest. "See you around."

"Yep." He tapped my window ledge and gave me a little wave.

Chapter 16

As I drove away, I wondered what skill and education were required to become a *real* reporter, one with an actual beat. Adam seemed only a few years older than me. Grayer, certainly, and reserved in a way that was hard to pinpoint, but I assumed that was a natural by-product of covering a rampaging serial killer for three winters.

Noticing my gas gauge was inching below empty, I pulled into a Munch-N-Go station, filled my tank, and trotted inside to pay and buy a bag of corn nuts. I'd been trying to kick the corn nut habit because they smelled bad. Also, I felt like corn was the bully of the grain world and wanted to start giving other foods and maybe even a legume or two more attention. Too bad the nuts of the corn plant were so delicious.

I was choosing between plain and ranch flavored—the latter being fairly poor marketing if you thought about it—when a conversation at the front of the store caught my ear. Some guy in an ill-fitting suit was trying to sell a line of candies to the woman behind the counter. It was his nasal accent that stood out.

"Salted caramels are our bestseller. We're famous for 'em."

"Where would I put them?" the woman asked. "I don't have any counter space as it is."

"Not to worry. Check this out!"

I inched away from the corn nuts so I could see what he was referring to. He held a tiered metal basket that he hooked to the cigarette pack dispenser over her head, where it dangled in previously unused space. Each level was stocked full of a different kind of candy. Saliva began to pool in my mouth.

"Wow," she said, and it sounded like she meant it. "Well, I'd have to talk to my husband first. Do you have a card?"

"I have one right here. Take some complimentary candies, too. I hope to hear from you soon."

The guy bent down to grab his materials, and I caught his profile. It was pointy, his generous nose and mouth close together at the bottom of his face and his eyes up high on his forehead. He wasn't disfigured, exactly, but if you rolled him in brown fur, he'd at least place in a guinea pig look-alike contest.

"Thank you!" the woman behind the counter said, unrolling a candy to pop it into her mouth. Her eyes closed as she chewed. "These are delicious. You drive safe now, OK?"

He'd been on his way out the door, but he turned back toward her, and I heard a smile in his voice. "Will do." And then he disappeared outside.

I grabbed the plain corn nuts and a pack of peppermint gum and made my way to the counter. "Gas on pump two," I said.

The woman smiled. "Nice weather, isn't it?"

I glanced outside. The day was gray, but it wasn't snowing and the roads were clear. "Sure." I pointed at the pile of caramels. "Are you going to start carrying those?"

"I don't know. I just got them. Want to try one?" She slid over a candy about the size of my pinkie finger, creamy brown caramel in a clear wrapper. The outside read "Chi-Town Candies Famous Salted Caramels" in fancy white script.

"Thank you." I tugged on each end of the wrapper and it untwisted. I popped the caramel into my mouth and went a little weak at the knees. It tasted of fresh butter and sugar with a hint of salt to keep it from being too sweet. "Oh. My. God."

"I know." She nodded, her eyes wide. "I think I'll be able to convince my husband we need these."

"Please do," I said. I paid for my purchases. By the time I reached my car, the salesman was gone.

With nowhere else to go, I headed home, deep in thought on the drive. How could such a large police and FBI force be trying to find the same man, with no success? Where would the killer strike next? My head was thick with the dark possibilities.

Mom wasn't home when I arrived, but she'd left a note that she was playing bridge with friends and would be back this afternoon.

That must have been where I'd seen her going earlier today, if it had, in fact, been her. I tended to Luna and Tiger Pop, both of whom seemed thrilled to be here, probably as a result of the shelf of treats Mom had bought for them, then fixed myself an early dinner of a cheese and pickle sandwich on wheat bread with a side of ruffled black pepper potato chips and tried watching TV, but I was too fidgety. I couldn't find a book that held my attention, either.

I considered redecorating my bedroom but realized that I didn't have the materials I'd need, specifically a sledgehammer and a bucket of Wite-Out. I was about to alphabetize the spice rack when Mom arrived home, glowing and humming.

I hadn't seen her like that in, well, ever. I crossed my arms suspiciously. "You must have won big at bridge."

"What? Oh, I did." She smiled. Her mouth seemed a little dry, her eyes a little red. I leaned in to sniff her. She pulled away. "Mira! What are you doing?"

"I saw you today, going into the alleyway in town," I accused. "That's where the drug dealer used to live."

She narrowed her eyes. "How would *you* know where the drug dealer used to live?"

"Everyone knew." I put my hands on my hips, unwilling to let her turn the tables. "You weren't 'playing cards' with the pot man, were you, Mom?"

She reeled back. "Mira!"

I shrugged. "Just asking. You seem extra happy."

She must have been joyful when she was younger. She'd told me stories about her friends in high school, being on the cheerleading squad, waiting tables after practice at her parents' restaurant. On the rare occasions when she talked about it, she remembered a lot of laughter back then.

Then, one day, my dad drove in on his motorcycle, got her pregnant, married her, and headed off to war. Her parents died shortly after he returned, my grandpa to a heart attack and my grandma to cancer. Mom had made the best of everything that came her way, but I didn't remember much laughing in our house growing up. Life's trials had sanded down her natural joy. So what had brought it back, if it wasn't drugs?

She patted my cheek. "Can't I just be grateful that my only child is home with me for the holidays?"

"I suppose." I realized I was acting overprotective, and on top of that, I was starting to feel itchy again. I spotted the little slip of paper I'd stuck on the corkboard, advertising the self-defense class. It started at seven thirty. I glanced at the clock. It was six forty-five. "I'm thinking of taking a self-defense class for women. It's at the Tae Kwon Do gym in Richmond." It was only a half-hour drive and would get me out of the house.

"Sounds wonderful," she said, removing her coat. "When does it start?"

"It runs from seven thirty to nine all week."

She turned away, but not before I caught the look of disappointment on her face. "I was hoping we'd have time to talk tonight, but I think a self-defense class is a great idea," she said, her voice strained. "It's important to be safe. You have fun."

"Thanks, Mom." I walked over and gave her a hug. "I love you, you know? It's just hard to have all this free time on my hands. I'm used to working two jobs. Having so little responsibility is making me antsy."

She kissed my cheek. "I could write you up a chore list if it'd make you feel better."

I was happy to see the twinkle had returned to her eyes, and I laughed in response. "That's a fantastic idea. You can pay me a quarter for each one I cross off."

I changed into sweats and sneakers, grabbed my boots in case I landed in a ditch and needed to walk somewhere, and drove off.

I didn't know what to expect at my first self-defense class, and my chest felt a little tight as I walked through the doors of the chiropractic clinic and followed the signs to the gym in the basement. Descending the stairs, I heard yelling and smelled clean sweat. The steps ended in a hallway that doubled back on itself.

This is the right thing to do. You're not a loser. There will be lots of women here who don't know anything about fighting, either.

I tried keeping up the mantra, but I found myself unable to take the right turn into the gym. I sighed. I'd been exposed to too many new situations and old ghosts in the past three days. I just didn't have it in me to subject myself to one more. I yanked my duffel bag close to my body and turned to ascend the stairs, feeling like a huge hairy failure.

"Chickenshit says, 'Mrs. Berns?'"

My head popped up. A tiny, shadowed figure stood at the top of the stairs. My heart soared. It couldn't be, could it? "Mrs. Berns?"

"Uh-huh. Thought so. Running scared, are you? That's what I told your mom would happen, as a matter of fact, when I called to find out where you were. She invited me to the house, but I said I needed to stage an inter-detention first. So here I am."

"Mrs. Berns!" I couldn't stop myself. I took the stairs two at a time and lifted her off the ground in an embrace, feeling like I was walking on air. I hadn't realized how much I'd missed her. "What are you doing here?"

She hugged me back and then pushed me away. "You ever been to Fargo? With my family? It's about as interesting as reading an aspirin bottle, except you're also in Fargo. With my family." She shook her head. "Couldn't get out of there fast enough. Figured I'd invite myself to your double-wide for Christmas. You're a lot of things, but boring isn't one of them. 'Course, when I found out you came back to Paynesville, I had to alter my plans slightly."

My grin threatened to separate the bottom half of my head from the top. Mrs. Berns was my best friend in the world, tough, funny, frisky, and always there when I needed her. Like now. "Did you tell my mom you'd be staying?"

"She insisted."

"Good." I pulled her toward the door. She was going to make everything at the farmhouse fun. "Let's get out of here."

She dug her heels in. "You *wish*. I didn't wear a sweatband for nothing."

Indeed, a 1980s-style braided headband held her dandelion-fluff hair into place and accented her bright-pink-and-aqua tracksuit and matching tennis shoes.

"Or your tracksuit?" I asked, pointing at it.

"Nah, had that on all day. Who's got time for zippers at my age? Now come on. Let's find out how to bruise us some testes." She pushed me back down the stairs and into the gym.

Chapter 17

The killer cruises past the house. The homeowners aren't around, haven't been for days at least. Someone shovels their walkway and cleans the snow off those hideous decorations, but the house stays empty. The yard is a cacophony of plastic candy canes, the home trimmed in red-and-white-striped lights. It's disgusting. Everyone else in town has had the decency to remove candy canes and snowmen from their property.

One who dresses like that brings it on oneself. It makes me so angry I want to push them down in the mud and look at them.

"What?" The killer looks over at the doll strapped in next to him. Her winter coat lies on the seat between them. It's warm in the vehicle. This car also smells like pinecones, thanks to the green, tree-shaped freshener newly purchased from the gas station up the road.

It dangles from the heating vent lever.

The doll continues to smile her smug little grin, not offering clarification. It's all right. The killer knows the words by heart. Auntie Ginger, her long brown hair pulled back in an immaculate bun, her dress perfectly ironed, would say those words every day after dressing her charges up to code. All of them, boys and girls, wore long strapless dresses and cheap long-haired wigs of the kind Cher made popular in the '70s.

Dress-up time, Auntie Ginger had called it.

Once they were all in costume, she'd pull the Barbie doll from her pocket, hold it in the air, and say with a smile, *You make me so angry I want to push you down in the mud and look at you.* This saying confused the killer as a child, who only visited Auntie Ginger in December. There was never mud outside then, only snow and ice. And that smile, as if she were paying them a compliment. Probably the saying was some southern bit of nonsense from her childhood. She had lots of those. She'd brought them with her when she'd moved to the Midwest, those and the orange begonias that she grew in a hothouse off her kitchen. Everything else she'd left behind and six feet under, she was fond of saying.

One who dresses like that brings it on oneself.

And then she'd choose one of the children she'd dressed up to go into the back room with her. The rest of them would play because they were kids and that's what kids did. And they didn't ask questions when the chosen child returned, eyes red and wide, a forgotten, bittersweet candy cane in hand.

The killer is gripping the leather-wrapped steering wheel tight enough to leave marks. This will not do. Looking backward brings pain. Better to look to the future and to save others from inviting that same agony into their lives.

The killer steers the car into the River Grove Public Library parking lot. It's time to create a new profile.

Chapter 18

The self-defense class had offered two surprises: the fourth-degree Tae Kwon Do black belt instructor was a woman, and I'd enjoyed the entire class. Mrs. Berns and I had missed the introductory session, where she'd covered commonsense topics like never walking alone and always carrying yourself assertively, locking your doors, and making eye contact with strangers, but she gave us a handout on those. We spent the rest of the class working on wrist releases.

Or, as Mrs. Berns called them, snakebites.

"See?" She'd grabbed my wrist with both hands and twisted each a different direction. "Snakebites."

"Not exactly," explained the instructor, Master Andrea, a worried smile on her face.

She was giving us one-on-one instruction to catch us up with the rest of the class. She wore a white martial arts uniform, and her black belt was embroidered with four impressive gold bars. She was about my height and age, brunette, but light on her feet and with arms like machine guns. I bet no one gave her the pitying looks I was receiving nowadays.

"Grab my wrist," she ordered Mrs. Berns, holding out her right arm.

Mrs. Berns obeyed. Quicker than I could blink, Master Andrea had her on the floor, face down, arm chicken-winged behind her back. The move had been silver-quick and oddly gentle, but I could see how Mrs. Berns's arm could snap like a twig in this position.

I leaned toward my friend. "Are you OK?"

She was beaming. "We're not leaving this building until I can do that."

Her wish was granted. By the time class was over, we understood the basics of takedowns as well as how to escape the hand-to-wrist grasp of the strongest man with a mix of speed, strength, and knowledge of angles.

When I woke up the next morning, my wrists were still a hot red from being practiced on, but I felt good about my newfound abilities.

"You look bright and shiny today," my mom said as I wandered downstairs, freshly showered.

I passed the first-floor crafts room at the foot of the stairs, which Mom had converted into a spare bedroom for Mrs. Berns. I heard her putzing around loudly on the other side of the door, muttering. She was probably feeling as sore as I was, though it was a good pain.

I smiled. "Class was great last night. We learned basic self-defense, and even got thrown a couple times. You should come with me and Mrs. Berns tonight."

Mom's eyes dropped. "I can't. I'm volunteering at church. We need to get ready for Natalie's funeral."

A cold ball rolled into my stomach. "That's so soon."

"The police released her body, and her parents don't see any reason to wait. I think they're so broken up that they're not seeing straight, and who can blame them?" Her face drooped with sadness. "The wake is this afternoon, Saint Augustine's, at two. You're coming?"

"Of course."

The glow from the self-defense class faded, leaving a somber black cloud. Mom offered me fresh-baked caramel rolls, but I couldn't stomach them. I tried to pass entirely, but she wouldn't let me leave without at least taking one for the road. I thanked her, gave her a hug, and hollered a goodbye to Mrs. Berns before heading to Willmar for PI training.

I arrived early. Only Mr. Denny and Kent were present. That reminded me that I had four more secrets to definitively match with their owners: someone who'd been fired but still continued to go to work, another with a prosthetic leg, a third who had a drinking problem, and a fourth on the FBI watch list. I'd have an extra hour between class and the wake. If this building didn't house a student computer lab, I'd run to the library and see what I could scare up.

The other five students stomped in within minutes, knocking snow off the bottoms of their boots. All of them appeared as solemn as I felt. They probably weren't going to Natalie's wake this afternoon, but there was no doubt that they were thinking about her, or the women in their lives who were less safe every day.

Mr. Denny, likely sensing the mood, got straight to business.

The class covered information gathering, field notes, and reports, plus a variety of case studies that we were broken into groups of two to discuss. I was paired up with Leo, and our assigned study revolved around a woman being stalked by an ex-husband who seemed to always know her whereabouts. An investigation revealed that he'd installed a tracker in her car while they were still married. While the material was compelling, I found it difficult to keep my mind off Natalie's murder.

Murder.

The girl I'd shared secrets and ghost stories with as a sixth grader was dead at the hands of a serial killer.

What would make somebody choose to kill a stranger minding her own business? As we moved from our pairs to a whole-class lecture, I tuned out Mr. Denny and began scribbling notes. What drove a person to kill? *Revenge. Money. Mental illness. Fear. Love. Control.*

I immediately crossed out "Money." From the little I knew of serial killers, that was an unlikely motive. Mental illness was more probable, though the precision with which the killer was attacking and the fact that he hadn't yet been caught suggested he was socially skilled. He was, by definition, unbalanced but not necessarily motivated by a chemical-based mental illness to kill.

I couldn't see how fear would be a motive, either, but I wasn't ready to cross that one out just yet. I supposed revenge against women was a viable option, as well as a need to control women.

"Mira?"

I glanced up, startled. Mr. Denny stood next to me, yesterday's test in hand. The rest of the students were standing and putting on their jackets.

"Sorry." I grabbed the test, surprised to see that I had answered 87 percent of the questions correctly. I gave him a weak smile and reached for my coat, my heart cold and leaden. Despite the plan I'd had when entering the class this morning, the last thing I now felt like doing was sitting in front of a computer and researching a silly secret exercise on my classmates.

I pulled on my jacket and headed into the bracing cold. It was too early for me to head to the wake, so I just slid behind my wheel and drove. I was surprised to find myself following Kent to the Sears parking lot, which I supposed was as good a place as any to go. I parked my car one row back and several cars over and watched him lock his door and jog to the front glass doors. He paused ten feet shy of his destination, turned, and stared straight into my eyes. I sucked in a breath when he made his way to my car. I rolled down the window when he reached me.

"This has to be boring for you, following me to Sears each day," he said. His cheeks were red from the cold, but his demeanor was relaxed.

"The first day was an accident." Since he'd made me, I might as well come right out with it. "You the one without a job?"

He shoved his hands in his pockets and stared off toward the Burger King on Highway 23. "Yeah."

"So you just go to class in the morning and hang out at Sears in the afternoon?"

"Yup."

My curiosity got the better of me. "Why don't you just tell your family you were fired?"

He shook his head, still gazing far away. "It'd kill my wife. We've got three kids in college, a mortgage. She doesn't need the extra stress. I'd rather tell her when I find a new job."

Chirpy Christmas music floated out of the mall. "What kind of work did you do?"

"Managed a factory. Twenty-seven years." He rubbed his bristly chin. "They downsized a month ago, shipping most of the business overseas."

I pursed my lips. "That's a crap deal. For whatever it's worth, I think you'd make a pretty good PI. You're tough to tail, and you figured out I was following you. I'll keep my ears to the ground for jobs."

"I'd appreciate that." He seemed to come back to himself. "Don't suppose you have a prosthetic leg?"

My laugh surprised me. "Sorry. I may have a drinking problem or be on the FBI watch list, though."

His eyebrow shot up. "No shit?"

"None. If you find out for sure, let me know?"

He offered me his hand, the faintest hint of a smile warming his eyes. "That's a deal."

I rolled up my window and drove to Natalie's wake.

Chapter 19

The Vrolstad Funeral Home parking lot was full. I ended up leaving my car on the street, two blocks up. The short walk was cold, the snow crunching underfoot, my gloved hands tucked up in my sleeves. Mourners trudged toward the conservative, gigantic, Craftsman-style building, their faces solemn, great puffs of frosty air billowing out of their mouths.

I'd attended only four wakes in my life: one for my grandpa and another for my grandma on my mom's side, one for a great-aunt, and my dad's. I'd been too young to really remember my grandparents' wakes. My great-aunt had been old when she died, and that event, while sad, had also been full of laughter and reminiscing. I couldn't recall the details of my dad's send-off, but I was reminded of the raw feel of it when I walked into Natalie's observance.

Someone tugged on my jacket. "You might want to pull your shoulders out of your ears and stop looking so scowly."

I was immensely relieved to see Mrs. Berns. "You did come! Is Mom here yet?"

"Over there." She nodded at a group of women holding each other. "The one leaning on your mom? That's Natalie's mother."

Mrs. Garcia appeared ready to collapse, deep, quiet sobs racking her. People stood on the periphery, at a loss, but my mom was on the front lines, embracing her and whispering into her ear as she caressed Mrs. Garcia's hair.

I felt tears in the corners of my eyes. "This is so sad."

"Sad?" The venom in Mrs. Berns's voice surprised me, yanking my gaze from Mrs. Garcia. "This makes me so mad I could eat fire. Some bastard is killing innocent women. I'd like to give him a little taste of his own medicine."

I knew what she meant, but the words came out automatically. "The police don't have any leads."

"That's what they always say. They have to say that if they don't want the killer to go into hiding. No, I'm sure they know more than they're telling us. In the meantime, we should see what we can do to help them."

"What? No way." I shook my head vigorously. "We're not getting in the way of the FBI. That's wild talk. We can help by staying *out* of the way."

"Mmm," she said noncommittally.

I couldn't get another word out of her. Her glance swept all the broken-looking people shuffling around the funeral home's giant foyer, stunned. Some of them paused at the photos of Natalie, a retrospective that started with Kodachromes of her dangling in a park swing as a toddler and moved up to the most recent shots of her playing with a black Lab, her gorgeous hair falling in her eyes as she smiled widely at the camera. The last image was so vivid that I could almost remember the sound of her laughter.

Those who weren't staring at the photos read the cards poked into cloying flower arrangements or made stilted small talk. You could tell who those closest to Natalie were because they appeared erased around their edges. Mrs. Berns followed without comment when I signed the guest book and slipped almost all my remaining cash into an offerings envelope.

When we entered the main chapel, I was horrified to spot the open casket across the room, a kneeling bench in front of it. I caught a glimpse of Natalie's cold, waxen profile over the coffin's edge. I suddenly couldn't breathe or hear. It was as if someone had clapped their hands over my ears and filled my mouth and nose with glue.

"Mira?"

Mrs. Berns gripped my arm, but the sensation was distant. I stumbled toward the coffin, pushing through the crowd waiting in a curving line to pay their respects. When I got close to the casket, I shoved my way to the front, feeling like I was floating outside of my own body.

There she was.

Horribly beautiful, her hair arranged around her like a doll's. Her sweet, unlined face and her closed eyes. That tiny nose that we'd agreed in sixth grade made her look exactly like Morgan Fairchild. If I only looked at the top of her face, I could believe she was sleeping. It was her mouth that gave away the dreadfulness of the moment. The red lipstick against the slackness of her jaw seemed almost obscene.

That mouth would never smile again.

She wouldn't laugh, or tease, or kiss.

I went from not breathing to short, huffing gasps. Pinpricks of light danced around my eyes. I reached forward for something to hold on to, but it was as if I were dropping through the floor.

Patsy came up from behind and squeezed my elbow. "Mira, how are you?" Her eyes were puffy and red.

I accepted her embrace like a life jacket, feeling returning to my body. I stayed put until I trusted my voice. "Terrible. How's her family holding up?"

"About like you'd expect."

I pulled back and reoriented myself to the room, deliberately turning away from the casket. Patsy stood patiently next to me.

Looking around, I was surprised that I recognized a lot of people from high school. I guess I was even more astonished at how much they looked the same. Trish Haselkamp, captain of the Knowledge Bowl team that went to state my junior year. Darren Fischer, perennial stoner and the guy voted class clown. In a corner stood Julia Dahlberg, who had been ridiculously popular and made everyone call her Jules starting in tenth grade. I'd detested her back then, my emotion a gummy high school putty of jealousy and admiration. Jules was still pretty and preppy, hair cut in a stylish, chunky pixie, and I was surprised at the brief pang of insecurity I felt looking at her. She was talking to Wyatt Miller, who'd been homecoming king the year Natalie had been queen.

Mrs. Berns pinched me.

"Oh, sorry. Patsy, this is a friend of mine from Battle Lake. Mrs. Berns, this is Patsy. I graduated high school with her."

"What happened to you?" Mrs. Berns asked me. "One minute you're standing next to me, and the next, you're running toward the casket like it's packed with Nut Goodies."

"Sorry." I shuddered. "I guess part of me hadn't believed she was dead until I saw the body. I had a little panic attack."

Mrs. Berns scowled, then turned to Patsy. "Maybe you can tell me something."

"Anything," Patsy said, smiling politely.

"Has Mira always been so timid, or is this a new development?"

"Timid?" Patsy shook her head, looking from me to Mrs. Berns in disbelief. "Her nickname was Maniac in high school."

Mrs. Berns nodded smugly, poking me in the arm. "Thought so. You let the fudge get scared out of you. Old you would have gotten pissed, not scared, looking at your friend in that coffin, and you would have been the first one to rush out and find her killer. Heck, the Mira I met last spring drank, screwed, and fought for what was right with the best of them. What happened to you?"

"I grew up." My eyes had wandered back in the direction of the coffin, against my will.

"You grew *scared*." She piffed and turned away from me. "So, Patsy, have you heard anything more about the killer?"

Patsy wiped the look of surprise at our conversation from her face. "Nothing new. Natalie's mom said her house hadn't been broken into, so police are wondering if she knew the killer. It might be their first break in the case, but it doesn't seem like a lot to go on."

"Yeah, that wouldn't help them much," came a gravelly voice.

We all turned to look at the woman who'd spoken. She was a presence, tall and heavyset, with short dark hair and thickly lashed, heavily made-up brown eyes. She also wore a smooth coat of taupe concealer and a blush that matched her coral lipstick. She was about my age, so all that makeup caused me to be immediately suspicious of her.

"Excuse me?" I asked.

"Sorry." She wiped her hand on her skirt before offering it to me. She wore crepe-bottomed clogs with white tights, which seemed incongruous against her flower-print blouse and calf-length denim skirt. She was either a nurse, a day care provider, or a cult recruiter. "I'm Quinna Bankowski. I worked with Natalie."

I shook it. "I'm sorry. What did you two do?"

"We were traveling nurses for the same company, based out of Minnesota. We worked all over the Midwest, though River Grove is home base for both of us. Or was, for Natalie."

"That explains your shoes," Mrs. Berns said. I jammed my elbow in her side, and she looked at me, surprised. "What? They look ugly and comfortable. Nurse shoes."

"You look familiar," Quinna said, focusing on me. Her gaze was an unnerving mix of calculating and intense. "Have we met before? What's your name?"

"Mira James, and I don't think so." I took a small step away. "I went to high school with Natalie, but I've lived in the Cities or Battle Lake since then."

"No, that's not it." She tapped her chin, then her eyes lit up. "I know! You were talking to the reporter and the FBI agent yesterday. I talked to them, too. A few times." She fluffed the back of her hair.

I gave her a look. "I didn't get out of my car."

"I'm pretty observant."

I squinted. "Do you live on the same block as Natalie? I didn't see you."

"No. I live on the other side of the city park."

She seemed immune to social cues and unaware that her behavior—seemingly stalking a crime scene—was odd. I wondered if she had social anxiety or was just weird. "Did you and Natalie hang out a lot?"

"Never." She shook her head vehemently. "Not outside of work. But I can tell you that all of Natalie's friends were decent, and she wasn't dating anyone."

She didn't offer any more information, and I could see Mrs. Berns and Patsy starting to inch away, too. "Well, I'm sorry for your loss," I said.

"You too." She rushed over to the wall of photos of Natalie, as if someone had called for her. She stood there alone, hands behind her back, studying the largest picture.

"There's a crunchy nut in every box," Mrs. Berns muttered. "Back to what we were talking about. Patsy, if we wanted to find out more about Natalie's recent activities, who here would we talk to?"

Patsy pointed toward three women about our age huddled near the coffin. "I met those ladies at two of Natalie's Coddled Cook parties. They're from River Grove and I think were good friends with her." Patsy's attention was drawn by someone over Mrs. Berns's shoulder. "Will you excuse me? I see someone I want to talk to."

As Patsy walked away, Mrs. Berns tugged me toward the trio.

"What questions do you have for them?" I asked as we navigated the crowd.

"What are *you* going to ask them, you mean. You're the private dick."

I stopped. "Remember you said you wouldn't call me that?"

"Not officially," she said. "Now focus. You need to get over your fear and start digging into this serial killer's business." She pushed me until we stood directly behind the women, and I let her because I didn't want to cause a scene.

I pretended to admire the nearest flower arrangement while Mrs. Berns peer pressured me with her eyes. I knew I'd have to ask the women something to get her off my case, but I didn't want to intrude on their grief and had no idea what they could tell me that the police wouldn't already have asked them.

". . . the orange begonia killer!"

My breath caught. *Another* killer? But before I could ask a question, Mrs. Berns had already elbowed herself into their conversation. "Orange begonia killer? Do tell."

Chapter 20

The three women exchanged embarrassed funeral laughs. The shortest, a woman about ten years older than me, finally spoke. "We were just remembering how all three of us and Natalie received orange begonia plants from a secret admirer five summers ago. We were saying we're grateful there was no orange begonia killer back then." She darted a glance toward the coffin. "Probably in poor taste to mention it. Events like this bring out my black humor."

"Remember how embarrassed we were to even tell one another about the flowers?" The woman speaking pushed her jeweled glasses up her nose. "We didn't want anyone to know we were into online dating, and then it turned out all *four* of us were!"

The short woman nodded. "What was that online service called? E-something. E-love?"

The third woman, who had been silent until now, smiled. "E-adore. It's how I met my husband."

"Not me," the woman with the glasses said. "The most I got out of it were some lousy dates and that orange begonia."

"Olivia, it wasn't that bad!"

Olivia shrugged. She seemed to think it'd been *exactly* that bad.

"Did you ever find out who sent the flowers?" I asked, insinuating myself next to Mrs. Berns. I'd kept quiet until now, though I'd wanted to comment on the name of the dating service. "E-adore" sounded like a Winnie-the-Pooh character, not an online human grocery store.

"No, though after we got to talking, we realized we'd all been matched with pretty much the same guys," Olivia said, wrinkling her nose. "Not a lot of choices in this part of the world. We figured we got the flowers from some guy who'd come across a begonia sale and was hedging his bets, but we never found out for sure."

Mrs. Berns nudged me. I followed her glance. Quinna Bankowski, Natalie's odd coworker, was two feet away, staring down at the top of the coffin. She seemed to be inching sideways toward us.

"I'm really sorry about your loss," I told the three women. "Could you do me a favor? Could you call me if you think of anything else out of place, something that might shed light on why Natalie was targeted?"

They nodded and each accepted pieces of paper that I'd quickly scribbled my name and my mom's phone number on. Mrs. Berns and I turned to leave before Quinna reached us and pinned us in another uncomfortable conversation. We hadn't gone three feet before I found myself face-to-face with Adam De Luca.

"Hello," I said.

He tipped his head in a distant, puzzled way, and then he placed my face with a name. "Mira! The one who told Briggs he was unformative." He smiled. "I told my editor the story when I called her last night. Gave her a good laugh."

Chagrined, I introduced him and Mrs. Berns while thinking of all the ways the orange-begonia story had gotten my blood humming. You could find out a lot by being in the right place at the right time. My encounter with Kent today was proof of that. So maybe Mrs. Berns was right, to a degree. Maybe we *could* uncover helpful information without putting ourselves in danger or getting in the FBI's way. We would be conduits of facts rather than investigators. "We heard today that the police believe Natalie knew the killer," I said to Adam. "Do you know anything about that?"

He scratched his neck absently. "I've heard that theory. I think it's unlikely, unless it was a copycat killer and not the actual Candy Cane Killer who targeted her. The odds of one man knowing all of these women, across three states . . . ah shit." He suddenly ducked his head like he didn't want to be recognized.

We turned around. Quinna Bankowski was staring at us, a short ten feet away.

"Watch out for that one," Mrs. Berns whispered to Adam. "She's as sharp as a marble."

"She's a death hound," Adam said in agreement. "You encounter that a lot in this line of work, unfortunately, people who are close to tragic death and want to profit off of it. Not in terms of money, of course, but fame. I've already interviewed her three times, at her request, and she's been hanging around the crime scene offering to help Briggs at every turn. He's ready to pull his hair out."

"Well, she's coming for you, which means it's time to skedaddle." Mrs. Berns grabbed my hand, and we fled not a moment too soon. A glance back revealed an uncomfortable Adam in Quinna's unblinking gaze. I couldn't imagine why he didn't just tell her to buzz off.

Mrs. Berns kept leading me all the way to the door of the main chapel and pulled me into a quiet spot off the foyer. The smell of lilies was intense. "Where's the nearest pay phone?"

"At the Amoco a few blocks over. Why?"

"You're going to call the FBI and tell them about the orange begonias."

I rolled my eyes. "You're not serious." I was getting on board with the idea of gathering information the police might have overlooked, but a five-year-old flower story seemed like a dead end.

She sniffed. "Any little bit helps."

"Random facts from five years ago do not help—they *hurt*. The FBI doesn't need us to waste their time. If we're going to assist, the first thing we need to do is stay out of their way."

She crossed her arms and settled in for a stare down. "If there's a connection, we'd be negligent not to let them know. If there isn't a connection, they can disregard our information."

She and I'd been here before. I knew it'd be easier to do what she asked than to fight her, and in the big picture, I had to admit that she was probably right. A legitimate fact wouldn't hurt. Let the FBI decide if there was anything to it. But first, I needed to say my goodbyes and offer my condolences to Mrs. Garcia and the rest of Natalie's family. The line to reach them was extensive, and the haunted look in their eyes when I finally spoke to them was almost too painful to bear.

When I shook Mrs. Garcia's hand, she pulled me into an embrace, whispered something sad and vague about making popcorn for Natalie and me during a slumber party, and thanked me for being a friend to her daughter. I wondered how she could remember me. Her brain must have been a blurry fog of pain shot with bright, unmoored memories.

No way could she hug all these women Natalie's age and not wonder, just for a second, why it was her daughter and not one of us lying in that coffin. I knew I couldn't, if I were her. My tears were flowing as freely as hers when I finally stepped away.

On my way out, I got an extra-tight hug from my mom, who told me that after she was sure she couldn't do anything more for Mrs. Garcia, she'd be spending the rest of the day playing bridge with friends.

After that, I drove with Mrs. Berns to the gas station and pulled out the business card Adam had given me yesterday once we reached the pay phone inside. I flipped the card to the back and dialed.

Agent Briggs was exactly as thrilled to hear from me as I'd expected. "What'd you say your name is again?"

"Mira Berns." The real Mrs. Berns, unhappy that I'd stolen half her name, somehow managed to twist my underarm skin through my jacket. I ignored the pain and told him the brief orange-begonia story. "We heard the story just now, at Natalie Garcia's wake. We thought there might be a connection between all four of them getting the same gift back then, and the killer and his candy canes and the three snowmen now." It sounded weak, even to my ears.

"Did De Luca tell you to call? Tell him we don't have time to chase any more ghost leads."

Click.

I hung up and shook my head. "I don't think he was too impressed."

Mrs. Berns shrugged. "It was a long shot. Better safe than sorry."

We were standing next to one of those hot dog treadmills, and I remembered I hadn't eaten yet today. Man, that meat smelled good. If it was, actually, meat. "It *is* a stretch between flowers and candy canes," I said, my brain going loose, "except . . ." Suddenly, the world dropped away, leaving just me and a huge, blindingly obvious possibility.

Mrs. Berns tipped her nose at me. "Except what?"

"Except it's *not* such a leap between online dating then and online dating now." My heart was hammering. "Think about it: If you wanted to find all the single, brunette women in an area, where would be the first place you'd look?"

"An online-dating site!"

"Exactly." My pulse was through the roof, but it eased up as I followed the possibility to all its natural conclusions. "But the police must have thought of that by now. Why wouldn't they tell all Minnesota women to pull their dating profiles?"

"I suppose they did, in a way. They've told women to be on guard against strange men and uncomfortable situations." She snorted. "Shows what they know about a day in the life of a woman. They might as well tell us to avoid doing more than our share of the housework, or having our opinions second-guessed."

I steered her back on topic. "But if all of the victims had online-dating profiles, wouldn't the media know?"

"Not if the police wanted to keep it under wraps. It seems like a good way for them to trap the killer, if they know that's where he's hunting."

I opened the gas station door and walked out, my hunger forgotten. Mrs. Berns followed closely.

"You know what we should do?" I asked.

"What?"

"Create our own profile." I threw myself into the front seat, waiting until Mrs. Berns was inside to continue. "Do a little fishing. We won't be in anybody's way, and if we find something suspicious, we can turn it over to the FBI."

Mrs. Berns buckled up next to me, a broad smile on her face. "There's the Mira I know and love! I knew you were in there somewhere under all that chickenshit. Now drive, Jeeves." She pointed out the windshield. "We've got a murderer to catch."

Chapter 21

The Paynesville Area Library on Washburne Avenue had one available computer. We signed in for it, planted ourselves in front of it, and called up the E-adore website. Plump, animated red hearts collided on the screen, raining a shower of tiny pink hearts upon the heads of a smiling couple straight out of central casting.

"Ugh." I had a theory that one should never shop online for leather pants *or* men. I could see why people would. It was lonely in these parts, and if you didn't meet someone at work or church, that left only bars and blind luck. There was just something about online dating that didn't fit me right.

"Why haven't I tried this yet?" Mrs. Berns shoved me out of the way to access the keyboard. "It's a smorgasbord of single men!"

"Hold those horses, missy." I wheeled my chair back in front of the screen and squeezed her out. "We're making a fake profile for a reason, remember? You can build your own flytrap on your own time."

"Party pooper."

With Mrs. Berns watching, I first posed as a man looking for women, ages twenty-four to forty-four, within thirty miles of River Grove, Minnesota. Forty-seven hits popped up. One featured a photo of a lady who looked an awful lot like Olivia, the woman from the wake who'd said she'd gotten only the orange begonia and lousy dates out of her online experience. In the photo, she wasn't wearing the jeweled glasses she'd sported at the funeral, and she seemed to have better cleavage, but otherwise, she was a dead ringer.

Quinna Bankowski was a few profiles below Olivia, looking perfectly normal. I scrolled down and flipped through a couple dozen more photos before I saw what I'd been dreading: a picture of Natalie, on a trip to the mountains somewhere, her friends' faces blurred out so only her smile shone through.

She looked young. Happy. Alive.

"That her?"

"Yeah." I pulled my hands away from the keyboard. "We probably shouldn't be doing this."

"Toughen up, buttercup." She tapped the screen. "You're looking at the reason we're doing this."

I swallowed past the lump in my throat and skimmed the rest of the women's photos. None of the others stood out. "We should probably print these. If the other two women who discovered snowmen in their yards are on these pages, we can be pretty sure how the killer is finding his victims."

I moved my cursor over the "Print" button. "I'll grab the printout," Mrs. Berns said. "You start building us a profile."

While Mrs. Berns went to the front counter to pay, I searched online for a generic headshot of a long-haired brunette in her thirties and uploaded it. My plan was to create an imaginary profile for a River Grove woman Natalie's age. That would allow me to scope the men she'd likely viewed. If any of them set off our alarm bells, we could approach them via our imaginary online persona and stand them up for a date in a very public place to get a closer look.

Mrs. Berns plopped in the chair next to me, a half dozen sheets of paper in her hand. "Got 'em."

"Awesome," I said. "What should our fake profile's first name be?"

"Veronica."

I raised an eyebrow but typed it in. "OK, Veronica lives in River Grove, is thirty-three, five six and 140 pounds, has never been married, loves to travel, and is a nurse. I'm gonna say she also likes Disney movies even though she knows she's too old, she enjoys crossword puzzles and naps, and her favorite holiday is Thanksgiving."

"He wouldn't be interested in her," Mrs. Berns said, arranging the papers so all the edges lined up. "Cuz she sounds like she's already dead."

I felt my cheeks flush. Except for being a nurse and liking Disney movies, that profile pretty much described me. OK, maybe I liked some Disney movies, too. "It doesn't matter. We're just looking for the men who come up as matches to someone with Natalie's same physical characteristics, job, and region. I'm betting the killer, if this is how he's tracking them, hasn't pulled his profile down. It'd draw too much attention to a single person. Makes more sense to just let the profile wither."

She was paging through the sheets in her hand. "Think he'd use his real picture?"

"Doubt it. He'd be caught by now if he did." I ran a spell-check of what I'd typed so far.

"You almost done?"

I nodded. "I think we've got enough for our profile." I clicked on the oval that said "Go Live!" Another screen popped up. I groaned. "It costs $14.99 to join for a month."

She riffled around her massive purse and came out with a credit card. "Do it."

"You sure?"

"I'm going to make my own profile anyways. I can just change around this one as soon as we're done with it." She smiled. "I saw some cutie patooties on here."

I plugged in her credit card numbers. They were accepted, and I tried the "Go Live!" oval again. The computer hummed, and an orgy of hearts capered on the screen. Mrs. Berns mused while we waited for our matches to show up. "They should make an online-dating site specifically for old people," she said.

I turned to her, surprised. "Would you go on it?"

"Not in a million years," she said, snorting. "You won't find me anywhere near a dating site where 'this is how the old ball bounces' is more than a saying. But it'd get the stale guys out of the pond so us women could get to the business of being wild. I even have a name for it: 'Carbon Dating.'" She cackled.

My mouth twitched. "That's pretty good."

"Don't I know it." She scratched her chin. "I might even share that idea with Kennie Rogers."

Kennie was famous for her questionable business ventures, and it was a testament to what a number Paynesville had done on me that I actually missed the woman. I was about to ask if I could get in on the ground floor when the hearts on the screen popped, one by one, revealing our matches.

"Look!" We had fourteen matches within twenty-five miles of River Grove. Two of them hadn't posted photos. Of the twelve profiles that did, one featured a familiar guinea pig–faced man.

Chapter 22

"I know that guy!" I said. "I saw him selling candy at the gas station in River Grove."

Mrs. Berns's brow furrowed. "Like a Girl Scout?"

"For a company. Like it's his career." I leaned into the screen. "Look here. It says his name is Sharpie and he's a traveling salesman who's living temporarily in the River Grove area and hoping to make it permanent."

Mrs. Berns snorted. "What kind of name is Sharpie?"

"It doesn't say, but he claims that he's got a good sense of humor."

"That's handy, with a face like that." She pointed at the mouse. "Print it out. What about the rest?"

I skimmed through the ones with photos and saw the usual: hunters who alleged they liked to cuddle and professionals looking for a woman who didn't like drama, size 6 and below only. They eroded what little faith I had in humankind, but none of them set off my radar, so I delved into the two profiles without photos.

Both were men aged thirty-nine, average height and weight according to their stats. The first, David, claimed to be a blue-eyed blond looking for a friendship. He stated that he had a good career and enjoyed motorcycle riding. The second was a guy who gave his name as Isaac and wrote that his hair and eyes were both dark. He stated that he was a well-read electrician who could make any date fun "in two shakes of a sheep's tail."

"What the hell does that mean?" Mrs. Berns said, pointing at the very sentence I was reading.

I shook my head. "I dunno. Maybe he likes to keep things lively? Everything else sounds normal. His favorite book is a John Adams biography, he watches the History Channel, and he says he's a good cook who doesn't mind doing the dishes." I sat back. "There's only one thing to do now."

"Set up a date with the pig-faced man and the two faceless gents?" Mrs. Berns asked.

"Exactly."

We typed a generic note extolling Veronica's imaginary positive qualities, trying not to snort with laughter when we got to the part about exercising:

> Hi! My name is Veronica, and I live in River Grove. I'm a nurse who recently moved to the area. I'm pretty athletic. In fact, if I don't work out at least five days a week, I go a little stir crazy! I like going out to the movies, or just a night in. I'm looking for a man who makes me laugh, someone who can show me the area. I'm leaving town soon for the holidays, and I'm hoping we could meet for a quick cup of coffee before then. Please respond ASAP. Look forward to hearing from you!

Before we had a chance to hit "Send," photo-less David came online and instant messaged us.

> **Hi! New here?**

I jumped, then glanced at Mrs. Berns.
She glared at me. "It's not rocket science," she said. "Type 'yes.'"
I did.

I like your photo. Want to meet for coffee tomorrow?

"Like shooting fish in a barrel," Mrs. Berns said.

We made plans with David to meet at the Fatted Caf, the coffee shop in River Grove, the next afternoon at one, which would give me time to drive over after my PI class and make it to Natalie's funeral afterward. We had no intention of actually meeting David, of course, but we wanted to see what he looked like, what he drove, and generally feel him out.

Plans made, we finished sending our message, directing one copy to Isaac and the other to Sharpie. We also printed out Isaac's and David's profiles and added them to the others we'd accumulated.

"I think that's all for now," I said. "Mind if I do some quick research for my PI class? It'll only take twenty minutes or so."

"Not as long as you use that computer." Mrs. Berns pointed to one on the other side of the carrel that had just opened up.

"Fine."

I moved over to the recently vacated one, digging in my jacket pockets until I came up with the folded sheet of paper containing my PI classmates' names and addresses. The office worker really had been generous. The addresses would cut down on my investigative time significantly.

I began by researching the "FBI watch list," something you only wanted to do from a public computer with no personally identifying information involved. I discovered that the list contained more than four hundred thousand names, and that I'd have more luck being invited to the White House for dinner with the president than finding out who'd landed on that list. I gave up on that line for now and logged on to the information database I'd bought a membership to the month before.

Once in, I ran the names of my PI classmates. The search only confirmed what I already knew: Gene's past addresses were all army bases.

Leo was a naturalized citizen originally from Albania. No documents told me that Edgar was cheating on his wife, but a recent sale of a chunk of land up north suggested something was shifting for him. I was reluctant to look into Kent's information. He really seemed like a decent guy.

I pushed through my squeamishness and was happy to see that, except for missing a recent mortgage payment, he was squeaky clean. The same couldn't be said for Roger, who'd earned four DUIs in the past three years. I guessed he was the drinking problem, which meant that I either was on the FBI watch list or had a prosthetic leg.

Shit.

I backpedaled and tried to rationalize my way out of this. More than one person in class could have a drinking problem, right? Mr. Denny might have been trying to trick us with his assignment. Maybe one student owned three of the secrets, and two of us had none. Sure, that made sense. I shut down my computer and strode over to Mrs. Berns. She closed out her screen as soon as she saw me coming.

I gave her the stink eye. "You're not looking at porn in a library, are you?"

"Naw, they wouldn't let me in. Those WWE sites are just as good, anyhow."

I let that slide and, given where her head was at the moment, asked a dangerous question. "If you had six men and had to figure out which one of them had a fake leg, how would you do it?"

"Hmm." She squinted at the ceiling as if giving the matter serious thought. "I'd probably release a whole pack of squirrels to see whose leg they crawled up first."

And . . . I got exactly what I deserved. "You hungry?"

"I thought you'd never ask." She restarted her computer and stood. "We just have time for a bite before self-defense class."

A thought struck me on the way out of the library. "I'm going to call Mom and see if she wants to meet us. She's playing bridge with some friends." I ran back in and requested a phone book from the librarian and permission to use her phone.

Her bestie Luisa picked up on the third ring.

"Hi, it's Mira. Can I talk to my mom?"

"Hello, dear. She's not here, I'm afraid."

I went back through what Mom had told me. Technically, she just said she'd be playing bridge, not who with. "So you don't have bridge scheduled for today?"

"Heavens, no. Wednesday afternoons we have Ladies Auxiliary. Bridge is on Thursdays. Besides, everyone's so shook up with poor Natalie's murder that we canceled for this week."

"Any idea who else my mom would play bridge with?"

"Honey, there is no one else. Your mom said she was going home to rest, and who could blame her?"

I held the phone stupidly to my ear. It wasn't possible my mom had lied to me. Had she forgotten which afternoon she played cards?

"So you haven't seen her since Natalie's wake?"

"No. Is something wrong?"

"Not really. We must have had our signals crossed, is all. Sorry to bother you." I hung up and tried my mom's home number. No answer.

Mrs. Berns had followed me back into the library and was leaning against the counter, waiting impatiently. "You look like someone pickled your face. What's wrong?"

"My mom. She's not playing bridge like she said she'd be, and she's not at home."

"Oh no! Has she also been shrunk by a toddler gun, and now needs to be babysat and spoon-fed?"

I sighed. "Point taken. I'm just saying that it's not like her to be so secretive."

"Parents." She shrugged. "You can't watch them all the time. You just have to trust that you raised them right."

I rolled my eyes, but not too hard because I wanted her to buy dinner.

After a modest but delicious meal of grilled cheese sandwiches and tomato soup at the Wishin' Well Café, Mrs. Berns and I traveled the ten miles to our self-defense class, where we learned how to take down an assailant attacking from behind or the front.

Of course, we'd need some warning that's what he was about to do, like, "I intend to grab you in a bear hug from behind," but I was confident we could take it from there: deep breath and elbows out, then drop to the ground, kicking for the knees and nuts.

Frontal attacks required a combination of the wrist releases, sweeping, and focused pressure on the attacker's breaking points. I wasn't sure how well it all would work if I was really under attack, but I liked the confidence it was giving me.

The class culminated in us learning how to make a fist. It seemed like a simple enough exercise: keep your thumb out, punch from the shoulder, connect with your knuckles. Many of us held back, though, or twisted our wrists at the last minute. Master Andrea would have none of it. She made us punch the bags again and again, until our knuckles were bruised and raw and our shoulders ached.

"Only punch when you mean it," she said as we left for the night, "and don't stop your momentum when you hit your target. Punch right through them."

Sounded like good advice.

I was certain that Mom would be home when we returned, but the large bay windows on the front of the house were dark, and the garage was still empty. I was getting worried, but I didn't know what to do about it. Mrs. Berns looked as tired as I felt. I fed, watered, and pet Tiger Pop and Luna while she got herself ready for bed.

I popped my head into the spare bedroom on the way upstairs. It was a cozy setup, an air mattress in the center of the room covered in soft blankets. Mrs. Berns was sprawled on the bed, eyes closed, wearing footie pajamas. "Do you have everything you need?" I asked.

"Everything except for dark," she said. "I'm beat."

"Me too." Problem was, I couldn't hit the hay until my mom was home.

"That was a hint, and not a subtle one," she said. "Turn the damn light off."

"Oh, sorry!" I left her alone and washed my face, brushed my teeth, and then lay across the couch, welcoming Tiger Pop into my lap. I had just decided on a *Cheers* rerun to distract me when the phone rang.

"Mom?"

A second of silence met my ear, followed by the sexiest voice this side of the equator. "Hey, Mira. How're you doing?"

"Johnny!" I sat up on the couch, blood racing to my extremities, a goofy smile on my face. My worries were temporarily forgotten. "How are you? How's Texas?"

He chuckled at my enthusiasm. "Great. Mom is having the time of her life, and I'm learning some southern gardening tips. I miss you."

My heart flooded with heat. "I miss you, too."

"I got your message."

"Excuse me?" The excitement at hearing his voice was replaced by confusion. "What message?"

He coughed discreetly. "The night before last. You called around ten and left a message on my home machine."

Hell. On. Fire.

I'd forgotten about drunk dialing him! What had I said? It was fuzzy, but I recalled something about wanting him and us needing to consummate our relationship. Had I even sung him a bit of "Feels Like the First Time"? Please god, no.

He was breathing oddly on the other end of the line. I realized I needed to say something. "Oh, that message. Um."

His breath picked up, and I thought maybe he was nervous, or angry. Then I realized he was trying to cover up deep chuckling. "You're laughing at me, aren't you?"

"No, I'm not," he said, laughing. "I haven't had a booty call in years. I'm flattered."

I cleared my throat. "I think I might have had too much to drink."

"I figured." His voice grew serious. "Are you staying safe? We've been watching the news."

"Yeah." I didn't want to tell him that I knew one of the women who'd been killed. He'd just want to comfort and protect me, and he wouldn't be able to do either from across the country. "Mrs. Berns is here, and we're enrolled in a self-defense class. I'm taking that PI course, too, so I'm learning all sorts of information on being safe and aware. Don't worry."

"Can't help it."

"Johnny, I—"

"Yes?" He sounded so hopeful.

"Nothing." I *did* love him. But the phone wasn't the place to forge that territory. "I need to go. My mom is out late, and she might call. I'd like the line to be free."

"All right." I could hear the disappointment in his voice. "Mom and I are flying back in six days. I'll see you then?"

"Wild horses couldn't keep me away." I meant it.

We hung up, and I tried to get back into Sam and Diane's playful banter but couldn't. Where was my mom?

I moved to the secondhand laptop—a gift from her church group—that she kept in her kitchen to look up recipes. I intended to follow up on the profile Mrs. Berns and I'd created. I logged on to E-adore. We had one message:

I'd love to meet tomorrow, but I don't drink coffee. How about I take you out to an early dinner at Tammy's Tavern on Highway 23?
Sharpie Trevino

Chapter 23

It was a little after midnight when Mom finally arrived home, claiming she was exhausted but wearing a mysterious smile. She said she'd been playing bridge with a new pack of friends and that they were a little wilder than her regular group. These ladies didn't have Auxiliary on Wednesdays, for one, and they didn't mind a little nip every now and again. After making sure she hadn't been drinking and driving ("For gosh sakes, I just had a sip!") and admonishing her to leave a phone number where she could be reached in the future, I stumbled off to bed, too tired to stay upset.

I was puffy-eyed and cranky for the fourth day of PI class. Kent tossed me a long look when I walked in but didn't say anything. I settled into my seat and watched the rest of the students move around the room, arranging their jackets on the backs of the chairs, going to the front to speak with Mr. Denny, settling in. No one appeared to be sporting a prosthetic leg, which made me unreasonably crabbier.

Mr. Denny focused on situation assessment, including personal safety, pre-surveillance research, and surveillance tactics. The personal safety information was basic and not nearly as effective as what I was learning in my self-defense classes, but I was fascinated by what he called tachypsychia. He explained that it was a human response to extreme stress that resulted in tunnel vision and a sense that time was either slowing down or speeding up, depending on your personal makeup. Either way, it could screw you if you were fighting for your life.

The best way to stay in the moment and save yourself, according to Mr. Denny, was to build your muscle memory of basic self-defense moves and to practice combat breathing. The latter, when explained, sounded just like deep breathing to me, but I wasn't the expert. I hoped I wouldn't need to use the information in any case.

With thirty minutes left in class, he ended his lecture by asking for questions. There were none. He nodded as if expecting this, then walked around to the front of his desk and leaned against it, arms crossed. "In that case, who wants to learn about serial killers?"

I shot upright in my chair. He had my complete attention.

"When I worked homicide in Minneapolis, I had the displeasure of being on the FBI task force assigned to catch the Weepy-Voiced Killer. Anyone remember him?"

Both Kent and Leo nodded. "It was the '80s, right?" Leo said. "The guy called after each murder to confess anonymously. Sounded like he was crying each time."

"Correct." Mr. Denny glanced out the window into the steely winter morning. "Most serial killers keep their crimes a secret. Then there's the outliers, the ones who feel the need to reach out. Some, like the Lipstick Killer and the Weepy-Voiced Killer, beg the police to catch them. Others, like the Zodiac and Happy Face Killers, communicate to gloat. Our Candy Cane Killer has not made contact with the outside world about his killings, but he does express many of the other standard traits of killers. Take out a pen and paper."

Mr. Denny gave us an overview of the gruesome world of serial killing in the twenty-five minutes remaining. According to him, most serial killers murdered for psychological gratification. They were usually males in their late twenties or early thirties and from a working-class or lower-middle-class background.

Frequently, they were victims of abuse as children. Some—but not all—of them exhibited psychopathy or sociopathy, both of which were usually demonstrated as selfishness and a lack of empathy or remorse. Psychopaths were methodical, often traditionally successful, and could blend into society, working normal jobs and, in many cases, maintaining a normal homelife, including a spouse and kids. Sociopaths, on the other hand, were usually more reckless and had difficulty forming relationships.

"Because psychopaths have taught themselves to wear a mask of civility," Mr. Denny said, "they are the most difficult to catch. They blend in with society and can be considered quite charming."

I shivered. "The Candy Cane Killer is a psychopath?"

He nodded. "Most likely. None of his victims have shown signs of sexual abuse, so we know he isn't a hedonistic serial killer or a power serial killer. That leaves two other kinds: visionary, those who kill because they hear voices telling them to, or mission-oriented, the killer who thinks he's making the world better through his actions."

My head swirled with information. None of it helped to pinpoint the killer, but it did result in me updating the motivations for the killings, which could come in handy in the online-dating research Mrs. Berns and I'd undertaken.

By the time I stepped out of the classroom, I had shaken off my lack-of-sleep funk, both scared and excited by the thought of today's mission: observe David, potential serial killer, from a safe distance. I picked up Mrs. Berns on my way to the Fatted Caf.

The twenty-minute drive northwest took us past snow-drifted fields and the occasional wind-seared tree. This was the part of the state where you could watch your dog run away for three days, according to the joke. After a bit of small talk, including Mrs. Berns telling me that my mom was teaching her how to crochet and she liked it (officially making Paynesville the most boring town on the planet), she got to the guts of the day. "What's the plan?"

"We go into the shop," I said, "order some coffee, find a seat, and watch for a man fitting David's description to enter at the appointed time."

"In that case, I brought you this." She yanked a blonde wig out of her purse. I almost drove off the road when I saw it. "I borrowed your mom's car so I could visit the costume store in Saint Cloud. You don't want him to confuse you with brunette Veronica."

"I don't want him to think I'm an inside-out Dolly Parton, either. I'm not wearing that."

"I thought you'd say that. That's why I brought this." She yanked another mass of hair out of her purse.

I didn't want to look, but the sleek black bob caught my eye. It had sharp-cut bangs and was very Louise Brooks. I forced my eyes back onto the road. "You could have put it into a bag. It's got a gum wrapper stuck in it."

"Thought you'd love it. I'll wear the blonde one, then."

I shook my head as I pulled into the Fatted Caf's parking lot. "We're going to a small-town coffeehouse, not Mardi Gras. We can't both wear a wig."

"Don't worry. I'll pull my hat on over it. I'll appear very tasteful."

I was doubtful. That misgiving was exacerbated after she yanked a makeup kit out of her bottomless purse and started applying blue eye shadow. Ten minutes later, she looked more like Madame, the puppet from *Solid Gold*, than tasteful, but I wasn't going to tell her that. I, however, felt kinda sexy spy-lady in my black bob. I hated to admit it, but I also felt like a real PI going undercover.

"Ready?" she asked.

"Please, after you."

"Thank you so much."

"Do you think the French accent is a little much?" I asked, getting out of the car.

She glared at me over the Toyota's roof, her cheeks bright with blusher. "Guess what?"

"What?"

"Shut up, chicken butt."

"Fine." I held the front door for her. The rich smell of roasted coffee and fresh-baked rolls was heavenly. It reminded me of the Fortune Café back in Battle Lake, a charming coffee shop, restaurant, and all-around hangout owned by my friends Sid and Nancy. God, I missed them and their normalcy right about now.

The Fatted Caf was packed with the lunch crowd, but it seemed to be mostly a takeaway joint. Three of the seven tables were open. I was surprised at how few stares we garnered. Was everyone here sight-impaired, or just polite?

"What do you want?" I asked Mrs. Berns when we reached the counter.

"Black coffee with a shot of Bailey's."

The barista appeared concerned, but I translated. "Two mochas, please, one soy and one regular. Medium. We'll take a couple of those chocolate chip scones as well." I reached into my purse for my second-to-last twenty. I had a credit card, too, but I didn't want to bust into that. Credit was a slippery slope.

I was getting my change when Mrs. Berns tugged on my sleeve. "Ver-oay ere-they," she said.

"Hold on. I'm paying."

"Ver-oay ere-they!"

I pocketed my change and gave Mrs. Berns my full attention. "Are you stroking?"

She held a large swath of plastic blonde tresses in front of her face, her eyes gazing demurely through the hair at one of the occupied tables. A blue-eyed blond guy in his late thirties or early forties was drinking a cup of coffee and reading a newspaper. When the door opened, he'd glance up before returning to his paper.

"David?" I whispered. I needn't have bothered. The Billie Holiday pouring out of the speakers contained each conversation in a pocket.

She nodded. "I ink-thay o-say."

"I preferred the French accent to pig latin, and I'm not sure why you're hiding behind your hair. He doesn't know us."

"Humph." She pulled back her locks and reached for the coffee we'd just been handed. She took a deep gulp and smiled with satisfaction. "Perfect. Now come on."

We threaded our way through a pack of people waiting for their to-go food and sat at the open table next to the man. He was shorter than his profile had promised, and a little thicker around the middle. His face was incredibly average, hard to pick out of a crowd or to find a feature to comment on. If he were a car, I'd always lose him in the parking lot.

"Lovely day," Mrs. Berns said to him.

He glanced over, startled. He smiled a slow, open grin. "Yes, ma'am. It is."

I didn't know what to make of the southern accent. It sounded authentic, far more appropriate than Mrs. Berns's French one. I tipped my head when he said hello to me.

"You're not from around here?" I asked.

"Nope. Moved here five years ago from Alabama. The only thing I miss is the weather." He rubbed the back of his neck. "If you don't mind me saying, you two don't look like you're from around here, either."

I snorted, and Mrs. Berns kicked me under the table. "I don't know what you're talking about. My sister and I have lived in the area our whole lives."

I glanced over my shoulder to see who she was referring to, then realized it was me. I kicked her back. "She doesn't mean we've lived in River Grove our whole lives," I said. "We're actually from Paynesville, just passing through on our way to Fargo. Do you travel a lot?"

He folded his paper to give us his full attention. "I'm afraid not. Moved up here with my wife. She passed away two years ago. Cancer. I haven't had the heart to do much other than go to work and go home. Not until recently, anyways."

"I'm so sorry," I said.

He shrugged in that way that people do when they have no answer but don't want to be rude. I suddenly felt like a jerk for wasting his time.

"Name's David," he said.

Bingo. It would have been polite to offer ours in return, but instead, Mrs. Berns asked him what he did for a living.

He smiled again. "Dentist. One of two in town."

I restrained myself from making a face. I realized dentistry was an honorable profession, but still, spending your day cleaning people's mouths? Gross. "So, do you have big Christmas plans?"

"Thought I'd volunteer at the local shelter. That's what I did last year. Gives me a rush to hand out food."

Mrs. Berns reached over and pinched him, hard.

He pulled back, his expression one of shock. "What was that for?"

"Just checkin' if you were real. Come on, Thelma. We've got that meeting to get to."

"Like I said, I'm so sorry," I told him, as she strode out the front door, stuffing what was left of our scones into a paper sack. "I hope you have a happy holiday season."

He gave a polite nod but overall appeared bewildered. I couldn't blame him one bit.

"Really?" I asked, once I was outside. "You have to pinch the widower? And since when am I Thelma?"

"You know the rules. I'm always Louise. As to the first question, I wasn't buying a thing he said."

"You're not serious." I opened my car door and slid over to unlock hers. She dropped into her seat. "A dead wife? That couldn't have all been a lie. Could it?"

She reached for her belt buckle. "You don't live as long as I have without recognizing a pile of horseshit when you see it."

"Serial killer–level horseshit?"

"Naw. Trying-to-get-laid-sized buffalo chips. Bet it works, too."

I went over the entire interaction in my head. Even on replay he struck me as genuine. Just to be safe, we drove out of the parking lot and across the street and waited. David left twenty minutes later, a ski cap on his head and a disappointed expression on his face.

He slid into a late-model silver Buick LeSabre. We followed him down the main drag, took a left on Ivy Street, and watched as he pulled into the RESERVED FOR DENTIST space in the lot next to the Dr. David Fleece Dentistry Office. I crossed him off my mental suspect list at the same time I slid off my wig. This trip had been a waste of time, minus the delicious coffee, and we now had a funeral to attend.

Mrs. Berns and I made it to Saint Augustine Church only moments before the service began. The parking lot was crowded, including a CNN van and two local news crews. We hurried past them and into the church, choosing two of the last seats in the crowded chapel's rear pew.

Natalie's family all spoke, sharing funny stories of her as a child, reminiscing on her dreams, speaking in trembling voices about how much they would miss her. The most painful moment was when her mom rose, walked over to her daughter's casket, and sang "Amazing Grace" in a voice so raw and pure that it sounded like crystal shattering. She paused at the end of her song, her dry eyes sadder than a thousand tears, and turned to address the congregation.

"She was my baby. I carried her, I nursed her, I put Band-Aids on her knees when she fell. I went with her to buy her first formal dress, I curled her hair for prom, and I had a dream of watching her get married someday. Her father and I loved her every second of her life, and I hope she finds peace in God's arms, because there will never be peace for me again on this earth."

The church was silent. The smell of incense and hothouse flowers hung in the air. Mrs. Garcia's husband rushed to her side. He was a small man, but he nearly carried her back to her seat. Her tears started then.

It must have taken immense self-control to hold herself together long enough to pay tribute to her daughter. Her racking sobs set off the rest of us. Even Mrs. Berns cried, which made her makeup run and somehow added to the effect of the wig she hadn't yet removed.

She and I didn't follow the hearse and mourners to the cemetery, though my mom did. It felt too intimate. Sixth grade was a long time ago, and I didn't want to take space from her closest friends and family.

Or, as Mrs. Berns pointed out, I was a coward who didn't want to visit the same cemetery where my dad was buried.

Both reasons were equally true, and they all led back to the same path: Mrs. Berns and me heading to an early dinner with Sharpie Trevino, a heightened sense of resolve in our hearts.

Chapter 24

"Don't stare," I told Mrs. Berns.

"This is what staring's for."

She had a point. Sharpie Trevino, the man I'd seen trying to sell candy at the gas station, had hopped up and stared hopefully at her and me upon our arrival but sat down, disappointed, when we removed our winter caps and scarves to reveal short black and long blonde hair.

I hadn't seen him head-on at the gas station, but here it was apparent he stood a few inches taller than me and weighed about the same. I'd put him in his fifties, maybe younger for the lack of gray in his wildly spiky, dark-brown hair. I also updated my initial thought that he was of guinea pig descent. He looked much more like a hamster. The only things missing were a jogging wheel and a set of whiskers.

"Still," I hissed. "We don't want to draw attention to ourselves."

Big words for Cagney and Lacey, back in their wigs and trying to blend in at Tammy's Tavern, a classic Midwest bar-restaurant. We were surrounded by dark wood paneling decorated with stuffed animal heads and bug-eyed fish.

In the far corner, a gas fireplace gave off a soothing glow under the watchful eyes of a twelve-point buck. Despite the flickering candles at every table, the bar-restaurant was dim, and an unexpected hazy winter storm was blowing in, making it preternaturally dark outside.

The hostess led us to a table about fifteen feet over from Sharpie Trevino, who continued to jump up every time the front door opened.

Mrs. Berns couldn't drag her stare off him. "He's got creepy ginkgo biloba eyes."

"I don't even know what that means."

"It means he's got something to hide, that's what." She turned her attention to the laminated menu. "Are you ordering deep-fried mushrooms? If you are, I want some."

"How can you think about food?"

She pushed back a blonde tress. "Last time I checked, we were in a restaurant."

"With a possible killer, and after just leaving the funeral of one of his victims."

She swatted me with her menu. "I know that. That's why we're here! Now get the mushrooms, and I'll order the waffle fries with cheese, and we'll share." She pulled a tissue out of her sleeve and blew her nose, then stuffed the tissue back in. Afterward, she straightened her acrylic wig and applied another coat of Coral Kiss lipstick a little outside the lines.

I couldn't pull my eyes away. "I believe I am witnessing the birth of a cat lady."

She ignored me. In fact, she didn't say another word until the waitress came to take our order. Mrs. Berns tacked on a draft beer, and I stuck with water.

"What do we do with Sharpie?" I asked, after the waitress left. Mrs. Berns didn't respond.

"One of us could strike up a conversation with him." Still nothing. I sighed deeply. "I'm sorry I called you a cat lady. And you have my permission to execute plan B."

She clapped her hands in glee.

The *B* stood for "Boobs."

Mrs. Berns had come up with the idea on the drive here. She wanted to fluff her cleavage and then hit on Sharpie. She claimed her lovely ladies had hypnotized men before. Once she had Sharpie ensorcelled, she'd casually find out where he'd spent Sunday night, the evening Natalie was murdered. I'd told her that was the stupidest thing I'd ever heard of, at which point she'd told me fine, we could go ahead and stick with plan A, with the *A* standing for "Ass, Mira, you are one." Still, I'd refused to back down, until now. It didn't hurt that Sharpie Trevino gave off zero danger vibes.

Mrs. Berns slapped the table. "Now we're cooking with Crisco! Hold on to your hat, cuz I'll be right back. I need to make myself look extra special."

That's exactly what I was concerned about. "Remember, don't tell him anything true about yourself, including your name. Just make small talk, then ask him what he watched on TV Sunday night or something."

She winked at me like she hadn't heard a word I'd said. Five nail-biting minutes later, she waltzed out of the bathroom, and I had to admit, she looked pretty good. She'd tied her fake blonde hair back, dialed down the makeup so it accented rather than spackled her beautiful wrinkles, and her boobs were front and center. She was a petite woman, but you wouldn't know it by looking at Lady and the Tramp, her nicknames for her breasts. Perfectly plumped in the vee of her sweater, they jiggled like a waterbed, drawing the attention of men and women alike. I was the only one who knew her secret, which was that she folded each boob over itself like an accordion to build the cleavage.

She strode to the front of the restaurant and grabbed a section of the newspaper from the hostess's station before making her way toward Sharpie. She was standing beside him when she dropped a section. Because they were only two tables away, I could catch most of their conversation, even though the restaurant was filling up.

"Ma'am," he said, reaching for it. "You dropped your paper."

Mrs. Berns fluttered her eyelashes as she accepted it. A commotion at the bar drowned out her response. I shifted my chair so I could better hear their interaction, but Sharpie's back was to me, so I also missed his reply. Whatever it was, she laughed at it before taking the chair across from him.

The front door opened, and for the first time since we'd arrived, Sharpie didn't glance at it or stand up. I had to give it to Mrs. Berns; she still had it in spades. She'd probably forgotten more about flirting than I'd ever known. She and Sharpie were still chatting when our food arrived, so I ate all but one of the mushrooms and had started in on her waffle fries when she finally made her way back to me. She was glowing.

"I am amazing," she said.

I raised an eyebrow, dipping a latticed fry into the ketchup. They were soggy but salty, just the way I liked them. "That's the truth. What'd you find out?"

She stared down her nose at our plates. "That I can't trust you with my food."

"No, about Sharpie."

She dropped into her chair. "We talked about the weather, and about baseball—he's a Cubs fan, just like my late husband—and I asked him if he'd made it to the River Grove tree-trimming on Sunday evening." She pointed at the front page of the weekly newspaper she'd brought back with her, and there it was, a headline story about the annual tree-lighting ceremony in the park.

"Quick thinking," I said.

She nodded and leaned in. "You'll really like this. Sharpie said he'd heard about the tree-trimming but couldn't attend because he was on the road selling candy."

"Not much of an alibi."

"Nope, especially when you know he's only using the hotel here in town as a temporary base while he scopes out a site for a factory his company wants to build in central Minnesota." She swatted my hand away from the fries. "His real home is Chicago. Where was the first Candy Cane Killer's victim found?"

"Chicago." The fried food suddenly felt heavy in my gut. "Holy crap."

She nodded smugly. "Exactly. We should call the FBI."

"Maybe we should wait until we hear back from the third guy from E-adore. Isaac. Then we can turn over everything we know and cut back on our chances of being labeled the girls who cry wolf."

She mulled it over. "I suppose you've had worse ideas. Now pass the ketchup. It's hard work being cute."

We finished our meal and left, but not before Mrs. Berns said good-bye to Sharpie, requesting his phone number and giving him a peck on the cheek when he handed it over. He'd been stood up by "Veronica," of course, but with Mrs. Berns around, he didn't seem to mind at all.

Chapter 25

It was a thirty-minute drive to the self-defense class, where we lost our wigs and changed into sweats before reviewing wrist releases and punching. After twenty minutes of that, we learned how to disarm an attacker wielding a knife, a gun, or a garrote. The last one seemed a long shot for Stearns County, unless the weapon was crafted of twine or jumper cables. The knife and particularly the gun defense felt more useful.

Master Andrea had everyone break up into groups of two and practice scenarios with the weapons, pair by pair. The first group went, with one woman slipping a knife around the neck of another. After the victim successfully disarmed her attacker, the second group went, this one with the attacker pointing a knife at her partner's chest.

After them came Mrs. Berns and me.

I stood in front of the class, pretending to walk along a dark street. Mrs. Berns popped out from behind a punching bag and waved an orange plastic pistol in my face.

"Give me your money!" she hollered.

I thrust my hands in the air, like I'd been instructed. I'd just watched two pairs of women enact almost this same exact skit. I knew the next step was to talk to my assailant, humanize myself, draw her attention away from her next move.

But I couldn't do it.

I was suddenly paralyzed, dunked in an ice bath, my mouth stuffed with cotton. It was just Mrs. Berns holding the fake weapon, and we were in a well-lit class, and I *knew* it was pretend. We'd been practicing self-defense here for three days now, and I'd been joking and enjoying it the whole time.

Suddenly, though, I couldn't stop thinking about the gun that'd been pulled on me in November. My assailant and I had been in the cab of a truck. He'd held a pistol, and he'd intended to kill me with it.

He'd failed, but not for lack of trying.

Funny thing was, other than some nightmares and overreacting to loud noises, I'd managed to keep the memory of that terrible moment at bay, always on the periphery, telling myself it was no big deal, and I'd succeeded right up until Mrs. Berns had pulled a fake handgun on me. Now, the memory flooded me like wet cement and nailed me in place.

"Mira?" It was the instructor. She stood beside me, and her voice was neither gentle nor harsh. "Talk to Mrs. Berns."

I blinked. I heard the words, but they didn't make sense. They were so far away and slow.

Mrs. Berns reached forward and grabbed my T-shirt. "You gonna make it easy for me, Spice Girl?"

It was a move we'd practiced one hundred times on the first day we'd come to class: someone grabs you, you grab them, and something about the physical contact pulled me back. I ignored the gun for the moment, placing my hand over Mrs. Berns's. My thumb slid under her palm, and my fingers grasped hers. I pulled her hand across my body, twisting as I went. The angle forced her forward and then down, and I slid into the vee between her arm and torso, not releasing her.

"A loose gun is a dangerous thing," Master Andrea said. I no longer knew where she was standing because my focus had become total. I hooked Mrs. Berns's right ankle with my left and propelled her to the ground. She fell with an *oof.* Once she was sprawled on the mat, I leaned over her back without releasing her hand and snatched the gun. I became aware of the pounding of my heart and sweat running down my sides.

Other sounds began to filter in: the ticking of the clock, a cleaning crew working upstairs, my ragged breathing. I offered Mrs. Berns a hand.

"That's more like it," she said, eyeing me as I helped her up. "I thought you'd choked."

I glanced at the class of twelve women. They were staring back. Master Andrea reached for the gun. She pointed it at me. "Again," she said.

On the drive home, Mrs. Berns didn't mention me freezing at the gym, and I wasn't going to bring it up. When we finally reached the farmhouse, we were exhausted but proud of our day's work. While Mrs. Berns chatted with my mom, I went online to see if Isaac had emailed our E-adore account.

He hadn't.

We all got ready for bed, including me putting fresh water in Tiger Pop's and Luna's bowls. My mom was spoiling them, and the house was littered with catnip mice and chew bones. They hardly cared whether I was around, but I didn't mind. It was the Christmas season, and everyone deserved to be spoiled by a mom. I had my foot on the bottom stair when the phone rang.

"Mira. It's for you."

"Thanks, Mom." I strolled into the kitchen and picked up the wall receiver, waiting until I heard the click of the phone being hung up in my mom's bedroom. "Hello?"

"James. It's Ron. I'm at the *Recall* office."

I glanced at the clock. "What are you doing there so late?"

He grunted. "Got a Christmas issue to put out, and my best reporter left town. Or haven't you heard?"

I smiled on my end of the line. "Did you call to share the gift of sarcasm with me?"

"No, I called because you have a present here. A flower."

My heart did a little skip. Had Johnny sent me something? "What kind?"

"I dunno. A live one."

I grinned, then paused. Johnny knew I was in Paynesville. He wouldn't send me flowers to the *Recall* office. A cold stone rolled down my throat. "What color is the flower, Ron?"

"Hold on." He must have put his hand over the receiver because I heard a muffled discussion before he came back on the line. "Orange. The wife says it's a begonia."

Chapter 26

The words punched me in the gut: *orange begonia.*

The flowers sent to Natalie and three of her friends five years ago by a mysterious online admirer.

The inspiration for Mrs. Berns and me to create an online-dating profile in the hopes of flushing out a serial killer.

A warning, clearly, telling me to back off. Or was I being told that I was next?

Ron assured me there was no card on the flowers, only a slip of paper with my name and no other identifying information. He said he and his wife had come back from a late dinner at the Turtle Stew and discovered the flower on the newspaper office's reception desk. He couldn't remember if they'd locked the front door. He heard the fear in my voice, but I didn't tell him what was going on. I needed to make a call.

With shaking hands, I found Adam De Luca's card. I flipped it over and dialed Agent Walter Briggs's number, any concerns about bothering him or passing on irrelevant information completely gone.

His phone rang once, twice, three times before switching over to a message. I told him to call me, that it was urgent.

It was difficult to return the phone to the cradle because it meant I had to deal with this now, on my own. Luna was at my side, whining at my agitation. I glanced out the windows. The earlier storm was gaining ferocity, and snowflakes swarmed around the yard light like a plague of locusts. I suddenly felt very exposed on this side of the bay windows and clicked off the kitchen light. I stood for a moment, listening to the howl and whistle of the wind, before stepping into the mudroom to check the front door locks. They were flimsy, but latched.

Too flimsy.

Someone knew that I knew about the orange begonias, and they also knew where I worked. That realization forced two facts: the orange begonias meant something, and I had put myself, Mrs. Berns, and my mom in serious peril.

The first rule of self-defense was to avoid dangerous situations. Too late for that, but I'd be damned if we were going to sleep here tonight. I hurried to Mrs. Berns's room and explained the situation in a fearful whisper. She understood immediately. She packed and started readying the animals for travel while I went to my mom.

No light came out of her room. I tapped lightly on the door and cracked it open. "Hey, Mom?"

She switched on the reading lamp next to her bed, smiling at me in confusion. Her hair was in curlers tucked under a sleeping cap. "What is it, honey?"

I didn't want her to know how deep we were in it. "Um, that phone call? It was the police. They're calling everyone, encouraging women who live in the country to stay in a hotel until the killer is caught."

"But there's three of us."

I wanted to turn her light off. It felt like a beacon, calling to the murderer, letting him know how many of us there were and where we stood. "Still. It'll just be for a night or two."

Her face crinkled in worry. "How will we pay for it?"

"I got a raise at the paper," I lied. "I'll cover it."

"Mira." She pursed her lips. "What's going on?"

"I'm worried, Mom, OK?" We needed to get out of here before the panic buried me. "There's a serial killer out there, and I don't want to lose you. We have to go. Now."

"It's Christmas soon!" She clutched her quilt. "We can't leave. I have pies to bake and cookies to decorate."

Outside, a tree cracked. It was a cacophonous snap, the echo of nature meeting wicked cold. I couldn't stand it any longer. I rushed around her bed and flicked off the light. "You have to trust me, Mom."

She relented, though unwillingly. My neck prickled as I watched her pack. Was the killer outside? Was he studying us now? It was difficult to leave my mom alone for even a few minutes, so once she was ready to go, I ran upstairs, tossed whatever was nearest into my bag, and hurried back to her.

We left the house together, Mom, Mrs. Berns, me, and Luna, with Tiger Pop meowling alongside in her carrier. I got them all situated in Mom's van before leaving the safety of the garage for my car. The walk across the drifting sidewalk felt like a death march. The freezing needles of the storm sliced at my cheeks, and I slipped on a patch of ice, nearly landing feet over neck. I caught myself, though, and started my car up just as the garage door rumbled open.

Outside, the wind howled as our convoy of two vehicles drove away from the lonely, now-dangerous house I'd grown up in.

Chapter 27

Convincing my mom that Mrs. Berns and I needed to head out from Paynesville's nicest hotel, the Relax Inn, to run errands at ten thirty at night was more difficult than getting her to leave her house. Since she'd bought into my argument that her home wasn't safe, she didn't want to let me out of her sight. Fortunately, she was too polite to argue for long. After extracting a promise from her that she'd lock the door with both the dead bolt and chain and peer through the spy-hole before letting anyone in, Mrs. Berns and I left.

"Who else knew about the orange begonias?" I asked.

"Those three women at the funeral, any random people they told over the years, Natalie, and you and me."

I pulled onto Highway 23 going west. "Who knew that *we* knew about the flowers?"

"Those three women."

"And?"

Mrs. Berns fiddled with the radio. "I didn't tell anyone, if that's what you're implying."

I shook my head. "You forgot one. Quinna Bankowski. She was standing so close when we heard the story that she was almost riding my shoulders."

"Forgot about her. Why would she send you an orange begonia? And how would she know where you work?"

"She'd google me. You type in my name and up come my *Recall* articles. As for why she'd send it, I don't know. Because she's a creeper?" We'd driven far enough for the coil to heat. I cranked the fan, sending a blessed wash of hot air over us.

"But she's not a serial killer. Women don't do that, right? It's gotta be David or Sharpie who sent you the begonia. We set 'em off by contacting them online and standing them up."

I sighed. "That idea occurred to me. I don't know how they'd know about the orange begonia, though, or that it was us who set up the fake profiles. Quinna is the only suspect who makes sense."

"Maybe we're not thinking like a serial killer. It could be we're dealing with someone who has access to information that we don't."

I nodded. I'd thought of that, too.

"We're heading to River Grove, aren't we?" she asked.

"Yup. I want to drive past Quinna's house to see if she's home. We might as well see what Sharpie and David are up to while we're at it."

I pulled into the next gas station that still offered a pay phone. We lucked out. They had a county phone book covering River Grove, and Quinna's and David's addresses and phone numbers were in it. I called Quinna first. No answer. Next I called David. He picked up on the third ring, and I slammed down the receiver. I scribbled down both addresses, and we left. The moon broke through the clouds as we traveled down the lonely road. The light created sharp, ominous shadows out of the few trees that we passed.

Fifteen minutes later and we were outside Quinna's house on the other side of the city park, the trimmed pine tree in the park's center lit up like a landing strip. The street was quiet, and except for occasional yard and Christmas lights, the houses were dark. Quinna's, a walk-out rambler, was no exception. The outside was austere, lacking decorations. Her walk was well shoveled.

"We should have brought a thermos of coffee," Mrs. Berns said. "This is going to be a long night. Plus, then we could have peed in it.

That's what you private dicks do, right? Pee in your thermoses so you don't have to leave the stakeout?"

I drew in a long breath through my nose. "Absolutely. And we use magnifying glasses to follow footsteps and look for telltale lipstick marks on cigarettes."

"Now you're talking," she said, smacking the dashboard. "I'm thinking about switching careers, you know."

I rubbed my face. "Other than harassing me at the library, you don't have a career."

"Exactly why it's time to switch. That PI class doesn't sound too hard. The trick'll be living long enough to get six thousand hours of supervised investigating in." She held her hands up as if reading a Broadway marquee. "Berns and James Investigations. What do you think?"

I turned away so she wouldn't see my smile. "Don't you think we'd drive each other batty if we had to work together all the time?"

I could hear the shrug. "Maybe. I just said I was thinking about it. We really going to sit in this car all night?"

That didn't sound like a great plan. "How about I peek in Quinna's garage to see if her car is there. If it is, we stay here all night. If it isn't, we check in on David and Sharpie."

I understood the dangers of approaching a dark house in a jumpy town. My form was clearly female, but a recent murder would make everyone dangerous. I decided to act quickly and with confidence. I marched up the driveway.

On tiptoes, I peered through one of the three ornamental windows on the garage door. The inside was dark, but a bit of light from the moon trickled in, revealing a two-car garage so stuffed with boxes and litter that you couldn't fit a ten-speed bike in there, let alone a car. If Quinna was home, she'd have to park in the driveway. I returned to the Toyota.

"She there?"

"Nope. And she looks like a hoarder. Her garage is full of junk."

"Messy home, messy brain," Mrs. Berns said. "On to the dentist's house."

David Fleece lived on the other end of town in a colonial with new-looking siding. Both his driveway and his sidewalk were immaculately shoveled. The interior of his house was dark. I parked the car across the street and left it running while I dashed up to his garage. This was the tonier part of town, and the four houses lining each side of the street had large yards. They were all as dark as David's. This was the type of area that the police would patrol regularly, and I wasn't sure how I felt about that. On the one hand, cops were better than serial killers, but not getting caught at all was the goal. The moon slid behind a cloud, which gave the whole block a surreal feeling.

The frigid air froze the insides of my nostrils as I jogged. I'd already observed that his three-car garage didn't have any windows, but I'd hoped to peek in a crack. No luck. She was sealed tight. I ran around the side and found a locked, windowless door leading into the garage.

I glanced to my right. A winding sidewalk led to David's front stoop. That door was decorated with a Boy Scout wreath, three plastic red balls hanging off a ribbon at the bottom of the green pine circle. It had a thin panel of glass running the length of it. I wanted to charge up and peek in. Just a quick dash and I could be up the three front steps and looking into his house.

What would I see? A tastefully decorated living room? A serial killer, staring back at me, a tiny smile on his face? The last thought froze my blood. I couldn't do it. I ran back to the car, resisting the urge to glance over my shoulder. I hopped in and locked the door.

"Spot anything?"

I shook my head and breathed warm air through my mittens to thaw my fingertips. "Couldn't see in."

"Doesn't matter. I've decided he's not our guy."

Mrs. Berns displayed far more confidence than I felt. There was something about missed opportunity that made me certain I'd passed on the golden ticket. "On to Sharpie?"

The River Grove Inn was a one-story, L-shaped motel a seven-minute drive from David's. It was located on the business end of town between the Copper Kettle Restaurant and an industrial building with a sign that read JACK'S FABRICATION. Most of the inn's rooms were dark and had a car parked in front of them, but neither Mrs. Berns nor I knew what kind of vehicle Sharpie drove, so we had no guess as to which room he was in. We knew the motel wouldn't give us the number if we asked directly, but I had an idea.

"How about we use your cell phone to call the motel and ask to be patched through to Sharpie's. If a light goes on at the same time we call, we know which one he's in. Plus, going through the front desk to reach him would mean he couldn't trace your number."

"Sounds good to me," Mrs. Berns said. "Here, you do it so I can watch the motel."

It was a long shot, but a lucky one. The tired-sounding woman who answered the phone put us through Sharpie's. After the first ring, a light blinked on in the fifth room from the main office. At the second ring, we saw a shadow pass in front of the curtain. The third ring brought an answer.

"Hello?" Sharpie sounded friendly, given the late hour. I supposed it was second nature, given how much business he must do on the phone.

I hung up. "He's home."

"Yup," Mrs. Berns said. "Room five."

Chapter 28

When the police ask him about it, the twelve-year-old boy remembers very little. He had been sledding with friends. Sure it was late, and of course they probably should have come home earlier, but the night had been perfect for racing down a hill: clear winter sky with stars so close you could almost touch them. Nights like that come only two or three times a winter, especially in the dead of the season, and you make 'em last as long as you can. That's what the boy tells the police.

Then the stubborn oak tree had cut the night short, at least for him. It refused to get out of his way, and he was flying too fast to maneuver out of its, and so they met at a high speed.

The tree won.

He'd gotten blood on his new scarf and his expensive Spyder parka. His mom would be so bent out of shape that she'd get that line down the middle of her forehead. That's what he remembers was on his mind as he sulked home earlier than planned and nearly ran into something else: Santa Claus.

Of course he knew it wasn't the real Santa. He was almost thirteen, for cheese's sake. It was just some guy, a little taller than his dad but his dad was a short man, dressed as Santa for the holidays. The guy had the whole costume down: black boots, red pants, and matching jacket trimmed in white, wide plastic black belt cinched over his bulging belly.

Was it a real belly? Hard to say. It was dark out except for the stars and moon, and he was worried about his bloody scarf. Man, his mom was going to be torqued.

Santa's face? It's even harder to describe. It was too shadowy to see much. The curly white wig and fake beard and mustache were so bright they almost glowed, and they took up most of Santa's face, but the boy thinks maybe he spotted a real mustache underneath, a dark one. Come to think of it, Santa had reminded him a little of Junior Hemmesch, the Orelock town mayor. It couldn't have been Junior, though, because Junior knew the boy's parents, and he would have tugged his beard down a little and winked if it'd been him.

No, this Santa wasn't Junior Hemmesch. He carried four wreaths, two on each arm. He ho-ho-ho'd when the boy almost ran into him. It was dorky, but in a funny way. The boy remembers smiling and agreeing to help Santa deliver the Christmas cheer. It didn't hurt that Santa had fished a twenty-dollar bill out of his wallet as soon as his right arm was free.

Did the boy still have the twenty dollars? Yeah, he supposes he does, but he worked hard to earn it, delivering the wreaths to four different houses, their addresses scribbled on a piece of paper. He's positive he no longer has that paper. He chucked it in the snow as soon as the last wreath was resting against the door of the fourth house, exactly as Santa had requested. He had enough to explain with the blood and the late hour without his mom coming across that scrap of paper.

The wreaths? They looked like regular wreaths, he supposes. Round, not quite as big as a car tire, green, with a big bow at the base. Wait, there's one more thing. His face lights up as he remembers. He really does want to be helpful.

The bow on each of them? It had a candy cane tied to it, one of those big ones, curved like a fishhook, red-and-white striped, and as thick as a sausage.

Yep, he definitely remembers that now.

A candy cane on each of them.

Chapter 29

I carved out all of forty-five minutes of sleep, and that was accidental. I'd drifted off in the parking lot of the River Grove Inn around 4:00 a.m., lulled to sleep by Mrs. Berns's rhythmic snoring. When I awoke with a start, a crick in my neck, she was still out, sucking in air like a Hoover with a hairball.

The interior of my car, which I'd been warming by starting the car every forty minutes and letting it run for ten, was frigid. I scraped the interior of the windshield and saw that the red SUV remained parked in front of 5, the light off in Sharpie's room. Letting Mrs. Berns sleep, I started the car and headed toward Paynesville after a quick spin past Quinna's and David's. Both driveways were still empty and both houses still dark. The evening was a stone-cold bust. I'd traded in sleep and comfort, and all I'd gotten in return was the knowledge that Quinna hadn't spent the night at home, David may have, and Sharpie never left his motel room.

My Toyota was the only car on the road. I plowed through tiny drifts forming like sand dunes across Highway 23. My eyelids felt coated with grit, and the lack of sleep and shifting snow played tricks on me. I tapped the brakes on three separate occasions to avoid an animal I was certain was darting in front of my car, only to realize at the last moment that it was nothing but a mirage caused by the blue hour and drifting snow. It took minutes for my heart to stop palpitating after each false scare.

Once in Paynesville, I felt bad about waking Mom to get into our room, but she'd followed my advice and used the chain lock. She didn't ask us any questions, but I saw her worried glance lingering on me. Mrs. Berns stumbled into the second bed, upsetting Tiger Pop. I took Luna for a quick pee and stopped at the front desk on my way back to try Agent Briggs again. I was sure he could trace the calls. I didn't care. I was tired, sore, and hungry. If I was going to be up at 5:00 a.m. because some sick creep had sent me an orange begonia, so was Agent Briggs.

He finally answered, his voice as grouchy as I felt. When I identified myself, he was none too pleased but agreed to meet me in forty-five minutes at the Fatted Caf in River Grove.

When I arrived at the coffee shop and yanked open the door, the deep, earthy smell of fresh-ground coffee beans perked me up slightly. I ordered a tall black coffee, and the barista studied me oddly. I knew I must look a mess, but a night without sleep would do that to a person. I recognized her as the woman who had waited on Mrs. Berns and me yesterday. Maybe she was wondering where my wig was.

Agent Briggs and another guy, both in those well-tailored coats that looked perfect for a foggy summer day in Seattle but painfully thin for a Minnesota winter, sat in a far corner. I could feel their eyes on me, but I wasn't handling this without coffee. I accepted the steaming mug and walked to their table.

"Ms. James?"

"Hi. Thanks for coming."

Briggs's eyes narrowed. "You said it was urgent."

I suddenly felt awkward. They were both so official, wearing their suits like armor. I realized I hadn't combed my hair or brushed my teeth yet. I ran a hand over my face, checking for crusty parts. "Mind if I sit?"

"Be my guest," the other gentleman said, sliding over. He appeared at least a decade younger than Agent Briggs. "I'm Agent Lee."

"Mira James." I misjudged the distance to the bench and dropped awkwardly, spilling coffee. Agent Lee offered me a napkin.

Agent Briggs's phone buzzed. He looked at it, then shot me an impatient glance without answering it. "What can we do for you?"

He turned his attention out the window just as I started to answer. It was rude, but I was too tired to react. I explained our theory that the killer was tracking his victims through online-dating sites, though I left Mrs. Berns out of it. I told him the orange-begonia story we'd heard at the funeral to illustrate how we'd developed our hypothesis and explained that I'd set up a profile, discovered Sharpie Trevino and David Fleece, and planned meetups with them.

I slapped down a copy of the dating printouts we'd gathered, the men's as well as the other women in River Grove with similarities to Natalie. I listed the facts I'd discovered about each guy, including where and how I believed Sharpie had spent the previous evening, though I didn't say how I'd gathered any of the information.

Briggs exchanged a look with Lee. They'd been silent up to this point, their faces impassive. "You tell 'em your real name when you met up with them?"

I shook my head. "No, and they didn't know it was me who set up the profile or contacted them. We just happened to be in the same place at the same time, as far as they knew."

I sipped my coffee, feeling the first licks of doubt. Briggs was clenching his jaw like he wanted to bust through his teeth. It was time I got to the point of the whole story, the reason I was sleeping in a hotel room with my mom, my friend, and my animals. "But last night, I received a threatening message."

Briggs sat forward in his seat. "What was the message?"

I drew a deep breath. "An orange begonia. Sent to the newspaper where I work in Battle Lake."

The air was hushed and heavy for a moment, just like it gets right before a storm. The silence was shattered by Agent Briggs's hearty and unexpected laughter. "A flower?"

I stared at him, shocked. I must not have explained myself clearly. "Not just a flower. An orange begonia. Don't you see? Either Quinna, Sharpie, or David must be involved. Our—my—investigation into the online dating triggered them to send a warning."

Lee regarded me from behind an emotionless mask. "How would any of them know about the orange begonias sent five summers ago?"

"Quinna overheard the story at the funeral. I don't know about Sharpie or David." I flushed. I'd had the same questions myself, but Briggs's laughter made me defensive. "How else do you explain orange begonias getting sent to me.so soon after I first heard the story and set up an online profile?"

"Long-lost admirer?" Briggs asked. His voice was condescending.

I suddenly felt ashamed, a four-legged creature putting on airs. I'd left the hotel this morning knowing that the flowers meant something. Now, talking to these two, that certainty seemed childlike. My voice, when I spoke, was low. "Can you just check who's bought orange begonias in the area, here or around Battle Lake, in the last couple days?"

Agent Briggs snorted. "This ain't *Law and Order*."

Lee glanced at his watch.

I curled into myself. "So you're not going to do anything?"

"We appreciate your telling us about this," Lee said. "I can assure you we follow all legitimate leads."

He was trying to placate me, but his message was obvious: *you've wasted our time.*

Briggs grabbed his gloves and the sheaf of papers I'd set on the table. "In the meanwhile, don't do anything else stupid, OK? No online dating, no meeting with men you think might be serial killers, don't cross at a red light, all that good stuff. Got it?"

I slid out of the way so Agent Lee could exit the booth. I didn't meet their eyes. I didn't want them to see the shiny tears being held back by pride.

Chapter 30

"Assholes." That was Mrs. Berns's verdict.

When I'd returned from my meeting with the agents, I'd found her waiting for me in the Relax Inn lobby. She'd said the room was too small with a cat and a dog and a mom and an old lady.

She'd called up friends in Battle Lake, who had in turn hooked her up with some "inmates"—her word—at the downtown Paynesville Good Samaritan Nursing Home. She planned to spend the day volunteering and visiting. I was fairly sure she'd have a full rebellion in swing by this afternoon, maybe even spring a couple of the spryer ones and take them up the street to Sir Falstaff's for a bump.

All she needed was a ride to the other side of town. After checking on my mom, who was on her way out the door for a quilting class, I loaded Mrs. Berns into my car and drove her to the nursing home, picking up our conversation where it had left off.

"Agent Lee had a good point," I said grudgingly. "We still don't have a good explanation for how Sharpie or David would have known about the orange begonias from five summers ago."

"You're the brains of this operation. You figure that out. There's some connection, you said it yourself. You just need to discover what it is. If you suss it out before Agents Poopyhead and Balls-for-brains, all the better."

I felt a sudden surge of anger toward the agents as I pulled into the nursing home parking lot. Unfortunately, it was too late to do me any good. I tried to clamp it down before it affected the innocent. "Get out of my car. I'm going to be late for my PI class, and I still have to walk Luna."

"Who suddenly peed in your cornflakes?" She gathered up her purse. "You're making me feel rushed."

"Well, you're making me feel slowed," I snapped.

A hurt look crossed her face.

"I'm sorry." I dropped my head on my steering wheel. "They treated me like a child. I just felt so stupid, you know? I hate it when someone does that to me."

She flicked the side of my head. It stung. "I've definitely seen you act stupid, but no one else can make you *feel* stupid. Trust me on that, and follow your instincts. They've always been good."

I knew she was right, but I intended to wallow in feeling bad for a little while longer. "What time should I pick you up?"

"Five o'clock. That'll give us time for a quick bite before our Toe Can Do class tonight."

I didn't have the energy to correct her, though I did accept her peck on the cheek before driving to Willmar. I arrived twenty minutes late for my fifth and final day of PI class. If I passed the cumulative test today, all that stood between me and my license was 5,960 hours of supervised investigating.

The only new topics Mr. Denny covered were writing a final case report and successful billing. The rest of the lecture was a review of everything we'd learned to date, which, as it happened, was a lot. We now knew the basics of managing and promoting a small business, finding cases, working with the police, surveillance, research, and investigative ethics. I was impressed with his organization and comprehensiveness as well as the amount of information a PI had to juggle on any given day.

The last hour of class found us in a computer lab, where we completed a multiple choice and true-false test. I was a fast reader, which made me a fast tester, even when I was crusty from lack of sleep. I completed all fifty questions in under twenty-five minutes, which left me the rest of the hour to research Quinna Bankowski, Sharpie Trevino, David Fleece, and the Candy Cane killings.

The bonus of researching someone with a name like Sharpie Trevino was that you could be certain every hit was the guy you were looking for. He was actually a co-owner of Chi-Town Candies, according to their website. I wondered why he was on the road. Surely, a subordinate could handle that level of marketing. Then again, if what he'd told Mrs. Berns was true, it would make sense for an owner to be directly involved in scoping out a new factory site.

I located his permanent address in Elgin, Illinois. I didn't uncover any criminal charges in his past, even after running his name through the paid database. No connections between Wisconsin and Sharpie existed, either, though he'd be hard-pressed to travel from Chicago to Minnesota without driving through the cheese state. I filed that information away and gave up on Sharpie for the moment.

David Fleece, DDS, showed up even more frequently online. The first hit was his current dental practice, the second the practice he'd left in Alabama five years earlier. He was also linked to his wife's obituary. She had died two years ago, exactly as he'd said in the coffee shop. The remaining hits all referred to his extensive volunteer work, including the Dentists Across Borders organization he'd started with his wife before she passed. The man was a saint, so much so that I'd be suspicious if I hadn't gotten a good vibe from him other than the little self-scare I'd given myself outside his house last night. I decided that had been entirely in my head, and I wrote him off once and for all as a suspect.

Quinna Bankowski's name pulled up fifty-eight matches, the most out of the three. After skimming them all, I deduced that two different Quinna Bankowskis existed. One lived in Florida and was retired, and the other was my traveling nurse.

She frequented AOL chat rooms, but her posted personal information was the basic name-job-state. Her chat room posts were scarce and mostly updates of online games she was playing, but her info page linked to a blog. I clicked on it.

The blog was titled *Cherry Pits*, and the red fruit decorated the borders of the page. The top post was dated two days ago, and its headline was What's Wrong with River Grove. The post complained about the lack of a movie theater, irregular road plowing, and mean people, among other grievances.

Below that was a post called What's Wrong with TV, followed by What's Wrong with Teachers, and What's Wrong with Health Care. I counted 127 posts, all of them complaints by their titles. According to the blog's info page, Quinna had started it two years ago last November.

The complaints seemed petty, for the most part, and none of them had comments. I saw only one title in the compendium that interested me: What's Wrong with Me. I clicked on the title and was brought to the blog post. It was empty.

"Time's up!"

Mr. Denny's voice goosed me. I'd been so focused on Quinna's blog that I'd forgotten where I was.

"Your tests have just automatically closed. Any unanswered questions will be marked incorrect, I'm afraid. We'll mail out your test scores and final percentage for the class within seven days." Mr. Denny clapped his hands, once. "It's been a good week. I hope you agree. Any questions before we call it a day?"

Gene was sitting at a computer near Mr. Denny. "The extra assignment," he said.

Of course. I'd given up on those questions after I'd realized I lacked the resources to verify whether I was on the FBI list and didn't want to knock on legs.

"Ah, yes," Mr. Denny said, eyes twinkling. "The extra assignment. You mean the secrets, right? How about this? I'll write them on this whiteboard. Each of you scribble down your guesses on a sheet of paper. I'll tell you immediately if you matched them all correctly."

I ripped out a piece of paper. Gene was ex-military, Leo Albanian, Kent unemployed but still going to work, Edgar a cheater. I guessed Roger, the guy who'd arrived late to class three out of five times, had a drinking problem. I put myself down as FBI watch list and Dale as having a prosthetic leg. I wrote my name on the top and walked the list to Mr. Denny, then sat back down until everyone else had done the same.

He smiled distantly as he read the answers. Once he'd gone through them, he addressed the class. "No one got them all right. One of you answered only one wrong."

We all looked at each other.

"Mira James, good work," he said. "Since no one answered them all correctly, you'll receive the extra points. Any questions?"

I was surprised, then happy, then, ultimately, so curious that my ears buzzed. How could I, or anyone for that matter, answer only one incorrectly? Seven secrets had to be matched with seven names. If one name was assigned the wrong secret, that meant another one had been as well. I waited until the rest of the class shuffled out and it was just Mr. Denny and me. I studied his back while he erased the board.

He seemed unsurprised to see me still in my seat upon turning. "A question, Ms. James?"

"Which one did I answer wrong?"

The grin spread slowly across his face like a sunrise. "That curiosity will serve you well in this profession." He lifted his foot onto the small table in front of him and hiked the leg of his pants to his knees. Underneath was a red-and-black argyle sock. Peeking over the top of that was a pink but plastic-looking calf. He knocked on it. It made a dull sound. "Fake from the knee down. Lost it in a motorcycle accident."

"I'm sorry." Those words were automatic. The next were not. "Isn't that cheating? To hide your secret in the pile, I mean."

He pushed his pants leg down, still smiling, and placed his foot back on the ground. "Not at all. It's the nature of the business. Assumptions are your enemy. You have to look at information from every possible angle."

I watched him line up the papers in front of him and stick them into his briefcase. "You've done this exercise before, haven't you?"

"Every time I've taught the class. Only twice has someone gotten them all right. Usually, students average about 50 percent correct. Rarely do they consider me. We often let a person's authority distract us, don't we?"

His final comment brought up a mental picture of Agent Briggs, which caused me to flush painfully. I'd let him use his position to intimidate and embarrass me. I pushed the thought to the back of my mind. "I guess."

He studied me. "There's something else?"

I cleared my throat. "Well, yeah. So I *am* on the FBI watch list?"

"Yes and no. You're not in the official terrorist database, or, obviously, on the FBI's Ten Most Wanted List. You are a person of interest, though."

"For what?"

He studied me. "You tell me."

Two nights of too little sleep, a humiliating morning, and seven months of dancing with dead bodies weighed me down. I asked rather than answered a question. "You found out about me being a person of interest through unofficial routes?"

He nodded. "I called in some favors. I do it for all the students, but rarely do I find an FBI connection."

I sighed. What great news. "Do you mind if I stay here for a little bit? I have some research I need to finish."

"Not a problem. Make sure the door closes behind you. It locks automatically."

I nodded my thanks and returned my attention to the computer screen in front of me. It took a full minute to realize Mr. Denny had stopped at the doorway and was considering me.

"What is it?" I asked.

He shook his head as if dismissing an idea, then seemed to think better of it. "I think you've got a gift, Ms. James. Let me know if you ever need my help."

"OK," I said, uncomfortable with the praise, especially since I hadn't even matched up all the secrets correctly in his little game. "Thanks."

He smiled, tapped the doorjamb, and left.

What a day it'd been, and it was hardly even noon. I closed out Quinna's *Cherry Pits* blog and returned to the Google main page, using "Candy Cane Killer" as my search term. The articles that I pulled up focused mainly on the White Plains and River Grove killings in Minnesota, with only a cursory mention of the Wisconsin and Chicago murders. I skimmed all those, but none of them offered me any new information.

Digging deeper, I located an article from two years ago with Adam De Luca's byline. It was coverage of the third murder in Chicago. The victim was named Betty Cyrus. An unopened package of candy canes had been found on a table near her murdered body. That wasn't the detail that caught my attention, however.

Instead, my eyes were drawn to a brief paragraph toward the end where the name of the Candy Cane Killer's first victim was mentioned: Monica De Luca, age thirty-seven.

Chapter 31

"Do you have family?" Adam De Luca asked me.

He sat across the table from me at Tucks Café in Paynesville. The restaurant was exactly as I'd remembered—a lunch counter with a pie case behind it, comfy booths covered in red Naugahyde, and the delicious smells of broasted chicken and homemade soup. Strings of red and green garland were draped across the pie case and over the doorways, and a small, fake Christmas tree sat in the window, strung with lights. We'd snatched a booth in the back, though the small restaurant was mostly empty. Adam appeared more haggard than when I'd last seen him, almost a perfect reflection of how I felt. The murders were getting to both of us.

"Just my mom and me," I said.

He thanked the waitress as she slid him a cup of coffee and a caramel roll. "Don't ever stop appreciating her. Family is all we have in this world. One day they're there, the next day they're gone."

I felt a pang of guilt. Appreciating my mom was the opposite of what I'd been doing ever since my dad had died. "Monica was your sister?" I'd called to ask if he could meet with me as soon as I'd read the article. He'd agreed.

"Yes. My sister, my best friend, my only family. She was the oldest. Our dad disappeared when I was still in the crib. Mom ditched out on us shortly afterward. It was Nic and me against the world. She basically raised me." He drank his coffee black. His caramel roll sat untouched.

The waitress began to clear the circular table next to us. A large party must have left shortly before we'd arrived. I raised my voice to be heard above the clatter of plates. "I'm sorry." I felt like I'd been saying that a lot lately.

He raised a shoulder in a noncommittal gesture. "Me too. I get sorry all over again every time I see other people go through what I did. Did you see the look on Mrs. Garcia's face at the funeral? That's shock so deep it knocks you out of this world for a while. I saw it all the time when I used to cover war zones. And I wore it on my own face when I found out about Nic."

I leaned forward, trying to get him to look at me. "Why do you do it?"

He blinked, surprised. "Do what?"

"Cover this serial killer. It must be torture for you. I'm surprised your editor lets you."

"Yeah, me too." He ran his hands through his hair and lifted his cup for more coffee. "She didn't, not at first. Said I couldn't be objective, that it wasn't healthy. Then the writer she originally assigned to CCK moved to LA, and I wouldn't let up."

"CCK?" I translated the initials as soon as the question left my mouth: *Candy Cane Killer.* "Oh."

He nodded. "I convinced her that I'd be obsessing about the case anyhow, so she might as well take advantage. By then, CCK had struck twice. My sister and a woman named Audrey Jordan. He killed twice more before he left Chicago. Do you know the wildest thing?" He tipped his head, a bitter smile on his face. "I was furious when he went underground that first time. How could we catch him if he stopped killing? That stupid fury lasted right up until he struck in Wisconsin the next December. That's when I decided I didn't care if I ever found out who he was, so long as another woman wasn't murdered. If he could just die a nameless death and the killings would stop, that would be enough."

I tried to imagine how difficult it would be to let go of the need for justice if someone I loved had been brutally murdered. "You still feel that way?"

"Yes."

He appeared so desperately alone for just a moment that I wanted to hug him. I obviously didn't know him well, but I could see he was torturing himself by following this case. I was reaching over to comfort him when his pocket chirped.

He reached in and yanked out a phone, holding it to his ear. "Yeah," he said.

I watched in amazement as five years were added to his face. Lines around his mouth deepened and his eyes sagged. He rubbed his hand over his forehead and leaned into the phone as if it were whispering to him.

"Jesus. Yeah. Got it. Yeah." He ended the call and fumbled the phone back into his pocket. He brought his eyes slowly to mine, and they looked like two holes drilled into his face.

"There's been another murder. Northern Minnesota. In a place called Orelock."

Chapter 32

Adam had no more information; he'd gotten the call from his editor, who'd gotten it from an FBI contact. He'd left immediately for Orelock, a town located approximately two hours northeast of Battle Lake. The killer would have had ample time to drop orange begonias off at the *Recall* office before driving north to seek his next victim.

I gathered Mrs. Berns from the nursing home and filled her in on the terrible news on our way to self-defense class. She was so struck with horror that she didn't even have a comeback.

It had all become too much.

By the time we arrived at the gym, everyone was talking about the news. The room was tense, a mixture of outrage and fear. Master Andrea, knowing she had no chance of getting the class started until everyone was focused, brought us into the workout room and clicked on the television above the treadmill.

". . . in Orelock, Minnesota. The town of 1,700 people is reeling from the news. At noon today, the body of Samantha Keller was found in her home. Police say the time of death was between midnight and four a.m. this morning. She was one of four women who received a wreath with a candy cane on it, delivered by a boy who said a man dressed as Santa paid him to drop them off. While the police have no suspects, they have taken a woman in for questioning. She currently lives in River Grove, Minnesota, the scene of the Candy Cane Killer's previous murder, though she's originally from Orelock."

I grabbed Mrs. Berns's arm. "Did you see that?" It had been just a flash, a split-second shot of a tall brunette with short hair being led into the Orelock police station.

"What?"

"Quinna Bankowski. She's their main suspect!"

Mrs. Berns considered this. "And the timing of the Orelock murder clears Sharpie. We watched him in his motel room until early this morning."

"You watched the inside of your eyelids."

Mrs. Berns smiled, immune to shame. "Good thing you're the private dick."

The rest of the newscast recapped what we already knew about the killings in Chicago and central Wisconsin. It ended with a panoramic shot of Orelock, a sleepy Iron Range town drifted with snow and dotted with snug houses and shops.

We all watched, shell-shocked or riveted. Nowhere was safe.

The instructor snapped off the TV. "Back to work," she said.

Chapter 33

Mrs. Berns and I were up at 4:00 a.m. to drive to Orelock. I felt guilty leaving my mom in charge of two animals in a hotel room, but she promised she'd be fine. Her eyes made it clear that she was worried about me, but she held her tongue. I knew she didn't want me to be a PI, couldn't understand why I wasn't happy being a librarian or an English teacher, but she was going to support me if it was the last thing she did. I thought back to Adam's words and vowed to be more appreciative of her.

It was too early to even be called morning, and the accumulated wear of three nights of little sleep made me twitchy. I kept seeing movement out of the corners of my eyes, but when I'd look, there'd be nothing there. We poured ourselves old coffee in to-go cups in the hotel lobby, tempered it with powdered creamer, and headed into the bracing cold.

Even knowing that it was fifteen below didn't prepare me for the slap of winter. My tips immediately froze as I raced to the car, holding the door open for Mrs. Berns. I was worried my Toyota wouldn't start, but I needn't have been. She was as reliable as the moon. I scraped the windows while she warmed up, and Mrs. Berns did the seat dance to try to coax heat to her extremities.

Every house we drove past was dark, and none of the Paynesville businesses were open. It was even more lonely once we hit the highway. Except for the occasional semitruck, it was only us and the drifting snow, hardly a building in sight. The sky pinked the farther north we drove, but the traffic never picked up.

The prairie of central Minnesota gave way to rolling hills and pine forests, which gave way to the stark landscape of the Iron Range. The lack of other humans on the road made me edgy, and Mrs. Berns must have felt the same, because we argued about everything from the radio station to the speed I was driving.

"That's black ice ahead."

I squinted. "You can't see that."

"Can too. You should slow down."

"I can't. We have too much to get done today." We didn't actually have a plan, more of a sense that we needed to be in Orelock. Still, not having a plan would take more time than actually knowing what we were doing, and I was itching to get to Orelock.

She flashed me her angry eyes. "You should learn patience."

"I don't have time for patience."

Mrs. Berns glared silently the rest of the way, not speaking again until we pulled into a gas station on the outskirts of Orelock. It sported only two pumps in front of a tiny building shaped like a 1970s space station. It was no larger than a bedroom, glass on all four sides. I could see the nametag on the shirt of the older man working inside, though I couldn't read it.

"Get me some M&M's," Mrs. Berns demanded as I pulled up to a pump.

I was too crabby. "If I have to get out of this car, you do, too."

I exited without waiting for her response. The biting wind whipped and stung while I filled the tank. It was cold all over Minnesota, but something about the northern cold felt like a personal attack, a keening to separate you from your herd.

Mrs. Berns followed me inside.

"$25.71," the clerk said when I made my way to his counter. I couldn't help noticing that his age spots were the same color as his eyes.

Mrs. Berns slapped a brown bag of M&M's on the counter. "And these." She reached into a hanging basket and palmed a pile of candy. "These, too. What are they?"

"Salted caramels," the man said, ringing us up. "$28.91."

"They look like butterscotch," Mrs. Berns said crossly.

His facial expression didn't change. "They're salted caramels."

"Hey, wait a minute." My moodiness melted away as I grabbed a clear-wrapped candy out of her hand. It read "Chi-Town Candies Famous Salted Caramels" in fancy white script. "These are the candies that Sharpie Trevino sells!"

The man behind the counter nodded. "Guy with a face like a rat? He dropped them off a couple days ago."

Mrs. Berns and I exchanged a glance, back on the same team. I knew we were both thinking that Sharpie sure did get around. I wondered just how certain the police were about the Orelock victim's time of death.

"Did you know Samantha Keller?" I asked.

The clerk put his hands on the counter and regarded us shrewdly. It was the first interest he'd shown. "No, but I know one of the other women who received the wreath with the candy cane. She said it was like being kissed by the Grim Reaper himself."

"What's her name?" Mrs. Berns asked.

He studied his fingernails. "I'll tell you for ten dollars."

"That's extortion!" Mrs. Berns said.

He shrugged, palms in the air.

She slapped a ten-dollar bill on the counter. It disappeared under his sliding hand. "Her name's Amanda Running. She's the daughter of the guy who owns this station. Lives over on Galena Avenue, gray house with blue trim. You can't miss it."

"Thanks." Mrs. Berns put another $18.91 on the counter, parsing it to the penny. "Have a nice day."

"Wait! Your gas and food was $28.91."

"That's how much I paid you."

"You only gave me $18.91. The ten dollars was for me."

Mrs. Berns gave him a disingenuous smile. "I don't care where you spend it, sonny." She grabbed my elbow and led me out, leaving the weasel clerk sputtering behind the counter.

When the door closed behind us, I yelled the obvious over the shriek of the winter wind. "Where Sharpie goes, death follows. Or is it the other way around?"

"It could be coincidence," Mrs. Berns said, sliding past the car door I held open for her. "He's in the state to sell candy and find a place to set up shop. You can probably find his caramels all over Minnesota."

She waited for me to get in to continue. "Plus, we know he was in his hotel last night when the Orelock woman was murdered."

"Do we? We never actually saw him."

"Did you get the license plate of the car outside his motel room?"

"Yup. We might need to set up another meeting with him to find out if that red SUV was really his."

"What if he has a partner in crime?" Mrs. Berns asked. "That would explain how he could appear to be two places at once."

I shook my head. "Possible, but unlikely. Serial killers almost always work alone."

Mrs. Berns cranked the heat vent wide open and held her hands in front of it. "We should have asked that guy for directions to Galena Avenue. Think I should go back in?"

I leaned forward in the driver's seat to see around her. The clerk was at the window, hands crossed, glaring at us. "Naw. It's a small town. We'll find it."

Orelock, like every other municipality in Minnesota, was festooned with Christmas decorations. Green garlands studded with white twinkle lights circled the telephone poles and light posts, with three-foot-high, bell-shaped ornaments sticking out from the top of each.

Downtown Orelock was too small for a stoplight, but it did have a four-way stop. I counted two diners, a hardware store, an accountant's office, a beauty parlor, and a Laundromat at the main intersection. "Reminds me a little of Battle Lake."

Mrs. Berns snorted. "Not nearly as charming."

She rolled down a window and yelled at a tall guy wrapped in down from head to toe. The wind had a loose end of his scarf and appeared to be using it to pull him forward. "Excuse me, where's Galena Avenue?"

He yelled through his muffler and over the wind, "First right, first right again."

"Thank you!" She rolled the window back up quickly. "Brrr. It's cold enough to turn balls into ovaries."

I nodded and tapped my blinker. The intense temperature made the roads a special kind of icy, so I braked well before the turn. I spotted a coffee shop, and Agent Briggs stepping into it. He wore a face like he was chewing on bad air. I instantly tensed up.

"There he is," I said, pointing. "The FBI agent. Briggs. We should stay out of his way."

Mrs. Berns adjusted the heater vent nearest her iced-over window, aiming it at the frost. "Really? You think we should avoid the man who treated you like shoe scum just yesterday for bringing him useful information? What's your position on driving in cars when we need to travel versus just leaning back in a chair and making revving noises? Think we should do that, too?"

I stuck my tongue out at her, hung a right on Galena, and was nearly to the end of the block before I spotted the gray house with blue trim. "There it is!"

I parked in front and leaned forward to get a feel for the place. "Are we just going to go in and talk to her?"

Mrs. Berns was halfway out of the car, a tiny force bundled in her blue winter jacket, scarf, and mittens. She was ringing the doorbell by the time I reached her.

"You don't think we should have a plan?" I asked, hopping from foot to foot to keep warm.

"We absolutely should. You're in charge of that."

I had my mouth open to object when the door cracked. The woman on the other side was about my age and height with brown skin and beautiful dark eyes. Her ebony hair was tied in a thick braid slung over her right shoulder. A TV blared a morning talk show in a distant room. "Hello?"

"Amanda Running?" I asked.

She narrowed her eyes and glanced behind her. The TV in the other room grew quieter. "Who wants to know?"

I looked to Mrs. Berns. She was smiling at Amanda and not about to offer anything. "My name's Mira James. This is Mrs. Berns. We're from Battle Lake originally, temporarily staying in Paynesville."

A child appeared at Amanda's hip and wound his hand around her waist. His T-shirt had a yellow Pokémon on it, and his soft-looking brown hair stuck up in every direction. "Mom, I'm hungry."

"Go back inside, you hear? You just had breakfast." The air still smelled like bacon. She returned her attention to us. "Look, it's been a long couple days. If you're trying to convert me, it's too late. If you're trying to sell me something, I'm broke." She started to close the door.

"Wait!" The wind whistled through the skeleton of an oak tree in her yard and sent eddies of loose snow across the front steps. "Look," I said. I wasn't sure what I wanted her to look at. She held herself like she was annoyed, but I spied fear around her eyes. She didn't need to know that I was a PI in training or a reporter for a small-town paper. She wanted to know why we were here and why she should care.

That left me only one path: honesty. "The Candy Cane Killer murdered a woman I went to high school with, and I think he's threatened me. We drove all the way up here from Paynesville in the hopes of finding out something to make us feel safe. We heard at the gas station that you'd received one of the wreaths with a candy cane on it, and we wanted to ask you some questions."

She stared, unblinking, for several slow seconds. Then she stuck her head outside and glanced around, the wind snarling the loose hairs framing her face. "Fine." She turned and walked indoors but didn't close the door behind her. Mrs. Berns and I followed before she changed her mind.

The smell of bacon was stronger inside, along with the odors of coffee and cigarettes. The front space was a living room paneled with the sort of faux wood that was popular in the '70s. Amanda tossed herself into a worn recliner and grabbed a pack of cigarettes. "I don't know anything. I woke up yesterday morning to bring Zach to school, and there was a wreath leaning against my stoop. I tossed it inside the house. That afternoon, police come door-to-door and ask about it. I gave it to them. I didn't want it."

Her son wandered back into the room. I put him at about five years old. "Not when I'm smoking, Zach Attack. You go watch TV."

"You were going to take me sledding," he said. If I were his mom, I couldn't have withstood the disappointment in those long-lashed brown eyes.

"Only when it gets above zero, I told you. Now go on, or we won't sled at all." He tossed us a furtive glance before scurrying into a back room.

"Was there anything weird about the wreath, anything written on it?" I asked.

"Nope, just a wreath with some berries, a bow, and a candy cane." She lit the cigarette and inhaled. "It was nice. Nicer than I could afford."

"How about footprints around it?" Mrs. Berns asked.

Amanda regarded her through the smoke curling out of her mouth. "You sound like the cops. I'll tell you what I told them: I keep my walk shoveled."

I could feel her retreating. "I know this sounds weird, but we think the killer is targeting women through online-dating sites. The woman I went to high school with was on E-adore. Can I ask if you were doing any online dating?"

The sudden tightening of her face followed by a quick glance to the room her son was in gave me all the answer I needed. She leaned forward in her chair, her eyes sparking. "That bastard is coming after women because they're dating? Christ." She took another pull off her cigarette, shaking her head in disbelief. "What am I supposed to do, stay inside my house all day? I didn't do anything wrong. I was looking for a friend, maybe someone to throw the ball around a little with Zach. I deserve to get my life threatened for that?"

Mrs. Berns put her hand up. "Just calm the heck down, missy. No one's saying you did anything wrong. He's the problem, not you."

"Was it E-adore?" I asked.

She nodded and stubbed out her cigarette. "They give you a free one-month trial in December." Her hand shook slightly.

"Do you know who got the other wreaths?"

"Sure." Her outburst had passed, and she suddenly appeared very tired. "It's a small town. Everyone knew Samantha, everyone knows me. Johnna and Rita are the other two."

We were getting full names and addresses when a knock came at the front door. It was one single rap, loud and ominous.

"Get down!" Mrs. Berns hissed.

Both Amanda and I looked at her in surprise as she hit the floor. "How about I just peek through the spy-hole instead?" I whispered.

Zach hurried into the room and tucked himself back into his mom's waist, a well-loved stuffed black bear in his hand. I tiptoed to the door and peered out.

Supervisory Agent Walter Briggs stared back at me.

Chapter 34

I instinctively dropped to the ground and crawled back toward Mrs. Berns. I knew Briggs couldn't see in the peephole, but something about his laser gaze directed right into it was unsettling.

"It's the FBI," I whispered. "Amanda, do you have a back door?"

"Yeah. Through the kitchen." She pointed the direction the boy had entered from. "You two in trouble?"

"Not if we can sneak out of here before he sees us," I said. "He's not our biggest fan."

She shrugged. "I won't lie for you."

"I wouldn't, either," I said.

"It's not lying if they don't ask you about it," Mrs. Berns said.

Amanda arched an eyebrow. She was done with us. Mrs. Berns fished in her purse for her M&M's and handed them to Zach. He looked at his mom, and when she nodded, he grabbed them and ran off again, a wide, sweet smile on his face. Then Mrs. Berns and I speed-crawled down the hallway, standing when we reached the cracked linoleum of the small but clean kitchen. We were halfway out the back door when we heard Amanda open the front.

We closed the door gently behind ourselves, walked into the alley, out into the street, and around to Galena. Agent Briggs's sedan was pulled up immediately behind my car. I had no illusions. He either recognized or had run the plates on my car, so he knew I was in town and had visited Amanda. I was OK with that. I just didn't want to run into him.

I started up my car, Mrs. Berns and I slunk low in our seats. We didn't speak until we were on the other side of town, searching for Johnna's and Rita's houses. We kept the conversation focused on navigating the back streets, both of us rattled.

Neither Johnna nor Rita was home, so we left a note with Mrs. Berns's cell phone number tucked in each mailbox and a request that they call us as soon as they could.

Not sure what to do next, we made our way back to the coffee shop that Briggs had entered less than an hour earlier. We were gratified to find creamy honey and cinnamon lattes and rent-by-the-hour computers waiting inside for us.

We took our coffees, freshly baked maple-nut scones, and bad attitudes to a computer, where we pulled up the E-adore site and began creating a profile for an Orelock brunette.

Chapter 35

The killer passed them as they pulled into the gas station, two women in a brown Toyota Corolla, older model, carrying road muck all the way from Paynesville.

Or, as it turned out, all the way from Battle Lake.

It hadn't been hard to track down her current address, job, and a list of family and friends, once she dropped her name. The killer had always been very gifted at research. It came with the job.

It had been much more difficult to locate her online ad. The profile was created last June on a cheap, no-name site. Her whole page was oddly worded, as if she weren't taking it seriously, and her photo was unflattering. It captured her from only the neck up, and a shadow across her face made it appear as if she had a large nose. She was much prettier in real life.

Still, she was advertising herself, and she had to expect buyers.

If you sell yourself short, be prepared to accept bargain-basement prices.

The killer's gloved hand is in the air, poised to strike the smug little doll strapped in the passenger seat. Had she just giggled? Her clothes are perfect, as always, but she's beginning to show the strain. A lock of curling brown hair has escaped her tight bun. It's no wonder, with the police swarming closer and closer, and now that nosy bitch from Battle Lake poking around.

"It was still a stupid move," the killer says, stealing a glance.

The doll only smiles.

"A damn mistake to send that orange begonia," the killer continues. "What did we gain? Scaring her? We could have accomplished that with a candy cane. The flower was too risky. Only a handful of people have heard that story. Now we're going to have to get rid of her, all because of you."

A house divided against itself cannot stand.

Tears are running down the killer's face. "That's not fair."

But when has it ever been fair? Killing Auntie Ginger ten years ago should have stopped the taunts, and it had, for a while. That memory of her shocked face as she regained consciousness to find that she was wearing a noose and perched on a chair, hands tied behind her back, still makes the killer smile.

One kick of the chair, four minutes of thrashing like a hooked fish, and it was done. The monster was dead.

Except the killer hadn't been able to leave Auntie Ginger behind.

The doll came with, just as a memento, a reminder of what could be survived. After all, it had been the doll, the cruel plastic plaything that Auntie Ginger pulled out of her pocket, that issued the actual commands to the chosen boy or girl at dress-up time. It was the doll, held in Auntie Ginger's hands and speaking with a falsetto version of Auntie Ginger's voice, who told the chosen child not to cry. It was the doll who exacted a promise from the children to never tell a soul.

It was the goddamn doll.

And how awful it was when the doll began to speak again, two years ago this December. It is the doll who orchestrates the terrorizing of the women and the murders, who always has, who reminds the killer every second of every day that there is no such thing as freedom.

The killer has to pull over. The pain is too much.

Chapter 36

"Do you want some?"

I dragged my eyes away from the computer screen. Mrs. Berns was offering me pink chewing gum with a secret center.

"I hate that kind," I said, shaking my head. "Chewing it makes me feel like I'm popping a blister."

She harrumphed, but out of the corner of my eye, I saw her slide the partially masticated chunk out of her mouth and slip it into the garbage.

We'd updated our E-adore profile so we could peer out into the online world as if we were a man looking for a brunette in Orelock. Unlike in River Grove, many of the women here had chosen to identify themselves only by usernames. Amanda, for example, called herself "LovetoLaugh1986." There was no way to discover if any of the other smiling faces belonged to Samantha Keller, Johnna, or Rita. I was trying to skim all the profiles to see if anything stuck out, marking them as victims, but none of them posted anything unusual.

Mrs. Berns was growing impatient with my research and demanded that I switch over and search for the guys who'd match with someone like Amanda.

"All right," I said.

I revised our Veronica profile, changing the name to Anne and the town to Aurora, an Iron Range village that we'd driven through right before reaching Orelock.

Next, I ran a search for men aged twenty-four to fifty-four within thirty miles of Orelock. There were only twelve, and none of them was Sharpie Trevino. Of those twelve, we immediately discounted the seven who had photos posted and began skimming the remaining five. We were on the third when I spotted it.

"Look!"

"What?" Mrs. Berns asked, pushing her cat's-eye reading glasses higher on her nose.

"This guy. He says he likes to go dancing, likes to travel, and can make any date fun 'in two shakes of a sheep's tail.' Where have we heard that bizarre phrase before?"

Mrs. Berns leaned back in her chair, her eyes sharp. "Isaac, one of Veronica's River Grove matches. What's he call himself here?"

"Isaiah."

"Not very imaginative. What about the others?"

Nothing stuck out in the remaining four. They all sounded like regular guys light on the helping verbs, which was to be expected in greater Minnesota. Though we both had a tingling sense about Isaiah, we reached out to all five of the photo-less men to be thorough. This time, we would spy on them but wouldn't interact. We'd decided to not make the same mistakes twice because, as Mrs. Berns said, there's so many to be made, why limit yourself that way?

We sent the same message to all of them. Two of the guys responded instantly, Floyd, who claimed to be a dead ringer for Sean Connery, and Arthur, who said he was a redhead who liked fish, beer, and naps. We asked both of them if they could meet us in this very coffee shop for lunch today, using our line that we had to leave tomorrow for a Christmas trip. They both said yes.

Isaiah and the fourth and fifth guys, Nathan M. and Phillip, didn't immediately reply. We would keep checking back.

"While we wait, I want to see what I can unearth about Walter Briggs." I'd made up my mind after we'd fled Amanda's. I hated feeling intimidated, and a good offense was the best defense.

"You're going to ogle an FBI agent?"

"Google, and yes, I am. He's a public employee, right?"

Mrs. Berns stood and pointed to the table farthest from my computer. "I'm going to be doing the crossword puzzle over there. Far away from your sketchy actions."

I let her go and plugged in Briggs's name. I pulled up a lot of noise until I added "FBI." I was instantly transported to his official bio:

> Supervisory Agent Walter Briggs is a member of the Behavioral Analysis Unit out of Quantico. He's been with the FBI for 32 years.

That helped me not at all. I clicked out of the official FBI page and, on a hunch, searched for Walter Briggs co-linked with Adam De Luca. A surprising number of hits came up. Briggs had been on the Candy Cane Killer case since the beginning and Adam not long after, and they'd become weirdly tied in cyberspace.

All but one of the hits were articles by Adam briefly referring to Briggs as the agent in charge. The exception was an article written about the second woman killed in Wisconsin, Evelyn Wable. According to the story, she was a relocated farm girl living in a medium-size city and working as an administrative assistant when she was murdered. Adam took an interesting aside toward the end of the article to offer a little more depth on the agent in charge:

> This case seems to have struck Agent Briggs, a native Midwesterner, particularly hard. When asked for a comment, he said only, "I have a daughter named Evelyn." The agent currently resides in Virginia, though he's been largely in the field trying to capture the Candy Cane Killer since his first strike in Chicago.

I sipped my latte. It was cold. I waved my hand at Mrs. Berns and called her over.

"What?"

"FBI Agent Walter Briggs is originally from the Midwest."

Her eyes widened. "You know what that means?"

I glanced left and right to make sure no one was listening, then leaned toward her. "No. What?"

"Nothing." She smacked my head. "Millions of people are from the Midwest. Now close down that screen before the FBI echolocates you and take a gander at who just walked in. I believe it's our local E-adore delivery, Floyd."

We were on the far side of the restaurant, both because the computers were located there and because it gave us a good view of everyone who entered. I turned to check out the guy who'd just walked in. He fit the online description and actually hadn't lied when he'd written that he looked like Sean Connery, if Sean Connery were five six and as bald as a monkey butt.

"Think he can fake a Scottish accent?" Mrs. Berns asked.

"You can't be serious."

Floyd got in line to order.

"I'm attracted to look-alikes," she said. "What can I tell you?"

"That you won't fraternize with the suspects. I think I see our second, by the way." A redhead had just entered. I looked down when he scanned the room nervously, sweeping his eyes over me and Mrs. Berns before standing behind Floyd in line. "Think they know each other?"

My question was so fresh it was green when the two of them started talking. The exchange was first friendly, and then they both cocked their heads at each other like quizzical chickens, and then heated words started flying. I heard "made a fool of" and "damn online dating," and then they both stormed out.

"I'd say yes," Mrs. Berns said. "They did, in fact, know each other, and now they know each other even better."

"Scratch them off the list," I said, doing just that. "If they're from around here, they're not our killer. It's between Isaiah, Nathan, and Phillip, and the smart money's on Isaiah. We can't stay in town forever, though."

"Not forever, but one more night." Mrs. Berns appeared smug. "I reserved a hotel room for us while you were noodling online, and I called your mom to tell her we wouldn't be back until tomorrow."

"Wow."

"I also told her you'd go to Mass with her tomorrow. It's the last Sunday before Christmas, after all. You can thank me later."

I grimaced. "That's exactly when I'll be thanking you. Much, much later."

"You're welcome," she said happily, ignoring my sarcasm. "We might as well get some Christmas shopping done while we're here. Come on."

Chapter 37

"Who knew a hardware store would have so many perfect presents?" she asked, one hour later. Her cart held a prepackaged snorkeling set, a windowsill garden kit, two-inch letter stickers that she intended to "rogue adorn" the front door of every friend in Battle Lake with, and various nails, tools, putties, and paints.

"I'm guessing only you and Tim 'The Tool Man' Taylor." I sniffed. "Maybe Luis from *Sesame Street*."

I usually liked the smell of hardware stores, the earthy, blue-collar perfume of metal, motor oil, and wood. After a full hour, though, I was so bored I'd begun to organize the shelves while Mrs. Berns pawed through bins for goodies. I was straightening a row of mucilage when the front door donged. I glanced up idly, then quickly yanked Mrs. Berns out of sight.

"Quinna Bankowski," I hissed, pointing toward the front door. The woman in question had just entered wearing a quilted black parka and a Swedish ski cap.

"What's she doing here?" Mrs. Berns whispered.

Quinna steered into the first aisle, giving us a good view of her back.

"Shopping for something to remove bloodstains? I'm surprised the police released her."

"They must have decided she's innocent, or didn't have enough to hold her on," Mrs. Berns said, freeing herself from my grip.

Boredom had made me reckless. "Only one way to find out."

I scuttled down the tools aisle, took a left at housewares, and another left at fasteners. Quinna was digging through a slide-out bin of flat-head nails.

"Quinna Bankowski?"

Her head whipped toward me, her eyes bright. She reminded me of a raccoon caught stealing garbage. "Yeah?"

I held out my hand. "Mira James. We met at Natalie Garcia's funeral."

She kept her hands in the nails. Her eyes narrowed. "What are you doing here?"

"That's so weird. I was wondering the same thing about you."

"This is my hometown. My mom still lives here. It's Christmas, right?" She finally pulled her mitts out and pushed the bin back in.

I noticed a wound across the back of her right hand.

"Cut yourself?"

She rubbed her left hand over her right without taking her eyes from mine. "Scratched myself on a nail. I was trying to help my mom put up Christmas decorations. Better late than never, right?" She finally broke eye contact and glanced back at the bin. "That's why I'm here. In the hardware store. To get more nails." She sounded suddenly rueful.

I was having a hard time keeping up with her emotional switches. The rolling thunder of an overloaded cart on concrete floors drew our attention. We both turned to see Mrs. Berns walking toward us.

"If it isn't the nurse with comfortable shoes! So, what'd the police want with you?"

Quinna glanced from me to Mrs. Berns, and back again. "About what you'd expect. I was in River Grove when Natalie was murdered, then I'm in Orelock when Samantha is killed. I went to school with Samantha, by the way. She graduated two years ahead of me. We weren't friends but I liked her." Quinna paused for a quick breath. "I didn't get up here until after she was killed, so they had to let me go. I was covering a late shift for a colleague. You two still haven't said what you're doing here."

I nodded sagely as if she had said something very wise instead of implied a question. "Well, it was nice running into you. I hope you have a merry Christmas. Mrs. Berns and I have an appointment to keep, so we'll be going now."

I glanced back as Mrs. Berns and I walked away. Quinna was standing in the aisle, her hands hanging loosely at her sides. The only light that came from her shone out of her eyes, which glittered as she watched us.

A tiny smile sat like a judge upon her lips.

Chapter 38

The only room available at the Voyageur Inn so close to the holidays was a space that was more closet than suite. It barely had room for a nightstand, a TV, and a double bed.

It was nearly midnight, and an inky, oppressive darkness weighted the air outside our window. Mrs. Berns was currently sprawled across 90 percent of the lumpy mattress, snoring like a Great Dane. Given how little sleep I'd had in the past three days, I should have been passed out from exhaustion next to her. Instead, I balanced myself on the lip of the bed and watched the ghost parade of memories floating between me and the window.

The first was my dad, of course. Jeff came second. We'd been lovers, briefly, in May. He'd arrived in Battle Lake promising excitement and stability in equal parts. He'd ended up with a bullet in his head, a victim of past jealousies and twisted perceptions. I'd discovered his corpse on the floor of the library, a book resting over him as if he'd fallen asleep reading. That murder seemed to ignite others, until I had a string of a dozen dancing ghosts, crying out, catching my eye, murmuring admonitions. I wasn't the reason they were dead, I couldn't be. It was simply bad luck that they'd died near me.

The ghosts kept whispering, though, and the loudest were the victims of the Candy Cane Killer, those women whose senseless murders were still unsolved. They were young, they were brunette, they looked like me. They woke up one morning, maybe worried about what outfit to wear to a job interview or whether they were gaining a few pounds or if they should get another cat or if their mom was going to survive her cancer scare.

Those thoughts, great and small, would swirl in their heads as they stepped out to conquer another day, doing their very best and maybe falling short, maybe promising themselves that they'd try even harder the next day. And they'd return home, and finally relax and remove the smiling masks they'd been forced to wear to make it through another day. Then, at last, home and comfortable in their own skin, they could dream their dreams in full glorious color, with no one around to judge.

But he was waiting.

With a knife.

Had the victims fought? They must have, at least one of them. Or maybe tachypsychia had suffocated each of them, dropping down like a lead apron, and they'd been frozen, watching their death approach, their blood draining before he even raised a hand.

Natalie, who as a sixth grader had legs halfway to her neck and buck teeth that turned her smile into an inside joke that welcomed everyone, my very best friend for one year, the girl who assured me at age eleven that she was going to go to college to be a meteorologist and find her husband but only if I also went with.

That sweet child all grown up had spent her last seconds on this earth in blind terror, a killer in her home, a senseless, inevitable end.

Had she yelled? Had she wished for ten more minutes of life so she could make sure everyone she cared about knew how much she loved them? Had she begged? If only I could see through her eyes in those last moments, share her terror to identify her killer.

I didn't sleep that night, I don't think.

Chapter 39

Nathan M. had emailed at exactly 12:23 a.m. our time, according to the inbox of our E-adore account. He wrote that he was currently in Mexico with friends on a two-week vacation and would be returning after New Year's. He said he'd be thrilled to meet with us then and had included a photo of himself on a beautiful white beach wearing a sombrero. It was enough to discount him as a suspect.

We'd also heard from Phillip, who instant messaged while we were checking out Nathan's response at the coffee shop, Mrs. Berns bright and shiny and me sucking down cup after cup of black coffee. I perked up when he wrote that he'd be thrilled to meet "Anne" here for breakfast.

We hadn't heard a peep from Isaac/Isaiah.

I ceded the computer to Mrs. Berns while I started in on the *New York Times* Sunday crossword puzzle, which, despite rumors, was not nearly as difficult as the Saturday puzzle. I'd positioned my chair so I was alongside Mrs. Berns but facing out, toward the door. I glanced up every time someone arrived.

I was penciling in "ort" for a three-lettered "piece of food" when the door opened. Through the large front windows, I'd observed an El Camino pull up. The driver parked between two pickup trucks and blocked the view of trees in the park across the street. This would be my first chance to see up close the man who'd emerged from the vehicle.

"Remind me again what Phillip is supposed to look like."

Mrs. Berns minimized a screen featuring something called a Hampster Dance and peered toward the E-adore page that'd been hiding behind it. "A huggable bear, not too tall and not too short, carrying a few extra pounds, forty-three. Dark hair and eyes. Divorced."

"Does it say anything about looking like he thinks he knows karate when he's drunk?"

Mrs. Berns swiveled on her seat and pulled her reading glasses down to the tip of her nose. "Wow."

The guy who'd just walked in was indeed about forty-three years old, average height, dark haired and eyed, and sporting a few extra pounds. In addition, he was wearing worn cowboy boots, acid-washed jeans with a bandanna tied around his upper thigh, and a Whitesnake T-shirt underneath his open Carhartt jacket. If I was not mistaken, a clunky pair of Ray-Bans perched on his buzz-cut head.

"The 1987 train has *not* left his station," I said, under my breath.

"I'm getting his number." Mrs. Berns was halfway out of her seat.

I tugged her back into place and forced her to join me in turning toward the computer before we drew Phillip's attention. "We had a deal. No fraternizing with the suspects." I tucked a loose string of hair up under my cap. From behind, it'd be difficult to guess my gender.

"Pshaw. He's no suspect. Look at him!" She threw an admiring glance over her shoulder. "He stands out like a sore thumb. No way would he go unnoticed."

"You can roll in him like catnip after the killer is caught."

She was correct that he didn't blend well, and the greetings he received from those already seated at tables suggested he was also a local, two facts that together made it even more unlikely he was our killer. There was always the possibility that he was an over-the-road trucker or had some other traveling job, since his online ad had left his occupation blank, but I had no idea how to find that out without talking to him.

"I think we've done our best here, and I have to free some of this coffee. Will you print out all the profiles, and then we can head back to Paynesville?"

Mrs. Berns nodded.

The bathrooms were down a long hallway. Both the men's and the women's were single-stall rooms, and the women's was locked. I leaned against the wall and closed my eyes for just a moment. Even with all the coffee in my system, I could just about drift off standing up.

"Holding up the wall?"

I jumped, banging my skull on the knotty pine knickknack shelf overhead. I turned, rubbing my head. Phillip was standing behind me, also leaning against the wall. His relaxed, overfamiliar posture made my skin crawl.

"I think the men's room is open," I said.

He smiled. From a distance, it would appear a harmless grin. Up close, I could see the swollen gums and excessively pointed eyeteeth.

"You don't want company?" he asked.

I made myself larger. "I'm waiting for the bathroom."

"You're a feisty one." He reached out toward my face.

Horrified, I swatted his hand away. Behind him, laughter bubbled out of the main café. Those people felt very distant.

"Relax. You have some crumbs on your chin." He smiled again, his eyes dancing.

"Don't you dare touch me," I spat. I couldn't tell if I was over- or underreacting. I pushed past him, to the warmth and normalcy of the main coffee shop.

"Come on," I said to Mrs. Berns.

She appeared ready to argue, but then she saw my face. She strode to the front counter to pay the computer's by-the-hour usage fee while I erased its history. I sensed rather than saw Phillip returning to the main room, but I refused to look at him until Mrs. Berns and I were on our way out. He was deep in conversation with a couple near the front windows and gave us only a passing glance. I was so busy trying to get my head on straight that I didn't notice Agent Briggs until my face was smushed into his chest.

Chapter 40

"Sorry!" I yelped.

He glared at me. The day was gray and frozen, much like his expression, the air so cold that the inside of my nostrils flash-froze. Between gritted teeth, he said, "Mira James. I thought I'd run into you, as we seem to be stopping at all the same places lately. You visited the Running household and got the names of the other women who received wreaths." It was not a question.

Over his shoulder, I spotted Mrs. Berns scurrying toward my car. When she reached it, she dropped to the ground and army-crawled to the passenger side.

"I'm a reporter, Agent Briggs," I said.

He reached into an inner jacket pocket and pulled out a Nokia. He removed a leather glove with his teeth and punched a few keys. "You are a librarian. You do freelance work for a Podunk newspaper consisting mostly of writing a food column featuring inedible recipes."

I tried to peer at the screen. "It doesn't say that."

He shoved his phone back in his pocket. "Let me save us both time. This isn't cute, this isn't a game, and you're not helping anyone. In this particular episode, the dead bodies stay dead. Get it?"

My cheeks burned. Behind me, the coffee shop door opened. The couple leaving were laughing but stopped immediately when they neared. They must have sensed the mood of our exchange. Was Phillip watching?

Briggs leaned in closer, so close that I could see the ice crystals forming on his mustache. "If you don't stay out of my way, I will have you arrested. If I see or hear from you again, *ever*, I will have you arrested. I'll make up the charges if I have to, and no one will question it. I cannot make my feelings on this matter any clearer." He continued to stab me with his eyes and then, abruptly, broke contact and entered the coffee shop.

I began to tear up. I told myself it was the cold and hurried across the street, head down. I unlocked the car and slid in. Mrs. Berns immediately followed, staying below the window line.

"What the Sam Hill was that about?"

My hands were shaking. "He's not real happy that I was at Amanda Running's house yesterday."

"Just you, right? He doesn't know about me?"

I let my forehead fall onto the steering wheel. "He didn't mention you."

"Thank god. He looked mad enough to kill. Don't worry, though. I'm sure he'll get over it." She patted my back absentmindedly. "What happened to you in the bathroom, by the way? Bad deposit?"

I sat back up. "I didn't even make it into the bathroom. Phillip met me in the hall and laid a whole pile of creepy vibes on me. He actually tried to touch my face."

"Ew." Her face screwed up. "I take back anything positive I said about him. He feel like a killer?"

"I don't know. I'm so tired that I'm not sure which way is up."

She pointed at the street. "I can tell you that way is south, and you better get driving. It's two hours to Paynesville, and you have to make it to afternoon Mass."

I was only too happy to oblige. The sky overhead was the color of hardening cement when we pulled out of Orelock. The roads were clear, but the news on the radio was grim. According to MPR, Minnesota was on a virtual lockdown. Women were told to call the police if they received any suspicious correspondence and to temporarily cease all online dating.

"The FBI sure changed its tune," Mrs. Berns said. "Didn't Angry Eyes Briggs pooh-pooh your online-dating connection just two days ago?"

I reached to turn the heat up, but it was already fully cranked. "Guess they couldn't ignore it any longer. Or they had made the connection themselves long ago and either found a way around all the lawsuits that are sure to emerge or decided putting all those women at risk wasn't worth the possibility of trapping him."

"What about our Isaac/Isaiah guy? What do we do with him?"

I sighed deeply. "He's definitely suspicious. Briggs doesn't take me seriously, unfortunately. During our little chat in front of the coffee shop? He said he'd have me arrested if he saw or heard from me again."

She made a frustrated sound. "So we just forget the profiles we printed out in Orelock?"

I signaled to pass a Sunday driver. "I think I'll just hand the information off to the police, or maybe to the reporter from Chicago, Adam, and he can tell Briggs."

"Good idea. Let's call the reporter on my cell."

I dug in my pocket for Adam's worn business card and handed it to her. She dialed and put the phone up to my ear when it started ringing. I heard three chirps before it clicked to his message.

Hi, this is Adam. Sorry I missed you. Please leave your name and number, and I'll call back as soon as I'm able.

"Adam, this is Mira James. Please give me a call when you get back, either at the Relax Inn in Paynesville or at this number. The cell belongs to a friend."

I handed the phone back to Mrs. Berns. "You know what's going to happen now, don't you?"

"You're going to pull into that gas station so I can pee?"

I shook my head but tapped my right turn signal and pulled into the station's parking lot. "Copycats and paranoia are going to take over. The whole state will be awash in tiny-minded people sending candy canes to enemies, and with every woman seeing threats under her bed."

And that'll be the least of our problems.

Chapter 41

As sure as eggs, we were pulling into Paynesville when the radio announced that the FBI tip lines had crashed due to a large volume of calls. It seemed to be a combination of people reporting the sinister appearance of candy canes and/or suddenly noticing suspicious behaviors in their neighbors. Agent Walter Briggs was introduced and offered a brief statement:

"The FBI is using all the resources at its disposal in order to capture the person the media has dubbed the Candy Cane Killer. We believe he has targeted women through online dating in the past, and we're requesting that women in the five-state area suspend their profiles until the killer is in custody. In the meanwhile, be assured that catching this person before he strikes again is our top priority. We also ask that any information regarding the killer be directed to your local police station until we can get the FBI tip lines up and running again."

His voice sounded gruff and serious, like always. It twisted my stomach. I pulled into the Relax Inn parking lot and shut off the car. "Are you going to Mass with me and Mom?"

"Nope." She smiled. "One of the many rewards of being God's chosen—a Lutheran." She fluffed her hair and stepped out of the Toyota. I followed. It felt at least ten degrees warmer than it had been in Orelock. "I figured I'd head back to the nursing home," she continued. "They can use my help, and if I dodder a little, the nurses think I'm one of the inmates and feed me. It's a pretty good deal all around."

"I can drive you."

"No thanks. It's only twelve blocks, and I need to exercise. I've been sitting in this soup can of yours for too long."

Something about her demeanor made me nervous, but *everything* was making me nervous, so I didn't argue. How much trouble could she stir up in Paynesville? It was daylight, and people were out and about. The gas station across the street was broadcasting Christmas music from speakers above the gas pumps. The sun was shining, and according to the local bank, the temperature was above zero. It was as safe as it was going to get. Mrs. Berns went one way and I went the other.

The Relax Inn we'd booked our indefinite stay in was small and locally owned and had been only too happy to take my Visa. I smiled at the teenager behind the counter and started up the stairs to our second-floor room. My mind was on the online-dating connection when I stepped onto the landing overlooking the lobby and took a left into the hallway.

A tall window at the end of the corridor let in dazzling sunbeams. My eyes needed a moment to adjust, and during that split second, it appeared as though a man was leaving my hotel room. My heart careened painfully off my rib cage. I blinked, and he began walking toward me. His shape blocked most of the sun, leaving his face in shadows. He was tall, and the outline of his hands appeared as large as clubs.

I stumbled backward, toward the top of the stairs. Glancing to my right, I saw that the teenager had left her station. I whipped back to face the man, my breath coming shallowly. Instinctively, I went into the fighting stance I'd learned in self-defense class.

Rather than attack, though, he passed me on the landing and started down the stairs. I saw him clearly for the first time. His hair was salt and pepper, and from behind, he didn't look nearly as tall as he had backlit against the sun.

"Excuse me." My voice was shaking. I gripped the railing. "Sir. Excuse me."

He turned, wearing a polite expression. He had a well-trimmed beard and mustache and smile lines around his warm brown eyes. I'd never seen him before in my life.

"Yes?"

"What room are you in?" I asked.

I thought I saw an atom of guilt or panic on his face, but I could have been mistaken because there he was, still smiling politely at me. "I was visiting a friend. Room 24."

The room directly across from ours. I shook my head as if clearing out cobwebs. "Sorry. Just, for a second there . . . never mind. Merry Christmas."

He smiled, and I thought I spotted a gold filling in the back of his mouth. "You too."

Chapter 42

Because we were heading into Christmas week, the Saint Joseph Catholic Church was offering Mass every four hours up until midnight, just like a holy *Rocky Horror Picture Show.* This, on top of all the Christmas services they had planned.

Mom beamed as brightly as a lighthouse to have me at her side during Mass for the first time since high school. I started out listening to the sermon with a bad attitude but warmed up when I realized it was one of the rare ones I loved, light on the Jesus guilt, with an extra helping of "do unto others." I was glad I'd packed dress clothes, or at least dress pants and a nice sweater, so that Mom didn't look like she'd done a bad job with me. I was so inspired by the priest's message of hope and love that I didn't mind staying after to be introduced to him like I was some sort of prize cow.

Plus, cookies were to follow.

I was standing in the basement, three napkin-wrapped gingerbread men in my pocket (I fully intended to share them with Mrs. Berns) and one frosted Christmas tree in my hand when Patsy walked over to say hi.

"Did you hear about the killing in Orelock?" she asked.

I wiped crumbs off the front of my sweater and nodded. "Are you and the kids feeling safe?"

"We are now." She hugged her elbows. "I moved us into my mom and dad's. The kids are on cloud nine, getting to hang out with Gram and Gramps for all of Christmas break. It's weird sleeping in my old twin bed, though, you know?"

I did. "That's where I was until Mom and I moved to the Relax Inn."

She stared at me, concerned. Her hair was down and curled, and she was wearing a pretty wool dress. The hair and outfit made her look very much like a mom. "Isn't that kind of crowded? Didn't you say you brought your animals?"

"Yup. I walked Luna right before we came here. It's cramped, but roomier than a coffin." I attempted a weak laugh, but the joke sounded painfully inappropriate even to my ears. Patsy politely ignored it.

"You should come out to Jules's tomorrow night. She's having a Yule party."

I choked on my cookie. "Jules Dahlberg? Ms. Snootypants?"

She cocked her head, a question in her eyes. "What do you mean?"

"She was always so stuck up in high school." I crumbled a little in the face of Patsy's bottomless kindness. It did feel childish to cling so tightly to old memories. "Or at least that's how I remember her. I'm sure she's way different now."

Patsy smiled brightly. "You two would get along great. She'd love to have you, I'm sure of it. She was saying how she wished she'd gotten a chance to talk with you at Natalie's funeral."

The invitation was kind, and I recognized the need to bury high school grudges, but I felt improbably committed to my vision of myself as the outcast. "I don't know. I don't want to leave my mom alone."

"You have nothing to worry about there. She'll be busy volunteering at the nativity scene here tomorrow evening, ten o'clock through midnight. She takes over for me. We both play Wise Men."

I couldn't help but laugh at the image. "OK, I'll see what I can do. Would it be all right if I brought a friend?"

"Of course!" Patsy spontaneously hugged me. "It's really nice to have you back, Mira. I mean that."

Mom was actually signed up to help at the church for the rest of today, too. I didn't remember her being so devoted when I lived at home. The church must have filled in the holes that Dad and I had left. She said I could either stay and help her stuff envelopes, or I could pick up some last-minute grocery items for the feast she was making as soon as we could return to the farmhouse. I didn't want to burst her bubble and tell her that we might be at the hotel for a very long time. Instead, I volunteered to grocery shop.

After I'd bagged the pumpkin pie filling, allspice, and cream of tartar, I felt restless. I returned to the hotel to exercise Luna. Both she and Tiger Pop were thrilled to see me. I brushed them both down before heading with Luna to a nearby park to throw the tennis ball. Her shaggy shepherd-mix coat kept her warm, and it was glorious to watch her strong, wolflike body leap into the air. After forty-five minutes of fetch, she sprawled at my feet, tongue hanging out the side of her mouth.

I brought her back to the hotel but didn't feel like watching TV. Instead, I drove to River Grove. I had no specific destination in mind and so cruised the streets, staring at decorations and lunar snowdrifts, wondering how a killer chose his victim.

The crime scene tape had been removed from the front of Natalie's home, but it looked cold and dark inside. I cruised past the candy cane–covered house, slowing as I passed. It hadn't changed. It was still loaded with the decorations and still made my stomach turn.

After I'd crisscrossed all of River Grove, I took off for White Plains. The drive was more than an hour. I didn't have a specific goal in mind there, either, though I thought to look for Sharpie's caramels when I filled up on gas. They weren't at the first station, or at either of the other two in town. The clerks at all three didn't remember anyone fitting Sharpie's description.

By the time I made it back to the Relax Inn, it was dark, and I was exhausted. A soggy snow had begun to fall. I took Luna for a short walk, the wind icing my eyelashes the whole way. She kept wagging her tail and looking at me as we strolled. I was sure she wanted to know if we were leaving the hotel for good. The room was cramped for a human but doubly small for two animals who couldn't leave on their own.

"Soon," I told her. She wagged harder.

When we returned, my mom was in the room, getting ready for bed. She told me Mrs. Berns had called to say she'd be spending the night at the nursing home. I had an inkling that slumber parties weren't allowed, but I was equally confident that Mrs. Berns would find a work-around.

Mom chattered happily about all the people she'd worked with that day, what their holiday plans were, how grand the nativity scene was going to be. Her voice was soothing. We both avoided discussing the killer or harder truths.

Chapter 43

The flurries are not thick enough to deter travel, but they do provide a natural camouflage to anyone out walking. The swirling winter crystals frolic under the candy-cane swathed streetlights, playing tricks on the eyes and promising a mythical white Christmas.

The killer strolls past the nativity scene twice, hands thrust deep in pockets. The snowflakes land with a dancer's precision on the thatched roof of the bower, others twirling to alight on the manger that will hold baby Jesus. The church rising behind it is grand, pointed spires racing toward the heavens and nearly disappearing into the night sky strung with stars as bright as chips of glass, but the nativity scene is something else. It's humble and plain.

Just as it should be.

The snow is nice, gentle and soft, but even without its disguising presence, no one will question the killer. That just comes with the territory. A car drives by and honks. It's a startling sound, and the killer jumps, only a little. The car careens around the corner and disappears. Probably teenagers on a joyride.

The doll is back in the killer's vehicle, a silver sedan, parked in front of a bar named after some literary character. Sir Lancelot? Frodo? The sedan is the killer's own vehicle.

It's too easy, these murders. It's making the killer complacent, almost, and still, it won't make any difference. No one has guessed it, not after three winters. One more erasure, and the killer will be done setting women straight for another year, at least.

Maybe done forever.

Setting women straight? No, you'll never be done with that. There will always be those who ask for it. Now, get to it. You came to clean out this town.

The killer's eyes narrow. How can she be audible? The car is blocks away. That's why the killer left her. The commands have become shrill, erratic, more demanding than ever. It makes it difficult to do what needs to be done. Still, she makes sense. The killer shouldn't waste any more time. Idle hands are the devil's tools.

TVs glimmer from the front windows of most of the houses. A group of carolers works their way down Mill Street, and their slightly off-key holiday warbling makes the night feel safer, somehow.

The tune is "O Come, All Ye Faithful."

The killer drops candy canes into two different mailboxes, four blocks apart, walking right up to the house for both of them. The Relax Inn will be more difficult, but in the end, the killer just walks directly inside, mounts the stairs to the second story, and hangs the candy cane over the doorknob.

The teenager in headphones at the front desk is so into the book she's reading that she doesn't even glance up.

Chapter 44

"Mira! Wake up. They caught the killer!"

I tried rolling away from Mom's persistent shaking, burrowing into the pilled comforter. Then I processed her words. Once I realized what she'd said, I sat straight up and stared at the TV at the foot of the bed. I ignored my reflection, all wild hair and bleary eyes, in the mirror to the left of it. "Turn it up."

My mother had been listening to the news quietly so as not to wake me but raised the volume immediately. Even Luna turned her attention toward the TV. Tiger Pop hopped off the bed, miffed that she'd been woken early.

The screen featured a reporter out of Minneapolis offering a recap. Under her, the words "Suspected Candy Cane Killer in Custody" scrolled across the screen.

". . . live in Agate City, Minnesota, where twelve women all received Christmas cards signed 'Dead by December.' Our news team has obtained a copy of one of the cards and is currently having it analyzed by specialists, but initial reports suggest that the handwriting matches that of the Candy Cane Killer, who left a note at the home of two of his Chicago and one of his Wisconsin victims. Local police report having a man in custody whom they caught delivering the cards. I repeat, police do have a man in custody who they believe may be the Candy Cane Killer."

My blood was pumping. I couldn't believe the good news—I'd begun to think that the killer was some sort of a demon, incapable of being caught. My mom dropped into the bed beside me and put her arm around me. On TV, a serious-looking twentysomething woman in full winter gear was pulled into the shot. People milled in front of a grocery store in the background.

"I have with me April Hahn, one of the recipients of the 'Dead by December' cards. Ms. Hahn, what can you tell me about this card?"

She shoved her blonde hair behind her ears and stared earnestly into the camera. "I found it outside my door when I went to grab the newspaper. I called the police right away. They have the letter now."

"What did it say?"

She glanced from the camera to the reporter and back to the camera. Her eyes were wide, blue and guileless. "It wished me a Merry Christmas and was signed 'With Love, Dead by December.' It had a picture of mistletoe on the front, and two candy canes underneath. The candy canes were crossed, like two Civil War swords."

The journalist nodded. "What did you think when you opened the card?"

"I was scared." It was simple and true, and spoke for every woman in Minnesota. Yet there was something odd about this whole newscast, something I couldn't get a bead on.

"Can you believe it?" my mom asked, holding me tighter. "They caught the monster. It's a Christmas miracle."

I squeezed her back and smiled uneasily. "Yeah. Um, I'm going to grab the morning newspaper at the front desk, OK? I want to see if they have any coverage of this."

My mom nodded happily and disappeared into the bathroom. I heard the shower start up as I tugged on the jeans I'd worn yesterday. I fastened a bra on beneath my pajama T-shirt and pulled my hair into a half-knot, half-ponytail array. I must have slept deeply last night to have messed my hair up to this degree, but I didn't feel rested. My sleep had been haunted by nightmares of sharp metal teeth and crying children. I shivered at the recollection.

Sliding the chain lock off and releasing the deadbolt, I yanked the door open. I was all the way through it before I realized I hadn't grabbed my room key. I'd need it if Mom was still in the shower when I returned. I stuck my hand out to stop the door from closing and automatically locking behind me.

The motion upset the candy cane that'd been hanging off the knob and sent it to the carpeted floor.

Chapter 45

The door swung shut and latched behind me. I couldn't move, could only stare at the candy cane against the burgundy carpet, the winning ticket in the Minnesota death lotto. It was an ordinary, garden-variety candy cane, the kind you buy at a grocery store checkout line on a whim this time of year. Six inches long in the straight part, elegantly curved, tightly wrapped in cellophane, red chasing white chasing red. The mascot of Christmas candy for more than a century.

Innocent, sweet, it sat motionless, a dozing snake waiting for me to reach, and then it would strike, flooding my veins with hot, minty poison. The floor began to heave, and I thrust out my hand to steady myself.

"Are you all right?"

Startled, I glanced to my left. A middle-aged hotel maid was reaching for a pile of tiny shampoos in her cart, her expression worried.

"Yes, I'm, uh, I accidentally locked myself out of my room, that's all. And my mom is in the shower."

A relieved smile warmed her face. "I can help you. Here." She tugged a key out of the massive ring at her waist and walked over to the door. "You're the one with a dog and a cat in there, aren't you? They've been so quiet."

"Thank you," I answered robotically. I reached down to grab the candy cane while her back was to me. It burned my hand.

"Let me know if you need anything else. Merry Christmas."

"You too." I stepped into the room and watched her figure retreat as the door swung shut between us. Luna nudged my hand, whining.

"Shh. I'm OK." I stroked the thick, coarse fur on her head. My mom was singing "Deck the Halls" in the shower, and steam plumed out from beneath the bathroom door. "They caught the killer, Luna. I'm just overreacting."

She whined again, and Tiger Pop even walked over to rub herself against the backs of my legs. I bent down and hugged her tightly. "You guys are right. Let's call Mrs. Berns and find out what she thinks. A second opinion is always a good thing to have."

I dialed "9" and then punched in her cell number. She answered on the first ring.

"Did you see the news?" she asked.

"Yeah."

She was quiet for a moment. "What's wrong?"

"I just found a candy cane on the outside doorknob of our hotel room."

"Holy hell. Are there candy canes on any of the other doors?"

I hadn't thought to check. I'd been too stunned. "Hold on." I set the phone on the table and walked over to peek out. The maid's cart was still outside room 24. All the doors had cardboard cutouts of Christmas scenes on them, which I hadn't remembered seeing yesterday. No candy canes. I came back to the phone and told Mrs. Berns.

"I suppose you don't want to call the FBI tip line?" she asked, her voice grim.

"You remember how they treated me about the orange-begonia theory and what Briggs said in Orelock. How do you think they'll respond if I tell them I got a candy cane on my door, along with other Christmas decorations, on Christmas week?"

"You have to at least tell the police."

She was right. I glanced down at my knees. They were still shaking. The killer had been caught; I'd just heard it on the news. The orange begonia and the candy cane were coincidences, harmless gifts easily explained. Or whoever had left them wanted to scare me. That made the person dangerous, even if they weren't a serial killer. "I'll call the police, but I don't want to spend another night in this hotel. It doesn't feel safe anymore."

"Good choice. I'll call around, get us another room, and be there within the hour."

We hung up, and I dialed the Paynesville Police Department. The female dispatcher was kind and professional. She took my name, my contact information, and my very brief story about the candy cane.

"It was smart to call," she said, "but the latest news is that the killer has been caught. There's a good chance the candy was just a harmless prank."

"That's what I'm hoping." I hung up and secreted the candy cane in my suitcase before my mom got out of the shower.

In the further interest of not scaring her, I lied when she stepped into the room. "We got a call when you were in the shower. The hotel double-booked our room for tonight and asked us if we'd move to another."

"You said no, of course. We're already settled here."

I shuffled my feet.

"Mira, is there something you're not telling me?"

It was the concerned mom eyes that undid me, but not completely. I was still too tough a nut for a total meltdown. "I know the news says the killer has been caught, but I'm still scared, that's all, and it feels better to move instead of staying in one spot."

She considered me, hands on hips, and finally nodded. I don't know how she reconciled my unreasonable requests, but she did, every time. We worked silently, gathering our clothes and boxing up the animal supplies. Mrs. Berns returned in under a half an hour, her cheeks pink from the walk over, to tell us that every hotel room in Paynesville and the surrounding communities was booked. Every single one, full to the shingles with families in town for the holidays.

Mom put her arm around me. "I know you're scared, hon, but I think this is a sign that it's time to go home. The killer is in jail. It's going to be Christmas in a few days. I want to roast a turkey and cook for us."

Mrs. Berns and I exchanged a glance. I heard the ghosts whispering.

"All right," I said. "Home it is."

It seemed as safe as anywhere else.

Chapter 46

Pulling over the little hill that hid my childhood house from the road, I was struck with a sense of déjà vu. I'd driven over this hill thousands of times, of course, but that wasn't it. I parked to the side so Mom could pull her van into the garage. Luna sprang out joyfully and leaped into the snow like a giant rabbit. Smiling, I began to unload the car, thanking Mrs. Berns for holding the door into the house for me. I set the bag of dog food and one of our bags of freshly bought groceries on the kitchen counter. We'd gotten the last thawed turkey in the store.

The answering machine blinked like a Morse code transmitter. "I'll check the messages."

Mom waved her approval, too busy bustling around the house and checking on plants and her Christmas tree to care about who'd called. While packing up the hotel, she'd talked nonstop about what a magnificent Christmas feast she was going to cook for all of us, including Tiger Pop and Luna.

Luna was currently running circles around the house with the focused glee of the Flash. Tiger Pop had immediately disappeared, something she'd probably wanted to do for days. Mrs. Berns was reacclimating herself to her room. I was happy at the thought of a bedroom door that closed, even if it led to my 1980s shrine.

I punched the play button on Mom's machine. The first message was from two days ago, and the voice was halting. "Hi, this is Olivia. We met at Natalie's funeral?"

I had to search my memory for a face to go with the name. Olivia was the one who wore jeweled glasses, the woman I'd discovered was still online dating when I'd gone searching for Natalie's profile. "You said to call if we thought of anything out of the ordinary relating to Natalie's death," she continued. "Well, I thought of something. Call me back." She left her number.

The second message had come in yesterday evening. "Mira, it's Adam. I'm calling you back like you asked. I'm in Agate City, and it's a madhouse here. They think they have the killer. Call if you still need something."

The third message was from Olivia again, left early this morning. Her voice was more assured this time. "It's Olivia. Call me."

Two more messages were for Mom, one reminding her to show up for the nativity scene tonight and another asking if she could cover a volunteer shift at the hospital on Christmas Day. I passed on both messages before calling Olivia. She didn't answer, and I didn't leave a message.

Mom, Mrs. Berns, and I spent the next two hours cleaning the house and listening to Mom chatter about everything she was going to cook. She said she was so grateful to finally have company for Christmas that she was going whole hog—turkey, stuffing, mashed potatoes, clover-leaf rolls, hot vinegar salad, and three kinds of pie for dessert. I liked the homey feeling of helping her to prep for the holidays, and having Mrs. Berns around made it that much nicer. Still, by early afternoon, the trapped feeling was beginning to set in again.

I sneaked off into my mom's room to use her phone in private and tried Olivia again. The phone rang five times. I was pulling the handset away from my ear to hang up when she answered.

"Hello?"

"Olivia? This is Mira James. You left me a message, something about Natalie."

A muffled sound came from the other end of the line. I realized she was giving someone instructions. She returned to the phone. "Sorry. I've got a houseful."

"I didn't mean to bother you."

"No problem. I'm probably the one bothering *you*. Something occurred to me, but it's sort of a long shot. It might be nothing at all." I heard the muffled noise again.

"Does someone need you?"

"I'm afraid so. Our cookies are burning. Do you mind calling back?"

My mom appeared in the room, a hopeful smile on her face. She was holding a box marked FAMILY PHOTO ALBUMS.

"I have a better idea," I whispered into the phone, so my mom couldn't hear me. "How about I come to River Grove? I can be there in forty minutes."

Chapter 47

After convincing Mom that I had to run a secret Christmas errand, I left her and Mrs. Berns to the domestic duties and headed out on the barren country roads. Inviting myself over to a stranger's house during the holidays, I'd cop to that. It wasn't the weirdest thing I'd done in the last week, however. And Mom and Mrs. Berns would be fine without me, probably even better, and I'd be back in time for supper and to watch *Santa Claus Is Comin' to Town*.

Mom and I had made a tradition of watching the show on Christmas week when I still lived at home. I had faint memories of my dad drunkenly yelling at Burgermeister Meisterburger for being such a monster, but after a while, he'd give up and stumble off into another room and leave me and Mom in peace to watch the rest of the show.

Believe it or not, it was a happy memory.

The radio informed me that we were in for a warm snap, above zero the whole week and no snow on the horizon. It'd be a perfect Christmas, weather-wise. We had about three feet of accumulation on the ground, soft sloping drifts of white that made every home look like a gingerbread house and every hill a sledding mecca. When the announcer promised to play only Christmas music until the twenty-fifth, I didn't even change the dial.

The candy cane on the hotel door had given me a jolt, but I'd informed the police, and in turn been told that they had good reason to believe the Candy Cane Killer had been caught. Olivia might have something interesting to tell me that would help police with their conviction of the guy, or she might not. Either way, she'd given me an excuse to leave the house just when my claustrophobe switch had been tripped.

I steered down the main street of River Grove and glanced at the directions that I'd jotted down on a sheet of notebook paper. Olivia had said to drive one and a half miles past the downtown intersection, take the first right, and she'd be the second driveway on the left, fire number 23837. Blue house, white outbuildings.

I located it without a hitch but had second thoughts when I pulled in. I counted nine vehicles in the circular driveway. I parked behind a silver sedan and let my car idle. Did I really want to interrupt a family gathering in search of possibly irrelevant information about a serial killer who'd already been captured? I decided I did not and put my car in reverse just as Olivia appeared at the front door, her jeweled glasses on a chain around her neck, a red-and-green apron wrapped around her waist. She waved me in. I sighed and shut off my ignition. *I should have at least brought some grocery store Christmas cookies,* I thought, as I made my way to the front door.

"You made it! I hope you're hungry." Raucous laughter bubbled out of the room behind her. I also heard the clatter of silverware on plates and smelled the most heavenly roasted ham smell. I didn't eat red meat, but that didn't mean my nose didn't work.

"I'm so sorry to bother you," I said. "I shouldn't have even come."

She tipped her head. "Nonsense. We have food to spare."

I smiled and shook my head. "My mom would kill me if I ate anywhere else but at her table this week."

Olivia gestured behind her. "I get it. My mom's the same way, only she comes to my house to do all the cooking now. My kitchen is bigger than hers."

I stood awkwardly on her front step. I didn't want to come in and have to make small talk with a bunch of strangers, but I also didn't know how to broach the subject of serial killers with her family eating holiday ham in the other room. She saved me the trouble.

"I suppose you want to know what I called about."

"If you don't mind."

"Well, I heard they caught the killer in Agate City, so this might not be anything." She stared up into the scudded winter sky. "In fact, it's probably stupid. It's just that you said to call if we thought of *anything* connected to Natalie's death."

"Yeah, I appreciate you reaching out," I said, hoping I was wearing my encouraging face and not my impatient face. I stored them right next to each other.

"OK, here it is." She moved onto the front step with me and closed the door behind her, lowering her voice. "You know how we told you about all of us receiving orange begonias?"

I nodded.

"Well, three of us went to the same day care back in the day. Not for very long. It was the summer between first and second grade."

I tried to process the words, but any way I mixed them, they didn't seem to carry much weight. "I don't understand."

Her expression screwed up, like she was staring backward in time. "The day care lady's name was Auntie Ginger. She went to our church. She seemed like the nicest woman, at least in public. She was mean behind closed doors, though."

"Like how?"

"She spanked, which wasn't unusual back then. She didn't stop there, though. A little boy pooped his pants once. He couldn't have been more than four years old. She made him eat it."

I recoiled. "What? She made him eat his own poop?"

"Not all of it, but a spoonful. Said that'd teach him to never do it again. Plus, all the kids there seemed constantly spooked—jumpy. I told my mom, and she pulled me out after two weeks. One of the other women you met at the funeral, Judy? Her mom and Natalie's mom were friends with my mom. They pulled their girls out, too."

"Natalie is originally from River Grove?"

"Her family moved to Paynesville in second grade. I think her dad got a job at a plumbing and heating place. Our parents stayed in touch, but it wasn't the same. She and I grew apart and then got to know each other again when she moved back five summers ago."

"You think this Auntie Ginger is connected to the serial killer somehow?"

Olivia shot me an apologetic look. "It's a long shot, I know. It's just that she was weird enough to really mess a kid up. That's how you do it, right? You mess with children when they're young and you turn them into killers." She leaned closer to me. "After our moms pulled us out, I heard rumors about what she did to kids, though she wasn't ever charged with anything. Icky rumors."

The way she said it made my skin crawl. "Icky how?"

"Abuse, some of it sexual. Pretty sick stuff."

I shuddered. People who hurt animals or children deserved a special spot in hell. "She lived alone?"

"More or less. She had some teenage relative help during the holidays, just during the month of December, I think."

"Boy or girl?"

"That's just it. I can't remember which, and neither can Judy. Maybe it was one of each?" She gave a halfhearted laugh.

"Is Ginger still around?"

"No, she died ten years ago. I heard she hung herself. Probably guilt." Someone hollered for Olivia inside, telling her the food was growing cold. She opened the door to yell back, then returned her attention to me. "That's it. Probably nothing, right? Three of us who years ago went to the same day care for a couple weeks got that orange begonia after we started online dating, and then five years later, Natalie gets the candy cane and is murdered. That's a reach by any measure, which is why I haven't told the police yet. Think I should?"

Ah, finally the reason I was here. She was looking for either confirmation that the connection was nonexistent so she could let it drop without guilt, or that it had a solid center so she could tell the police without the risk of seeming hysterical. Well, better her than me. "I'd call and report it. Let the police decide if it's worthwhile or not."

She looked as if a huge weight had been lifted. "That's what I thought. Hey, you sure you don't want to come in? My mom makes the best eggnog in Stearns County. I think it's the brandy."

"No thanks. I better be getting home before my mom worries. Happy holidays."

"You too." On the way through the door, she yelled down the hall, "There better be some mashed potatoes left!"

I crunched over the snow to my car. When I reached my door, it occurred to me that I hadn't asked where Auntie Ginger had lived. I didn't know what it would have gained me, but I wanted to drive past the house on my way back and make sure it wasn't the candy cane–laden monstrosity.

I glanced at the closed front door. No, it wasn't worth interrupting their meal twice. I slid behind the wheel and drove home.

Chapter 48

"I am as full as a python in a rabbit farm."

Mrs. Berns and I were reclining on the couch, the last strains of Fred Astaire singing "Santa Claus Is Comin' to Town" fading on the TV. Mom was in her bedroom, preparing for her shift as a Wise Man. I poked Mrs. Berns's belly with my pointer finger. "You *do* kinda resemble a snake digesting a rabbit."

Mrs. Berns didn't respond. She'd made the comment to buy herself time to process the story I'd just told her about Auntie Ginger. I hadn't wanted to mention it when my mom was listening, and this was the first alone time we'd had.

"She sounds like a devil," Mrs. Berns said, picking up the conversation where we'd left off. "We had a woman like that in Battle Lake. Can't remember her name, but families got wind that she was locking kids up during the day and not feeding them if they cried. Ran her out of town. Should have tarred and feathered her first."

"Creepy." I shuddered. "I don't see how there's any connection between that story and the Candy Cane Killer, though, unless Auntie Ginger created him with her abuse. But then why would he start killing in Chicago?"

"People move." Mrs. Berns burped. "Is there any of that pecan pie left?"

"You don't need any more pie."

"Nobody *needs* pie. Besides, I could die in my sleep. Might as well go to bed happy."

I couldn't hide my smile. "Fine, I'll get you a piece." I rolled my belly off the couch and followed it to the kitchen. "I can't tell you how glad I am I never tried online dating," I hollered from the other room.

Mrs. Berns responded, but I couldn't hear her. I popped a caramelized pecan into my mouth, served up her pie, and carried it into the living room.

"What'd you say?" I asked.

She accepted the plate. "I said, you did too try online dating. Remember the profile Gina created for you back in May?"

My heartbeat froze.

Mrs. Berns mistook my horrified stare for a confused one and continued. "You ended up on a date with that professor? Remember?"

The question was, How could I ever have forgotten? My pulse returned like thunder. I hadn't created the profile myself, but I'd gone on a date as a result of it. "That ad can't still be up there, can it? I've never received any emails."

Mrs. Berns chewed thoughtfully. "But you never did, did you? Even from the professor. Gina must have entered her own email address."

"Jesus." I strode over to my mom's computer to see if I could pull up the ad. I thought I remembered the host site Gina had created it on, but the internet wasn't cooperating. "I can't connect."

"In that case, I recommend eating pie."

My stomach was roiling. "What if the killer saw my online ad?"

"They caught the killer, remember? Anyhow, it's been up for seven months. Another day won't matter."

I drew in a deep breath. I wanted that ad removed, now. "Maybe Jules Dahlberg has internet."

"Who?" Mrs. Berns asked, handing me her licked-clean plate.

"Jules Dahlberg. She's a stuck-up girl I went to high school with, and she's having a Yule party tonight. Patsy invited me. We could go, and I could try getting online there."

Mrs. Berns removed her cat's-eye glasses and reclined fully on the couch. "Look, I'm doing an impression of a sleeping old lady. Pretty realistic, huh?"

"You're not going to make me go to that party alone, are you? It'll be full of people I went to high school with, people who hated me."

She pulled down the afghan draped over the couch and tucked it around her body. "Only jocks, prom queens, and dumbasses hang on to high school this long. Everyone else goes on to better things. Go. Confront your past. Get over yourself."

I wanted to stick my tongue out at her, but her eyes were closed. I settled for giving her and then Mom a kiss on the forehead and the animals a petting before I left into the night.

Chapter 49

I sat in my car for fifteen minutes working up the courage to go in. During that time, I replayed most of high school on a speed reel. My freshman year, rolling and pinning my jeans at the ankle so they appeared tapered, curling my mall bangs, trading friendship pins, learning to type on an IBM Selectric, eating fish sticks and white-bread-and-butter sandwiches for hot lunch and thinking it was pretty good, messing around with a Ouija board at a friend's house.

Sophomore year, saving up for Guess jeans and Benetton shirts, sneaking out after a basketball game to drink Bartles & Jaymes blackberry wine coolers, getting Ogilvie spiral perms, making honor roll but still sneaking into Mr. Tigner's classroom at night on a dare to steal chemistry tests, my dad dying in a horrible, public car accident.

Everything changing.

I remembered people distancing themselves from me, whispering about me, judging me. Cliques formed, broke up, reshaped, and I was outside of every one of them. I'd show up at school, and only Patsy would hang out with me.

Jules Dahlberg, with her trendsetting clothes and ability to talk to the teachers like an equal, was the worst of the bunch. She couldn't even be bothered to say hi in the halls after my dad died. The school and town pushed me out, and I'd left gladly as soon as I'd graduated. Now I was back, and what the hell was I doing sitting outside Jules's house?

"Boo!"

·I jumped so high that I cracked my leg on the steering wheel. I glared at the face pressed against the driver's side window. I recognized Kyle Kamel, a farm boy who took a lot of teasing for smelling like livestock, always needing to rush home after school to do chores, and never being seen without his cowboy boots. He put an end to all that when he beat the resident track star in a sprint our senior year. While wearing his cowboy boots. That made him underground cool, which still hadn't been cool enough to crack Jules Dahlberg's clique. What was he doing here?

Kyle made a circling motion with his hand, and I rolled down the window. "It *is* you. The rumors are true. Mira the Maniac has come home."

"Hey, Kyle." He'd grown his hair out and gotten his teeth fixed. He actually looked kinda hot. What a strange world. "How're you doing?"

"Happy to get away from the family for a bit." He leaned his elbows on my door. "How about you?"

"The same."

He tipped his head toward the house. "You afraid to go in?"

I followed his gaze. It appeared to be a regular old two-story colonial with tasteful brown trim and white shutters, decorated for the holidays with a solitary string of snowflake lights over the door. Inside, however, was the embodiment of nearly every insecurity I owned.

"Yeah," I said, realizing how odd it felt to talk to Kyle like a friend. I couldn't remember ever saying more than three words in a row to him. I guessed I hadn't broken that record yet.

"Come on." He opened my door and offered me a hand. "It's only scary the first time."

I took it gratefully and let him lead me toward the house. He opened the door and pulled me gently inside. A wall of familiar sounds and smells hit me—1980s music and keg beer.

I was expecting something out of a *Carrie* prom scene, but hardly anyone even glanced at us. I counted nearly thirty heads in the cramped room, and judging by the footsteps overhead, there were plenty more guests upstairs. The chatter of cross-conversations was noisy, but not loud enough to drown out the Depeche Mode. I felt a hint of a smile as I followed Kyle through the crowd and into the kitchen, where he poured us each a plastic cup of beer from the towel-wrapped keg. I was traveling back in time.

"Is it weird to be doing this legally?" he asked, giving me a wink with the cup. "Takes some of the fun out of it, I've always thought."

"Mira!" I followed the voice and spotted Patsy through the crowd. She wove her way toward me. "You made it!" She hugged me.

"It's my first Yule party." I indicated the guests laughing and chattering. "Who are all these people?"

She looked around, smiling. "I see you reacquainted yourself with Kyle. About half of the rest of the people are from high school, too, most from our class but a few younger and a few older. The rest are spouses, significant others, or Jules's work friends."

Kyle cuffed my shoulder. "You're in good hands now." He disappeared into the crowd, completely at ease. My mental high school diorama, perfectly preserved all these years, was cracking.

"Isn't he a hottie now?" Patsy asked. "He's single. Likes to play the field."

"Kyle Kamel?"

"I know!" she said, giggling. "Hey, come say hi to Jules."

She grabbed me before I could resist, leading me to the basement stairs and down. I received a lot of smiles and greetings on the way, but as we reached the rec room floor, the memory that I'd been trying to suppress since I pulled into Jules's driveway fully bloomed.

Me, on the chartered school bus, traveling to a Knowledge Bowl meet. It was my junior year, and I'd dropped out of every other activity in the wake of my dad's death. My favorite teacher, Mr. Butler, had convinced me to take part in just one more meet. He was concerned and wanted to pull me back into life, I could see that. I knew it wouldn't work, but I couldn't bring myself to turn him down, so I'd agreed to rejoin the team for the regionals in Annandale.

We'd lost, which hadn't bothered me. What had was the bus ride back, when Jules coined the nickname "Manslaughter Mark" to refer to my dad. It was high school behavior, wicked mean and pointless. After a few minutes of teasing, the other kids on the bus moved on to another topic, likely the amazingness of Duran Duran or the newest happenings on *Days of Our Lives*, but I'd carried that hot nugget of pain with me every day since then. Usually, though, it was a lot further back in my mind.

"Jules! I told you Mira would come."

Patsy dragged me so I stood directly in front of Jules Dahlberg. She was even more beautiful than she'd been in high school. Her short, dark hair was spiked in a playful pixie style, perfectly accenting her slanted green eyes and heart-shaped face. Her smile was blinding. She was petite but large-breasted, and for a moment, I had a flash that a younger Mrs. Berns must have looked very similar.

Jules didn't hug me, but she didn't kick me, either. "Maniac Mira James. How the hell have you been?"

"Fine." I took a deep pull off my beer. It was deliciously bitter, not unlike me at the moment. "You?"

"I'm great. Except we were just discussing what a bitch I was in high school." She moved so I could see her cadre gathered behind her, the three sycophants who'd shadowed her every high school move. If Jules wore purple eye shadow, they bought out the supply at the Ben Franklin store. When Jules loved U2, they split up which members of the band would marry whom. "God, you couldn't pay me a million dollars to go back to that time and place."

I scrutinized her doubtfully. "You were the most popular girl in high school."

"Don't think so." She shook her head, her smile fading. "That was Natalie." The mood within earshot immediately dropped, but Jules continued. "I was probably the *meanest* girl in high school, though. Made up nicknames for everyone, started terrible rumors. Patsy, do you remember when I told everyone you were pregnant because I was mad that you had the same Guess sweater as me?"

Patsy laughed good-naturedly. "That one didn't stick. You'd have had better luck convincing everyone that I was becoming a nun."

Jules shook her head. "Still, I was evil."

"You gotta forgive yourself, Jules," Patsy said. "I'm sure we'd all be the same if we lost our mom our junior year."

"What happened to your mom?" I asked, speaking before thinking. The direction of this conversation was making me jittery.

"Cancer." She frowned. "But this is supposed to be a Yule party, so let's stop with the gloom. I'm issuing a blanket apology, and then we can move on." Jules held a can of Sprite up to me in a salute. "I don't remember having anything to apologize to you for, though. You were always so cool and collected, even after your dad died. You seemed like you were above it all. Man, did I want to be you."

She tapped her can into my cup and made her way toward the Ping-Pong table on the far side of the room, where a mock argument had broken out.

I stood exactly as she'd left me. I couldn't have been more stunned if I'd just been crowned Miss America. Jules Dahlberg had been jealous of *me* in high school. She thought I'd been coasting above it all. Jules Dahlberg, the woman whom I'd spent more than a decade resenting for her arrogance, had actually lost her mom her junior year, and I'd been so caught up in feeling sorry for myself and imagining the world against me that *I hadn't even noticed*. I wanted to crawl into a hole.

Emily, one of Jules's former gang, came to stand by me. "This your first Yule party?"

I nodded dumbly.

"It's a lot like a Christmas party," she said, "except Jules isn't religious anymore. So, instead of exchanging presents, we all write down something we feel bad about or want to let go. Then we tie it to a Yule log and burn it on a bonfire. Some of the guys are getting it ready outside right now. Do you need a pen and paper to write down any regrets?"

I finally found my voice. "Do you have a notebook and all night?"

She laughed, but I wasn't joking. Mrs. Berns had been exactly right. Well, almost exactly right. Apparently, jocks and prom queens could let go of high school. It was just the dumbasses like me who let the bad memories fester or, worse, thought of no one but themselves. I had some serious mental adjustments to make.

It was both exhilarating and terrifying.

I reached for the pen and paper Emily handed me and was eagerly writing down the first of many bad thoughts I intended to let go of when Kyle appeared at the top of the stairs.

"Did you hear?" he asked in his booming voice. The conversations in the rec room quieted to a buzz. "It's on the news right now. The guy in Agate City wasn't the one. The Candy Cane Killer is still on the loose."

Chapter 50

Jules led me through the hot crowd. The atmosphere was palpably different, not subdued like I'd expected. Almost fierce. People leaned in close, flinging threats like knives around the room, promising what they would do to the serial killer who'd taken one of their own and still walked the streets.

Kyle was the loudest. "I hope that freak visits me. I goddamn *wish* for it. I'll roll him in candy canes, candy canes and gasoline, and then have him eat a match."

Victor Stratman, star of the class of 1988 cross-country running team and still built like a six-foot-six pipe cleaner, one-upped him. "I'd saw off his feet and feed them to him. Then I'd ask him if he wanted to run away."

A cold stone lodged itself in my throat. Jules grabbed my shoulders and steered me into the second room off the main hallway. It was blessedly quiet in her dark office. She took a seat at the desk pushed against the far wall.

"Sounds like we've got a mob forming." She circled the mouse on its pad, and her computer screen lit up like a cave fire.

"They're just letting off steam." The noise level was rising, and I closed the door. I'd begged her for internet access as soon as Kyle made his announcement. "Right?"

"I'm sure. How bad did you need to get online?"

I crossed the beige Berber carpeting. The room was empty except for a bookshelf full of photo albums and the computer desk cluttered with paper. It had the feel of recently being emptied, and I wondered who'd moved out. "Why?"

She swiveled in the office chair to face me. "Internet's down. Happens all the time in the country. Stupid dial-up."

She turned back to face the screen, the green glow reflecting off her. I stood over her shoulder as she clicked on the internet icon one more time for good measure. I couldn't miss the AA pendant draped over the side of her monitor. My mom had started attending Al-Anon after my dad's car accident, to "get perspective," she'd said. She owned and still wore a very similar necklace.

Jules caught the direction of my gaze. She held up her can of pop. "Sober three years."

"Congratulations."

She rotated the chair so we were facing each other, inches between us. I stepped back.

"So really, what have you been up to?" she asked.

I reviewed the image of Paynesville that I'd been holding like a rotten black jewel for over a decade. "Living in the past, apparently."

She smiled. "You get tired of that pretty quick when you don't leave your hometown."

"I suppose." I glanced out the window. The yard light cast a dismal glow over unbroken snowdrifts.

"Your mom still doing OK?"

"Yeah." I looked back at Jules. Her expression was intense. "Your dad?" I asked her.

"Sure, I suppose. He moved to Florida, got a new wife." She blinked rapidly, breaking her concentrated stare. It was a relief. "What'd you want the computer for, anyways?"

To delete my online-dating profile and remove the candy-cane-colored target from my back. "I want to find out if there's any new information on the killer."

She drew in a deep breath and nodded. "Patsy mentioned you did detective work now. That must be exciting. I always knew you were going to break out of this place."

We regarded each other, her sitting and me standing. Between us were our dead parents, the classmate we'd recently and brutally lost, dreams ground into dust and then rebuilt, maybe to be kicked down again. I leaned through the years, impulsively, and hugged her. She hugged me back. I stuffed my slip of paper in her pocket. "Burn this for me tonight, will you? I need to go home and check on my mom."

She nodded.

We were both dry-eyed, two seasoned soldiers.

Chapter 51

The heat poured out of the Corolla's vents, but it didn't penetrate my crust. Inside, I felt as cold as the winter moonscape hurtling past my windows.

I'd known the moment the too-young, too-blonde Agate City woman appeared on the news that it wasn't the Candy Cane Killer who'd targeted her and her town. She wasn't his type. I hadn't been able to or had not wanted to put a name on that niggling awareness when I'd first watched the interview, but there it was.

The killer was still hunting.

Suddenly, I couldn't reach home fast enough. I pressed my gas pedal as low as I dared, racing like a fiend across the ice-glassed country roads.

When she'd put up her outdoor decorations last week, my mom had twined berry-speckled garland around the mailbox. The bristled green caught my headlights, and the bloodred berries reflected it back. It was just an instant flash, and then I was in the driveway, pulling my car into the familiar spot in front and to the right of the garage.

A half moon floated in the cloudless sky, turning the clawed edges of winter trees black. The night felt lonely. It made me think of the week I took up jogging in high school. Determined to look as anemic as the batch of cocaine-thin models who saturated my generation in its formative years, I'd created an ambitious plan that involved setting my alarm for 5:30 a.m. to run three miles every morning and eating only saltines until suppertime, when I'd shovel down whatever my mom served so as not to raise her suspicions.

I'd instituted this plan in October of my sophomore year, the air crisp but not cold. At 5:35 a.m. sharp, I jogged down the dirt roads, the heartbeat of my Adidas tennies impossibly loud against the hard-packed gravel. I was the only person in the world, my ragged breath setting my pace, two breaths out, one in. Two breaths out, one in. It took three days to realize that I liked sleep better than jogging, but that peculiar sensation of being abandoned in a cold world resurfaced at times like this.

Luna met me at the door, which had been left unlocked. I'd need to speak to my mom and Mrs. Berns about that. The locks on my mom's house weren't much, but they were better than nothing. "Hey, girl. How are you? Did you have a fun night? Do some scrapbooking?"

She wagged her tail vigorously but did not make a peep. She understood the hour. I scratched her ears and under her chin.

"I'm just checking to make sure Tiger Pop didn't stick any 'kick me' signs on you," I said, running my hands along her back. She pushed happily against my leg, begging for more.

I removed my boots on the front carpet. Mom had swapped out the worn rag rug for a welcome mat featuring Santa waving from atop his sleigh. I tiptoed to Mom's room, smelling the delicious memory of recently baked cookies. Her door was partially cracked. I peeked in.

Her sleeping form was backlit by the moon trickling in the windows. I cocked an ear and caught the steady rhythm of her breath. She'd made it safely home from the nativity scene. I closed the door and repeated the routine in Mrs. Berns's room, though I needn't have bothered. She snored like a liquor-soaked sailor. I was halfway up the stairs, walking lightly, when I turned back around. The internet was probably still down, but I needed to check.

Tiger Pop found me while I was waiting for the computer to warm up. She jumped on my lap in a rare show of affection. She nestled down and began purring immediately, preemptively, daring me to do a bad job petting her. I rubbed the spot just in front of her tail, and she turned sassy, spinning onto her back and grabbing my hand in her paws, sheathing her claws but holding tightly with the soft pads.

"Oh, the tiger has me! Help!" I whispered, scratching her belly. She bit my hand, but gently. A development on the screen caught my eye. I was online.

"You're my good luck cat," I told her quietly. "It's your four lucky kitty foots." I grabbed one and shook it for effect. She bit me harder this time, then stretched nonchalantly.

I took my freed hand and moved the mouse over the Netscape icon and began scouring my brain for the name of the site Gina'd signed me up for. Cheap Love? Free Love? Love Gratis! That's what it was. When she'd first told me about creating my profile on the site, after the outrage had worn off, it'd occurred to me that the site builders had been wrestling above their weight class with that name.

I'd never actually visited the Love Gratis home page and was surprised at how tacky it looked compared to the sleek graphics of E-adore. The layout was a stale business-style template, the colors various shades of DMV brown, the font cheap and loud. Good thing I didn't intend to be here long. I clicked on "men looking for women" and was told to punch in the location as well as age and weight of a woman I was after.

"Very nice," I muttered. "Age and weight as criteria for finding a life mate. Same thing you look for in an astronaut and cheese." Tiger Pop stirred in my lap, kneading my thigh briefly before sinking back into a kitty coma.

The computer hummed, pulling up seven women's photographs. One of them was me. I looked like I was auditioning for a witness relocation program, one that hid lonely ladies with big honkers.

"My nose isn't that big," I swore to Tiger Pop as I clicked on the handle Gina had given me: Mirabelle.

My ad was short and sweet. I had an English degree, was working as a librarian, and was looking for a smart guy who didn't hunt. If only she'd known she was tagging me as killer bait when she posted this profile. Well, there it was, my worst fears confirmed. I was about to close down my profile when a tiny blinking circle in the upper right of the screen caught my eye. I rolled my cursor over it, and a pop-up box asked if I wanted to look at men who were interested in me.

That sounded like a slippery slope that led directly into a candy land of insecurity, shame, and regret. Unfortunately, I was only human, and a weak one at that, at least when it came to chocolate-covered nuts and curiosity.

I clicked.

I was instantly punished.

The first "looker's" profile included a photo of him in all his mulleted glory leaning against a deer corpse underneath the screen name DuckLover69.

FreeMustacheRides must have been taken.

"This, Tiger Pop, *this* is why I don't date online."

If not for the inquisitiveness that was the monkey on my back, I would have stopped there. Instead, I scrolled through all twenty-seven of the men who'd examined my profile in the last seven months. That's when I realized my inbox was empty. That led to the realization that the only thing worse than being checked out by a creep was to be found wanting by that same creep.

I decided to believe that Gina had deleted all the incoming messages, noted that none of the twenty-seven used the phrase "two shakes of a sheep's tail" or anything like it in their profiles, and then I made my profile invisible because I couldn't figure out how to remove it entirely.

I shut down the computer, feeling draggin'-stones tired.

The shrill complaint of a phone woke me. I shifted in bed without opening my eyes. My mouth tasted like feet smell, and the scratchy wool of a hangover cradled my brain, though I hadn't even had a sip of my beer the previous night. I rubbed my scalp and stretched, which was when I realized I was in the far corner of the bed. I opened my eyes to find Luna sprawled across the hand-stitched quilt and the sun pouring in.

"I'm telling Mom," I complained to her furry back.

She thumped her tail.

The phone stopped ringing. I nestled back under the cozy blanket and tried to recollect why I felt so logy. Not liquor. Was I sick? A systems check said no. That left only accumulated exhaustion from strange beds and late nights on top of monumental stress. The killer was out there, which meant at least one more woman was going to die.

"Honey? Are you awake?" my mom hollered.

"Yeah," I yelled back. Jimmy Page gazed out of the poster on the far wall, all splendor and bombast in his velvet jumpsuit, a Gibson Les Paul slung low across his slender hips. It was proof I'd had some taste back in high school.

"Telephone," she said.

I was tempted to overthink all the ways my body was protesting being awake but knew that would be a long and fruitless route. Instead, I stood up so fast that I got dizzy and made my way downstairs.

"Morning, sleepyhead!" Mom warbled.

"You look like deep-fried shit," Mrs. Berns informed me cheerfully.

I walked past both of them into the kitchen and picked up the phone. "Hello?"

"Mira? This is Adam. You called me and then never followed up." His voice was crackly, and I thought I caught the echo of a sportscast in the background.

"Are you on the road?" I asked.

"On my way back from Agate City," he confirmed. "There's nothing here but a copycatter and some very pissed-off folks. You heard, right? The guy who sent the threatening notes wasn't the Candy Cane Killer. He was your run-of-the-mill stalker, released from prison two days earlier and using the serial killer as cover to harass women. Anyhow, what can I do for you?"

Mom bustled merrily in the kitchen, her face a study of quiet joy. She was in her element. Mrs. Berns appeared to be knitting in the living room, a testament to the thickness of domestic bliss in this house. I didn't want to interrupt it by filling Adam in on what'd gone down in Orelock.

"I was hoping I could meet you for coffee this morning."

Mom's eyes shot up in a moment of disappointment, but she covered smoothly. "Just for a quick cup," I continued. "I know it's the holidays, and you probably have someplace to be."

"I'm Jewish," he said. "I can be in Paynesville in an hour."

Chapter 52

Overhead, the sky was a clear blue sheet of unbroken ice. The cold sun glinted off the unforgiving crust of snow that made up the arctic landscape. Despite the light, and the fact that it was almost Christmas, it felt like a dangerous time to be out. I took the turns carefully and kept the car below forty-five miles per hour. I didn't even want the radio on for fear that it would break my concentration.

Adam and I'd agreed to meet at Carlisle's gas station, which had a little coffee nook in back. I intended to tell him about Isaiah/Isaac and my conversation with Amanda Running. I'd be lying if I didn't also admit that I was hoping he'd share the latest information on the killer.

He'd sounded tired on the phone, but his voice hadn't prepared me for his appearance when I located him at the back of the gas station. His skin had the gray pallor of ill health, and his cheeks sagged. When he turned at the sound of his name, his eyes were dull.

"Mira." He waved at the industrial coffee brewer behind him. "Can I recommend the spiced pumpkin latte?"

I smiled politely at his attempt at humor. The coffee bar consisted of regular, decaf, creamer powder, and sugar. "No thank you. Are you feeling all right?"

He was leaning on the counter next to an opened sausage and biscuit container. He'd taken apart the whole sandwich but not eaten any of it. "I've been better."

I wasn't sure how far to push it. If he had the flu, it could be helpful to commiserate with someone, but I guessed this was more about being reminded of his sister's death and the helplessness of his position. I opted for the neutral route. "Anything I can do?"

"Not unless you know who the Candy Cane Killer is."

I took the opening to describe my and Mrs. Berns's online-dating foray in River Grove. After that I shared our experience in Orelock from beginning to end, including running into an unhinged Quinna in the hardware store and spotting Sharpie's caramels at the gas station. Adam shook his head distantly while I talked. He also picked at his sandwich but never brought the food to his mouth. When I was finished, I waited for him to ask questions. He seemed lost in thought, oblivious to his surroundings.

"They know he's targeting women through online-dating sites," he finally said.

"I figured that when the radio warned women to hold off on any online dating. Do you think the fact that both Isaiah and Isaac used that same 'two shakes of a sheep's tail' line means anything?"

He ran his hands through his hair. "I think you should trust your instincts. Have you brought this to Briggs?"

My cheeks flushed. "No. He's not my biggest fan. He basically told me to stay out of his way or suffer the consequences."

"Sounds like Briggs." Adam drew his hand into a fist and almost knocked his sandwich package to the ground. He caught it just before it fell. "He seems to be losing a lot of the info that I've been passing on to him, as well."

My throat hitched. "Like what?"

"Like the fact that the killer lived in River Grove at one time."

I thought of Olivia, and what she'd said about Ginger the day care monster and the mysterious young relative who visited her over the holidays. "How do you know?"

"This case has been my life for two years." He laughed, but it was a hollow bark. "I have resources and leads that the law won't listen to. So

I stay out of Briggs's way when I can, gather the story, and try to feed info to the FBI through Briggs's partner."

I thought of Mr. Denny's lesson. *Don't let someone's authority distract you.* Who better to misdirect a major investigation than the lead investigator? And who had a better excuse to be near every murder scene than the agent in charge?

"Why don't you write about that in one of your articles, how Briggs is putting up barriers to the case being solved?" I asked.

Adam ran a shaking hand through his hair. "My sister loved Christmas," he said. His eyes glittered with unshed tears. "Ironic, right, with us being Jewish? But it was her favorite time of the year. It's one of the greatest fucking ironies of my life that I can't be in this month without thinking of her murder."

I didn't know what to say, so I said nothing, my chest tight.

He seemed to collect himself after a moment. "I'm sorry. I'm too close to the case, right? So you asked why I didn't put all that in an article. Here's why. If I call out Briggs, if I air my suspicions that he's not doing everything he can to solve this case, then I become the bad guy and I lose access to my sources. The way it is now, I have contacts on the inside. If I push Briggs too hard, that'll stop. But what Briggs doesn't know is that this case is very near to being solved. The killer is gonna be caught."

He said the last part with such fierce assurance that I didn't know if it was fantasy talking or if he really did have inside information. "You think he's going to kill more before they get him?"

"Four deaths in December is his pattern. A leopard can't change his spots. He'll try, but if I'm right, he won't succeed."

"What do you know?"

He looked at me sadly. "Nothing I can talk about. But I can pass on your Isaac/Isaiah research to Lee, Briggs's partner. He'll know if it's something they can use. In the meanwhile, I suggest you spend the rest of the holidays appreciating your family. They're all we have."

He turned so quickly that he almost knocked over a woman balancing two quarts of milk, a can of green beans, and a box of Stove Top stuffing in her arms. She dropped the stuffing, but he didn't stop. I leaned to grab the red box and placed it back in her arms. That's when I noticed Adam had left his cell phone next to his massacred sandwich. I snatched it and ran after him. I didn't see him out front and dashed around the corner of the building. He was entering a silver sedan parked next to the dumpster. I jogged and reached him just as he was unlocking the car door.

"Adam! You forgot—"

He whirled, his face a mask of such raw pain that it took my breath away. He rearranged his features and positioned himself between me and the car. "What is it?"

"Your cell." I handed him the black phone, almost unable to look him in the eye. I'd never seen someone so vulnerable in my life.

"Thanks," he said gruffly, taking it.

We stood awkwardly for a moment, and then I walked to my car without saying another word.

Chapter 53

A beautiful, unexpected, fairy dust snowfall began as I drove home, so light that it was almost invisible except for the way it changed the shape of the air. The dancing sparkles would have provided the perfect Christmas cheer, except I felt terrible for Adam. I'd sensed his pain was far too deep and wide for a virtual stranger to touch, but I still felt like I should have made things better for him somehow.

His grief was still with me as I pulled into the driveway, but it began to give way to something warm and solid the minute I entered the door. The symphony of smells brought me immediately back to every good memory of my childhood: roasted turkey, garlicky mashed potatoes, cinnamon-laced pumpkin pie, warm, crusty bread fresh from the oven.

My mom had started what she called the Three-Day Feast tradition when I was five years old. She operated on the belief that one day wasn't enough to celebrate God's grace, plus she wanted us to be free to volunteer on Christmas Eve and Day, so she cooked enough food for an army three days before Christmas. We ate like royalty that night and opened presents, then had delicious leftovers for the next two days.

This was the first time I'd been part of the Three-Day Feast in years.

The smile my mom gave me was blinding when I entered.

"Sorry about that errand," I said. "Can I help with anything?"

She rubbed her hands on her apron and returned to ricing the potatoes. "The best thing you can do for me is to stay out of my way."

I grinned because that, too, was part of the tradition. My mom liked to cook, and she worked alone. I gave her a peck on the cheek, stole a crispy bite of succulent skin from the settling turkey before she could swat my hand, and went in to check on Mrs. Berns. I found her seated in front of the laptop.

"Have you been in the kitchen lately?" I asked her.

"Nope," she said as she tapped at the keyboard. "After a little polite hemming and hawing, your mom finally came out and told me that she likes to run the cooking show herself. I don't know why she was hesitating. If there's anything one woman should be comfortable telling another, it's 'get the hell out of my kitchen.'"

I walked forward to see what was on her screen. "What are you working on?"

She quickly minimized the view. "Hasn't anyone ever told you it's impolite to read over someone's shoulders?"

I was waiting for the glare that was sure to follow, but she didn't meet my eyes. This sent up an army of red flags. "You're not looking at online porn in my mom's house, are you?"

She crossed her arms and turned to face me. "Nope. Nothing uglier than two strangers having sex. If God had meant for the world to see all that, He would have put our wedding tackle on our heads and our ears in our pants."

I put up a hand in an effort to stop the visual from settling into my brain, but she'd been too quick. I winced when it hit home. "Then what are you doing?"

"Maybe I'm Christmas shopping."

"This late in the game?"

"Some good deals out there."

"You're probably right." I glanced over my shoulder. "Oh, Mom sent me in here to tell you that our Day One feast is ready, and she doesn't mind if we start with the pie."

Mrs. Berns was out of her seat faster than a greased sneeze. I didn't hesitate, sliding into her seat in a single hot second. One click brought up the E-adore site and Sharpie's grinning face. A blinking heart in the upper right-hand corner indicated that Mrs. Berns's account had an incoming message. I accessed it, and as the words of the message filled my eyes, the blood drained from me:

> **Hey, spunky lover. Sunday was amazing. Can't wait to see you again. With Christmas cheer, your Cyrano de Bergerac**

"You lie like a sack of shit," Mrs. Berns accused from the doorway. "Your mom said we don't eat for another half an hour. Why would you lie to a pie-deprived old lady like that? You *want* to go to hell?"

I pushed myself to the side, revealing the computer screen. Sharpie's photo stared at her from across the room. She immediately went into defensive mode.

"Look, just because he travels for work doesn't make him a serial killer. I'm telling you, I'm good at reading people, and old enough to know BS when I smell it. Sharpie is a good guy."

"You were the one pegging him as a killer after you talked to him in the coffee shop!"

She considered this. "True. But then we camped outside his hotel room, and he never left. That's when I got to thinking that I sure liked the sound of his voice back in Tammy's Tavern. And the way he looked at me."

I crossed my arms. "You don't know a thing about him."

"I know he's part owner of a candy company in Chicago. He's currently staying in River Grove as his base, selling candy and researching the feasibility of opening a factory in the area—low taxes for new businesses, cheap labor. I know he has no family except an ailing mom in Minneapolis and a sister in Boca Raton. If he can make a deal for a factory in Minnesota, he can settle down here and be closer to his mother." She leaned forward as if to tell me a secret. "And I'll tell you what, I know one more thing. That nose is *not* false advertising."

The last disturbing image she'd planted in my head was replaced by another. "All I asked for was you to wait until the killer was caught."

"Pooh." She put her nose in the air. "I'm trusting my intuition and living my life. I'm old enough to have earned that."

She was right. But still. "I'm worried about you, that's all. It's a dangerous time to date strangers."

Mrs. Berns walked over and ruffled my hair. "It's always a dangerous time to date strangers. A woman doesn't want to make stupid decisions, but she can't live in fear, either. Trust me. Sharpie's solid."

"Does he know you live in Battle Lake?"

"Yup, and that I'm staying here for the holidays. He's not afraid to travel for love." She winked. "We have a date later tonight."

I didn't like it. It might not be fair, but I'd tagged Sharpie as a questionable guy. I didn't want to admit it might have something to do with his appearance, so I didn't and instead focused on the facts. He was from Chicago, the home of the original Candy Cane serial murders, and he'd traveled to at least two of the towns in Minnesota where a murder had taken place. I'd be willing to bet he'd spent his share of time in Wisconsin, as well. The most I could do was keep a closer eye on Mrs. Berns and hope that Adam conveyed our leads to Briggs's partner so he could check out Sharpie Trevino.

"Fine, but could you do me a favor and not have any sleepovers? At least not until the killer is caught. I'd owe you big-time."

Mrs. Berns scowled, muttered something about closing the barn door after the chicken has gotten out and the egg has been laid, but in the end, she agreed. I shut down the computer and began to set the table, using the treasured lace tablecloth my mother had received from her grandmother, my great-grandmother, on her wedding.

It was well used, almost transparent in spots, and represented holidays. When the tablecloth came out, good times were sure to follow. Mrs. Berns had bought and chilled some champagne, so she popped the cork and served us each a glass. It wasn't long until we were giggling, lugging platters loaded with food from the kitchen to the dining room.

The meal was spectacular. I was glad I'd spent all the years stretching out my stomach so I didn't have to pass on thirds. The turkey was so moist that it melted, and Mom's stuffing was made from scratch, a perfectly seasoned, savory comfort food. Butter melted off the fresh bread, filling the chewy cracks and running down my arm. The creamed peas were the texture of mush and so delicious that I wanted to roll in them. We were so busy eating that we gave up talking until my mom remembered that she'd forgotten to say grace.

"And it's almost Christmas!" She had a hand to her cheek, her expression shocked. "Can you believe it? I have so much to be grateful for this year, and I didn't even bother to thank our Lord."

Mrs. Berns raised her champagne. "Thanks, Lord." She drained her glass and took another scoop of dressing.

My mom's smile was momentarily strained. She crossed herself and clasped her hands. "Bless us, Oh Lord, and these thy gifts which we are about to receive from thy bounty, through Christ, Our Lord. I would like to thank you for the food, the company, my wonderful daughter, and for taking good care of my husband in heaven. I miss him every day."

I'd closed my eyes out of habit at the start of the prayer, but they flew open at these words. My mother's face was serene. Had she really just referred to my dad, and even said she missed him? What a strange thought. I'd spent so much energy pushing down any memory of him that I couldn't imagine choosing to think about him regularly. I felt a click inside me, and then a slow swelling of something I couldn't identify. I offered my own prayer to distract myself.

"Yes, thank you for the food and the company. I hope that everyone I love will stay safe and make good choices." I stared pointedly at Mrs. Berns.

She stopped refilling her champagne glass. "And I hope that everyone I love will grow up and mind their own beeswax. Amen." She resumed pouring.

Mom stared at us, confused, and decided to return to her food. Mrs. Berns and I did the same. Eventually tryptophan, the great sedater, turned the blood in our veins to a hot, slow stew. We worked together to clean up after dinner, and once all our leftovers were packed and a massive pot of turkey stock simmered on the stove, we retreated to the living room to open presents.

The windows were festooned with twinkle lights. The soft snow outside had picked up its pace. Delicate flurries blanketed the world in white. Mom put on a Bing Crosby Christmas CD before joining us on the couch.

My mom and Mrs. Berns opened their presents from me first, at my insistence. My mom loved the gardening book I'd bought her. Mrs. Berns was surprised and then beamed as brightly as a lighthouse when she unwrapped the fedora that I'd found for her at a vintage clothing store in Willmar. She adjusted the jaunty feather in its brim and dropped it onto her head. The hat fit perfectly and made her look as cool as a cat.

"These are for you two," Mrs. Berns said, handing my mom and me each a delicately wrapped box. My mom opened hers first. Inside was a cameo brooch, a white silhouette against a coral-colored background and wreathed in ornate gold. My mom gasped.

"It was my mother's," Mrs. Berns said.

My mom immediately handed it back. "Thank you, but I can't possibly accept this."

"It's an honor to give it," Mrs. Berns said simply. "You raised one of my best friends in this world, and I'd like to give you a little something to thank you."

My eyes grew hot. My mom didn't bother to stop the tears flowing down her face. She pinned the brooch to her collar and looked at me with deep love.

"You're next," Mrs. Berns said.

I pulled the ribbon off my package. A hard black stone sat nestled in the bottom of the box. I pulled it out. It had a greasy feel. "Was this your father's?" I asked, holding it up.

"Nope," she said, shaking her head confidently. "That's a lump of coal. Didn't want things getting too sentimental. Better luck next year!"

My mom gasped in horror, but I smiled and placed the top back on the box. I loved Mrs. Berns more for giving me the coal than for giving my mom the brooch. It showed how well she knew me. "Thank you."

"You two next," my mom said. She handed Mrs. Berns and me each a red rectangular box, the kind that JCPenney sweaters usually come in. We both unwrapped ours at the same time. Mine held a hand-knit scarf created from the softest emerald-toned cashmere I'd ever felt. I held it to my cheek and almost purred. "Thank you."

"You're welcome." Mom beamed proudly.

Mrs. Berns's box also held a scarf, though hers was done in the bright oranges that she preferred. They were both absolutely lovely. Next, Mom gave Tiger Pop a sock full of catnip and Luna a peanut-butter-flavored rawhide bone tied with a red bow. Everyone was happy, the room itself a box of contentment wrapped in Christmas cheer.

Mrs. Berns chose that moment to leave for her date with Sharpie. I recognized that the warm glow on her face wasn't just from time spent with me and Mom. She had a genuine crush on the guy, and I had a hunch that she'd been spending more time with him than at the nursing home the last two days.

"You remember the wrist lock?" I asked her, referring to the self-defense move we'd covered on our first day of class.

"I do, but I favor the nut-splat, followed by the eyeball popper and then the throat punch. Don't worry, ninny. I'm a smart woman." She patted my head. "I'll be back by one, deal?"

"Deal." I thought I caught her and Mom exchanging a *she worries too much* face, and I couldn't believe it. As far as I was concerned, Minnesota women were currently operating in a war zone. There was no such thing as worrying too much. I walked to the bay window to watch Mrs. Berns drive away in my car, which doubled the anxiety I felt.

"C'mon, Mira," my mom said, motioning me away from the window. "Let's play cribbage."

We'd played so many games back when I was in high school that we'd needed to replace the pegs. It was our together time, when we'd talk about her day and mine. Our games had dropped off after Dad's accident, by my choice, I imagine, but they still held a warm memory.

I allowed myself to be distracted as she retrieved the hand-polished wooden game board from the closet. It was over this board that I'd told her all the secrets girls told their moms until they turned fourteen or so and decided their mothers could never understand a teenager's complicated life. I smiled as I ran my hand over the smooth surface. "When was the last time you played?"

"Not since you left," she said. She cut the cards and shuffled them with a whirring snap. "But don't worry. I've still got tricks up my sleeve."

She won the first round. I won the second. We were on our rubber match when I ran up to the question I'd been too scared to ask and threw it at her before I could change my mind. "Do you actually miss Dad?"

A deep furrow appeared between her eyes. She arranged her cards, then rearranged them all back. "Every day."

My mouth grew dry. "Even after what he did to us?"

She set her cards on the table and looked at me with her clear gray eyes. I was startled at the number of wrinkles around them. She looked closer in age to Mrs. Berns than to me. When had that happened? "Your dad made mistakes. He also loved us. Do you remember the October weekend he packed you and me up in the station wagon and drove us to South Dakota? I think you were in fourth grade, and you'd come home crying because you had to write a report on Mount Rushmore and didn't know what to say. We toured the whole park, and he spent the money he'd been saving for a motorcycle to cover the motel and gas."

Her eyes had a faraway look. "You earned an A on that report," she said.

I dug a little and remembered that trip, though faintly. It must have meant more to her than it had to me. "Why'd he drink so much?"

She sighed. "His dad taught him that. He also beat him every day of his life, until your dad ran away from home and joined the navy as soon as he was old enough. I consider it a great achievement that he never raised a hand to either of us. He loved you completely, honey. For that, I will always love him, and I'll always miss him."

I knew he'd had a tough childhood. I'd heard bits of it all through mine. I still didn't understand why he chose to drink so much when his life finally got good. I shuffled my cards.

"There's something else I need to tell you, sweetheart. Something I've been meaning to talk to you about for a while now."

Her voice was laden with regret and an odd note of excitement. The combination made me uncomfortable. I was grateful when the phone rang. "I'll get it," I said, hopping up.

Luna followed me to the kitchen, her bone in her mouth.

"Hello?" I said.

"Hello. I'm looking for Miranda James."

"Speaking."

There was silence on the other end for a moment. "This is Agent Briggs. We need to talk."

Chapter 54

His voice had an urgency that chilled my skin. "What is it?"

He sighed on the other end, followed by a shuffling of papers. The faint whisking noise echoed oddly, as if he were in a large empty space. "You heard that they got the wrong guy in Agate City."

It wasn't phrased as a question, so I continued to hold my breath.

"You're not making this easy on me, are you?" The background noise ceased. "I'm sorry I came down on you so hard in Orelock. You were in my way, no doubt about it, but this case has gotten under my skin and I overreacted. I don't even know who I am some days."

The odd familiarity of the exchange was unsettling. "Have you been drinking?"

"Hey, happy holidays to you, too." He either chuckled or coughed. "Here it is. De Luca told me about the Isaiah/Isaac guy you found online, and I need to hear everything you've got on that. *Everything.*"

"What exactly did Adam tell you?"

That chuckle-cough again. "That you posed online in Orelock as a woman whose physicals met the killer's MO, just like you did in River Grove. In both towns, you came across a profile of a man without a photo, with different handles and physicals, but with a similar phrase used in both profiles, something about sheep shaking their tails."

"That's right. That's the meat of what I know." I'd wanted him to hear the information and to take it seriously. I hadn't expected him to call me. Mr. Denny's advice hammered in my head: *Don't let someone's authority fool you!*

"You sure that's everything?" he demanded. "This is important."

I teetered on a line so thin it was a shadow. Something in the light camaraderie of his voice was all wrong. I was also hyperaware that he wasn't my biggest fan, and that he seemed the type to shoot the messenger. In the end, though, the possibility that he really was the good guy and close to catching the killer forced my hand. "I know that the Candy Cane Killer lived in River Grove when he was younger."

The silence on the other end was so profound that it was nearly a vacuum. "Hello?"

"Who told you that?" His voice was deep, as dangerous as an iceberg scraping the underside of a boat.

I didn't want to get Adam in trouble or compel him to reveal his sources. I also couldn't sit on information that might help this case, and if what Adam said was true and Briggs didn't know it, he needed to.

"Adam. He didn't tell me his source."

A crackle of a walkie-talkie shocked its way through the line. On the other end, Briggs's voice went from dangerous to urgent. "You're there with your mother?"

"Yes."

"Lock your doors, stay away from the windows, and don't let anyone in. I can be there in twenty minutes."

He was barking into his walkie-talkie as he slammed down the phone on his end of the line. I hung up mine, my body light with fear. It was the exposed dread of a lightning-slashed nightmare, the kind where you wake drenched in sweat and paralyzed as all the terrors of the night shamble toward you, and you're too scared to call for help.

Only I very much needed to find my voice and get my mom's attention so we could escape. It had all just clicked into place, right there on the phone.

I finally knew who the killer was, so help me god.

Chapter 55

"Mom?" It came out as an empty husk of a sound.

"Mom." Still a whisper. It was no good. I'd have to force my legs to carry me to her.

Outside the kitchen window, the yard light reflected a tiny plate of illumination off each snowflake. They swirled in a dancing confusion, miniature searchlights fighting a black night.

Against all predictions, a Christmas storm was descending. I could see nothing beyond the hill that hid the road. Black trees rimmed the house, remnants of a windbreak planted when this had been a working farm. Their branches moved in the blustery weather like skeleton fingers, and their trunks hid and manipulated shadows.

The nearest neighbor was more than a mile away.

Luna nuzzled my hand. I glanced down. She was staring at me with a fierceness, telling me she was by my side, and she wasn't going to leave me. Her faith spurred me to action. I shuffled forward, into the dining room. Mom had taken up her knitting while I was on the phone. She set it down when I spilled into the room.

"I hope you're prepared to lose the rubber match!" she said. The happy expression fell off her face and clattered to the ground when she caught sight of me. "What's wrong? Is it Mrs. Berns?"

"We have to get out of this house right away. We need to take your van. Don't ask questions." My tone was mechanical.

She stood and crossed the room, planting her hands on my shoulders. "No. You're going to tell me what's going on. Finally." Her voice was firm.

Oddly, I gained a mote of strength from her command. "I know who the serial killer is, and he's on his way."

Her eyes widened, but she chose action over words. She ran to the kitchen to grab her purse, searching for her keys. I followed, my brain racing. How much time had I spent with the killer, how much information had I given him, not even suspecting? The hints to his identity were little things, certainly, but little things that when added up were overwhelming.

Who else had been at the scene of every murder? Who had overheard me finding out about the orange begonias at the funeral home before threatening me off the case with a flower shipped to the *Battle Lake Recall*? Who'd specifically called me at home when I'd asked him to call me at the hotel or on Mrs. Berns's cell, indicating he was tracking my whereabouts? Who else could travel near the murders without causing suspicion?

Who'd said to me, only hours before, "a leopard can't change his spots," a phrase almost as clunky and dated as "two shakes of a sheep's tail"? And finally, who'd told me a piece of information so rare, so intimate, that only the killer and possibly the FBI agent about to capture him would know it?

We often let a person's position or authority distract us, don't we?

Adam De Luca was the Candy Cane Killer.

Dammit. I'd allowed myself to be so intimidated by Briggs's judgment that I hadn't told him information I should have been feeding him all along, regardless of how unprofessionally he'd behaved. Adam was unraveling—everything about his appearance at the gas station today had proved that—but I was certain he wasn't going to quit until he'd murdered his fourth victim.

The fact that he'd told me the secret about the killer-who-was-Adam growing up in River Grove made clear that he didn't intend for me to live long enough to reveal it to anyone else, and that he was banking on my fear of Briggs and my ability to sit on secrets.

Briggs was gambling that he could beat De Luca here. But Mom, the animals, and I couldn't wait for that.

Except Tiger Pop wasn't answering my call.

Mom had her keys in hand. Luna was sticking close to me.

"Leave Tiger Pop," my mom said.

I shifted my scared eyes to her. She also looked frightened, but resolute.

"She's a cat," she said. "She'll be fine. We'll come back for her tomorrow. Come on, honey."

She was right, but I couldn't leave her behind. As if on cue, she appeared around the corner, her tail quivering. I scooped her up.

"Grab a knife," I said as we made our way to the garage.

Mom slid a chef's knife out of the block without slowing her forward movement. Master Andrea had made it clear in the self-defense class that any weapon you hold can be used against you, so don't grab it unless you know how to wield it or have no other defense. I figured the latter described my mom.

The attached garage was cold, but flipping on the single overhead bulb revealed that it was also nearly as clean as my mom's house. The lack of clutter and shadows was a relief. If we could just all get in the van and get the windows and doors locked, we were safe, even if we had to crash the car through the garage wall to escape. Outside, the wind howled.

"Hurry," I told my mom.

She slipped into the driver's side. I opened the side door to let Luna in, and closed it.

That's when the lights went out.

Chapter 56

My breath escaped in a *huff*, as if I'd been punched in the stomach, and I dropped Tiger Pop. I blinked rapidly, trying to adjust, and slammed my back to the van. I heard only a silence so absolute it was like death.

My mom opened her door. "Mira?"

"Close it, Mom. Close it, lock it, turn on the lights." I had my fingers curled under the icy metal of the door handle when the shadows shifted in front of me. A crushing blow followed, numbing the arm that held the handle. Strong hands caught me by the hair as I fell toward the ground.

Time and sound slowed. I tried to remember the name Mr. Denny had given this sensation, but then that thought slipped away like an eel. I heard Luna snarling and thrashing against the van's door. My mom was yelling, but it seemed very far away, each wave of sound splitting and arcing around me.

A tiny filter of snow-spangled moonlight slipped through the cracks of the garage, allowing me to make out his shape. Muscled. Male. The smell of cinnamon chewing gum. I shot a hand in the air, hoping to connect with flesh, but it glanced off my captor. I twisted to free myself, and a big chunk of hair ripped from my head.

I could hold only one thought: *Draw him away from Mom.*

I stood and charged through the door that led from the garage to the mudroom. I hesitated for only a moment. I knew I shouldn't enter the house—I'd be trapped—so I ripped open the outside door and charged into the night. The ground was icy, and I fell to my knees. Loud breathing tore the air, slow and distant but somehow echoing like a hammer pound in my head.

Was it his? Mine?

I struggled to my feet and charged across the snow, but he was faster. He hit me from behind. We rolled to the ground, his arms squeezing me like a constrictor. I couldn't draw a breath. The paralysis was settling onto me just like it had at the gym. Why fight? It would be over quicker if I just let it happen, and this grinding terror could finally end. He'd already murdered eleven women, one of them his own sister. I was no better than them, no smarter, no quicker. I wasn't going to get away. I thought of my mom, and Mrs. Berns, and it made me sad that I'd be leaving them. My vision blurred, then narrowed, and I felt almost sleepy.

And then, to my great surprise, a yell rose from somewhere deep in my gut.

I didn't scream for anyone, or out of fear. I yelled because it hurt, and I was suddenly angry, and it turned out I *did* want to fight after all.

The noise reset time and sound.

My head flew back, cracking him on the nose. He swore and loosened his grip for a moment. That's all I needed to pull away. I twisted and connected again with his now-bloody face, with my forehead this time. He recoiled from the force of the headbutt and kicked at me, grazing my wounded arm. We both stumbled to our feet. Greedy flakes of snow swirled around our bodies and stuck.

I was facing Adam De Luca now, within arm's reach. Our chests heaved in ragged, tearing breaths. His face was an evil slate of blankness, the only life in it the blood coursing down from his cracked nose. His eyes were vacant, shifting glass. He looked not like Adam but like someone wearing an Adam mask.

Metal glinted in his hand.

I swung, and my punch went wild. Momentum pulled me down as he stabbed toward my chest. My unexpected shift robbed the knife of its target. The blade burned through my coat and the flesh of my upper arm instead. He must have thought I'd taken the cut in a vital area, because he let down his guard for a split second.

Catching myself before I hit the ground, I used the technique I'd learned in self-defense class to make a rock out of my left hand. I repositioned my weight and stood, hurling my fist toward his throat, a bullet from a gun. It connected. He made a noise like an air mattress popping, then fell to his knees. Drops of blood from his broken nose startled the snow around him.

A brutal growl from the direction of the garage drew my attention. Luna, a raging wolf creature, appeared in the door my mom held open. She charged in a four-legged blur. The force of her pushed Adam from his knees to his back, and she stood on him, her weight pinning him as he tried helplessly to reach his crushed throat.

The world became suddenly loud, a roaring wave of finally freed sound crashing around my ears: my searing, sharp breaths, my mom crying, Luna's feral growls terrifying even to me. After amplified sound came the pain. My right arm throbbed, and the coldness I felt washing over my hand was my own blood gushing from me. Exhaustion—empty, desperate tiredness—followed the pain.

I wanted it to be all over. I wanted someone to rush in and drag the bad guy away, tell my mom it was all going to be OK and to get me to a hospital. But that wasn't going to happen. Nobody was going to do that for me.

"I need rope, Mom." My voice was hoarse. I might have been screaming the whole attack.

She stood in the doorway for a moment with her hand clutched around the knife, the whites of her eyes as big as eggs. Her mouth kept opening and closing. Luna snapped at Adam's face, and the slicing click of her teeth woke my mom from her shock. She disappeared into the garage and came out with a circle of clothesline.

I took it in my left hand. "It's all right, Mom." My voice sounded unfamiliar.

My arm was stiff, my hands beginning to claw from the cold. I rejected the pain, begging Luna off Adam. She moved but kept her snout to his head, her teeth bared, a low rattlesnake noise in her throat.

I rolled Adam onto his stomach. He was still scrabbling for his throat, but his movements were weakening. I knew I'd probably crushed his trachea and that he might be dying. I wasn't willing to risk my mom's or Luna's life to save him.

I tied his wrists behind his back, and then I passed out.

Chapter 57

"How long had you known he was targeting women through online dating?"

"Since the third murder," Briggs said affably. "We're the FBI. Unfortunately, millions of people are dating online. De Luca struck four times in Chicago and was gone. By the time we figured out it was the same guy in Wisconsin, we only had two weeks to capture him, then he stopped killing. We were quicker in Minnesota. As soon as he struck in White Plains, we were there. Our specialists were running phrase-recognition software on all online ads and came up with the 'two shakes of a sheep's tail' connection about the same time you did. It was the only slipup De Luca had."

I shifted in the hospital bed. "That English degree finally paid off."

The statement was meant to be ironic. I had a dislocated shoulder and, in the same arm, fifteen ugly stitches holding two sides of my brachium together. The left side of my face was swollen and as bruised as a dropped apple. My pain level probably would have been a twelve on a scale of ten if not for the delicious Vicodin they'd been feeding me. As it was, I felt like I'd been hit by a motorcycle rather than a bus.

Briggs grunted. He and his partner were paying me a courtesy by being here, and he'd made sure I knew that. He also carried himself like a chained man set free. Three winters on this case, and the murderer had finally been caught. Briggs could go home to his family.

"That's all you had to go on?" Mrs. Berns said skeptically. "After two years? What's 'FBI' stand for—'fully brainless imbeciles'?"

I kept my face smooth, but it wasn't easy.

Agent Lee also looked like he was struggling to keep the smile off his face, but Briggs studied Mrs. Berns with eyes that'd probably forced life-hardened gangsters to confess. "Our profilers knew that our killer had been a foster kid, and we'd just found out that a River Grove woman who ran a day care had her grandson and granddaughter spend every December with her. The rest of the year, they lived in foster homes. Both the River Grove and White Plains victims attended that same River Grove day care as a child."

Olivia called the FBI, I thought, *and the FBI did their work.* I owed these people.

"The foster kids' grandmother and the owner of the day care, Ginger Lewis, was a brutal psychopath if there ever was one. Unofficially, of course. None of the charges against her ever stuck, but if one-third of them were true, she was the devil on earth. We'd unearthed the killer's connection to her and nearly had a name when I called you. Only me, my closest people, and the killer knew he'd lived in River Grove at that time. When you told me De Luca had shared that nugget with you, I knew he was our man, and that you were gonna be his number four."

I remembered Adam's doll eyes as he swung the knife at me. "What set him off? Back in Chicago, I mean."

Briggs ran a hand through his bristly hair. "As near as we can tell, he started online dating in Chicago two years ago and came across the profile of his sister. Because of things Auntie Ginger had done to both of them, he had very strong feelings against women exposing themselves in public in that way."

"He'd prefer we hid?" Mrs. Berns asked acidly.

Briggs shrugged. "I'm not the killer. I don't think it was like that for him, though. He seemed to think he was protecting the women from something worse by killing them. Auntie Ginger must have done a number on those kids. We'll never know for sure, however, as she hung herself a decade ago, though we have reason to believe that De Luca had a hand in that, too. It might have been his first killing."

"How'd he choose his future victims?" I asked.

"His sister, I already told you about. The others, with the exception of the two who went to Auntie Ginger's day care, seemed to be random women he found online who had features similar to his sister's."

I adjusted in my hospital bed. "That's how it starts, I guess, by thinking you know what's best for someone else and imposing your will on them." I tried to remember the last time I'd had a pain pill. The stitches in my arm were beginning to throb. "Did he tell you all that? How he chose his victims, and that he wanted to protect us by killing us?"

Briggs walked to the window. I hadn't been conscious when he'd shown up at my mom's house last night. She'd told me that she couldn't bear to leave me passed out near the killer, and so she'd held me there with Luna, trying to bind my wounds and rouse me so we could go inside to phone for help. She'd heard the sirens before she'd seen them, lonely, howling whoops echoing across the empty country roads.

Two police cars and a sedan had shrieked into her driveway, men and women exiting, guns drawn. It was Briggs who'd flipped the killer with his foot and studied his face for a moment before performing lifesaving CPR on him.

A female police officer was the first to reach me. Mom had to restrain Luna so the officer could assess my wounds. She'd finished my mom's work of stanching the bleeding in my arm while Agent Lee called for an ambulance. I came to shortly after that, but in a distant way. I remember the violent cherry snow cone my blood had made of the landscape. Adam's blood was mixed in, and the thick metal smell of it amplified by the pristine winter air had made me throw up.

My mom had cried a lot, holding tight to Luna. They'd bundled Adam into a different ambulance from me, but we'd both ended up at Paynesville Hospital, a surprisingly large and modern facility. Adam had two armed officers guarding him. I had Mrs. Berns and my mom. I was definitely coming out ahead.

"De Luca's not talking, literally and figuratively," Briggs said. "You stapled his throat pretty good with your left hook." He walked over to me and leaned in close, suddenly, fiercely. "I'm proud of you, kiddo. You did what you needed to save yourself. And I owe you one."

He paused as if he were going to say more, then stood abruptly and looked around the room. "Any other questions? I've got work to do."

I fumbled at the loose threads in my brain. "Are you really originally from the Midwest?"

"Des Moines," he said.

I filed this away. I had to admit—only to myself—that I'd considered him as a suspect at one point. "Sharpie Trevino was not connected in any way to the case?"

"Sharpie Trevino is what he appears to be," Agent Lee offered. "A business owner and traveling salesman—an honest one, without a record."

Mrs. Berns shot me a smug look, which I brushed off.

"Was Quinna Bankowski really working the night Samantha Keller was killed?" I asked.

"Yes."

I considered the creepy look she'd given me when I left her in the hardware store. "What was she doing in Orelock the day after Samantha was murdered?"

"She's a ghoul," Briggs said, echoing Adam's word choice.

I shivered.

"Was De Luca really Jewish?" Mrs. Berns asked.

"Nope."

"Jesus Christ," she said. "Is nothing sacred?"

Agent Lee actually laughed at this. Briggs flipped his card on the table beside my bed. "You know where to find me if you need me," he said, and he started to leave, his broad back nearly blocking the light shining in through the door.

"One more thing," I called after him.

He stopped, but did not turn.

"Am I on the FBI watch list?" It wasn't that I didn't believe Mr. Denny, just that I didn't *want* to believe Mr. Denny.

He turned, his face carved from stone. "If you weren't before, you are now." Then he made the cough-laugh sound that I realized was how he expressed humor.

When he strode out, Lee followed.

"They seem nice," my mom said. She'd been stroking my hair on and off all morning.

"Can you stop it, Mom?" I said, light annoyance in my voice.

It was nervousness. Sometime in the middle of the night, after the painkillers had settled me into a nice, purple buzz, she'd revealed that she'd been dating a guy named Hank for more than six months. He was a good man, she'd said, a regular churchgoer, a retired plumber, a widower with three grown children.

His was the apartment I'd seen her slip into the day I'd left the Paynesville newspaper offices. He owned a house in Florida and rented an apartment in town, where he'd come in the summer to fish and catch up with friends. Once he'd met Mom, he decided to stay year-round. I also learned he'd been in the hospital waiting room since shortly after we'd arrived. She'd called him while I was getting sutured, and he'd come right over in case she needed him. I'd agreed to meet him after the agents left.

"Sorry," my mom said. "It's not every day that I see my daughter get sliced by a serial killer."

I laughed against my will. "Was that sarcasm?"

She put her hands in the air, palms up. "What can I say? We all change."

I nodded, chewing on those words. "I'm ready to meet Hank." I hoped he didn't resemble my dad. That would have made me sad for some reason I couldn't name.

I needn't have worried. When he entered, a worried expression dominating his face, I realized Hank as the broad-shouldered, salt-and-peppered man with the gold filling whom I'd passed on the stairs in the Relax Inn. He looked nothing like my father, who'd been a small, quick Irishman. Hank was actually quite handsome, and solicitous of my mom in a way that warmed me from the inside out. We made slightly awkward small talk for about thirty minutes before the discharge nurse entered. Mom and Hank stood outside to give me some privacy while I got examined.

"Hank seems decent," Mrs. Berns said in a suspiciously normal tone. "A little boring, but that's not a bad thing. For someone like your mom, I mean."

I looked away as the nurse changed the bandage on my arm. Some blood had seeped through the mummy wrapping, leaving obscene red patches that crusted to a deep burgundy on the edges. "I agree."

"You know who else is decent?"

"You?" I asked doubtfully.

She flicked me in the forehead. "Johnny Leeson. You call him yet?"

I sighed. Man, had I wanted to. Almost as much as I'd wanted to break up with him. He was too good a guy to chain to my roller-coaster life.

"I can read your thought bubbles," Mrs. Berns said. "They're pitiful. 'I'm a dumbass' only has two *m*'s, by the way."

"What do you think he could do if I called him? Worry? He's all the way away in Texas."

Mrs. Berns crossed her arms. "'That's how it starts, I guess, by thinking you know what's best for someone else and imposing your will on them,'" she said, mimicking what I'd recently told Briggs about Adam.

"No fair, throwing my words back at me. I'm on prescription painkillers!"

"Don't rub it in," she said. "The rest of us have to make do with liquor and coffee."

The nurse finished changing the bandage. Her movements had been gentle, but the wound still pulsated. It'd be painful to drive. Hell, it was going to hurt to get dressed.

"It *would* be nice to have help," I said, in a quiet voice.

She clapped her hands gleefully. "That's a girl. I actually called him around two a.m. His plane landed an hour ago, so you should expect to see him soon. I promised him you'd do the no-pants dance with him as soon as you're healed, by the way. If you go another month without screwing that guy, I'm giving up on you."

The nurse wore her poker face perfectly. "Sorry to interrupt," she said, "but you're good to go. You'll want to give that arm as much rest as possible. Make an appointment with your regular doctor to get the stitches removed in seven to ten days, and call us if the pain in your shoulder or arm gets worse or the stitches start to feel hot or swollen. Here's a care sheet that outlines what you'll need to do to keep that wound clean and dressed."

I took the sheet and the extra bandages she offered and let her help me out of bed. I felt a little woozy, but happy to be standing. My shirt had been cut away from me on the scene. I wore the hospital gown top, which would have to do for now. And in a move that should be practiced among only the best of friends, I let Mrs. Berns help me into my jeans.

"Wouldn't kill you to buy these in your size," she grunted, yanking them over my hips.

"I *am* a size 8!"

"Maybe your feet. These hips need a little more dancing room." She buttoned the top clasp and zipped.

"Thanks. You're a good friend." The emotion in my voice surprised us both.

She cocked her head, studying me. "I guess that makes two of us."

Mom and Hank glanced up as we walked out the door. Mom beamed at me as if I'd just awoken from a coma. "Here," she said.

"Hank brought you a spare jacket. It'll be roomy, which is probably best with your arm."

"Thanks," I told him sincerely. "Could you do me one more favor?"

"Anything," he said. I liked the concern in his eyes.

"Could you take Mrs. Berns home and check on my animals? I have something that I want to do with Mom before we head back to her house."

Everyone shot me a quizzical glance, but to my great relief, no one questioned me.

Mom and I stepped into the frosty morning, and the whole world looked as if it'd been scrubbed and decorated with a clean batch of snow. A couple walked by across the street, pulling two giggling children in a blue plastic sled.

It felt wonderful, clean, bracing. I sucked in deep lungfuls of fresh air, trying to purify myself from the inside out. I let Mom put her arm gently around my waist and guide me to her van. I made sure I was looking away from her face when I told her the destination. I didn't want to see her expression. I wasn't ready to cry just yet.

The cemetery sat on the edge of town, a neat little plot of land surrounded by wrought iron fencing and gracious, sleeping oaks. The narrow road through it was freshly plowed. We parked at the chapel and started walking.

Natalie's grave was mounded over the top, so fresh that it didn't have as much snow as the rest. I set the red roses we'd bought at the hospital gift shop on top. It constricted my heart to stand at her graveside, but it wasn't the only reason I was here. I kept walking until I reached my dad's gravestone. It was plain gray quartz.

MARK DANIEL JAMES, it said, deep grooves etching the years he'd been alive. I hadn't seen it since the day we'd buried him.

"Hey, Dad," I said, my voice cracking. My mom stood directly behind me, and I could hear the warm sound of her tears. "Sorry I haven't visited."

I thought of what I'd written on the scrap of paper I'd handed Jules, the feelings or memories or mistakes I wanted to burn so I could start the year fresh.

I'd scrawled one word: "FEAR."

"I guess I just stopped by to say that I could use you around, you know? I miss you."

The hot tears flooded my face, more than a decade's worth of wet, scared hiding. Hiding from my past and hiding from the good things life offered me because I'd been afraid I didn't deserve them.

I'd been wrong, all that time.

Epilogue

It's scary to finally bury your dead; you get so used to hauling them everywhere that you don't know who you'd be without them. I'm proud to say that I sent a lot of ghosts to rest that Christmas week in Paynesville, fears and warped memories that I'd been carrying around for far too long. I even let my mom hold me as we both cried next to my dad's grave. Later, I walked toward my new life, feeling bruised but strong.

Mrs. Berns invited Sharpie and Mom invited Hank over that night, and when Johnny showed up, we had a comfortable evening of quiet laughter, everyone holding those they loved a little tighter. Johnny was lean and gorgeous, tanned from his trip to Texas, and smelling masculine and clean. He was solicitous, not smothering me but making sure I was as comfortable as possible.

Over champagne for those not on painkillers, Sharpie shared the good news that he'd just cut a deal to build his new factory in Willmar. I immediately gave him Kent's contact information, and Sharpie said he'd be thrilled to hire an experienced foreman to work for him. Hank and my mom held hands all night, sneaking glances into each other's eyes and sharing looks so personal they would have made me blush if she didn't seem so happy.

Later that night, after Sharpie and Hank had left and Johnny was crashed on the couch and Mom and Mrs. Berns were in their beds, I tiptoed downstairs. I couldn't sleep. I was too tired, my mind racing, my arm aching.

Johnny was awake, too. I took him by the hand and led him back to my childhood bed. His eyes were questioning, hopeful, tender. I touched his cheek. He brushed his lips against mine. The spark was instant and hot. Trembling, I kissed him, feeling the hardness of his body pressed against mine.

His hands glided over my body, but I felt him holding back, taut with passion yet worried about hurting me. Finally, he laid me gently on the bed and undressed me, never taking his eyes from mine. Then he unbuttoned his flannel and pulled off his white T-shirt, revealing his muscled chest.

Next came his button-fly Levi's, then his plain blue boxers. He stood over me, naked, the most glorious, sculpted picture of desire I'd ever laid eyes on. His shoulders were broad, his hips lean, his stare hungry. I smiled. I couldn't help it. This was really going to happen— and under the watchful stares of Jimmy Page and Kevin Bacon, no less.

"Are you sure?" he asked. A muscle twitched in his chest.

By way of an answer, I tugged him on top of me, whimpering only slightly when I had to adjust my arm. He smelled like sandalwood and love. He kissed my face, my neck, my body, whispering the sweetest promises.

When I couldn't stand it any longer, I pulled his face to mine and whispered, *"Yes."* I felt rather than saw his smile, moving slowly across his face and then down the length of him.

Except for my stitches and my mom sleeping downstairs, it was honestly as I'd always imagined it: love, rockets, and bliss. He held me in his arms afterward, and we talked in giggling whispers until the sun rose, despite my exhaustion.

I finally drifted off in midsentence, the morning light streaming through my curtain. I fell asleep with a smile on my face.

About the Author

Photo © 2023 Kelly Weaver Photography

Jess Lourey writes about secrets. She's the bestselling author of thrillers, rom-com mysteries, book club fiction, young adult fiction, and non-fiction. Winner of the Anthony, Thriller, and Minnesota Book Awards, Jess is also an Edgar, Agatha, and Lefty Award–nominated author; TEDx presenter; and recipient of The Loft's Excellence in Teaching fellowship. Check out her TEDx Talk for the true story behind her debut novel, *May Day*. She lives in Minneapolis with a rotating batch of foster kittens (and occasional foster puppies, but those goobers are a lot of work). For more information, visit www.jesslourey.com.